THE *Love's Journey*® SERIES IN SUGARCREEK

Bertha's RESOLVE

BY SERENA B. MILLER

Find more books by Serena B. Miller at ***SerenaBMiller.com***

Find her on Facebook, ***FB.com/AuthorSerenaMiller***

Follow her on Twitter, ***@SerenaBMiller***

The town depicted in this book is a real place, but all characters are fictional. Any resemblances to actual people or events are purely coincidental. Serena B. Miller is not a medical professional nor legal advisor. Any references to medical or legal advice and procedures is purely for entertainment purposes.

Scripture references are from the Holy Bible, King James Version (KJV). The Holy Bible, New International Version®, NIV®. Copyright © 1973, 1978, 1984 by Biblica, Inc.™ Used by permission of Zondervan.

Most foreign words have been taken from *Pennsylvania Deitsh Dictionary: A Dictionary for the Language Spoken by the Amish and Used in the Pennsylvania Deitsh New Testament* by Thomas Beachy, © 1999, published by Carlisle Press.

Author photos by Angie Griffith and KMK Photography | ***KMKphotography.com*** - Used by permission.

Cover & Interior design by Jacob Miller

Published by L. J. Emory Publishing

Love's Journey is a registered trademark of L. J. Emory Publishing.

First L. J. Emory Publishing trade paperback edition September 2020

ISBN 978-1-940283-52-4

ISBN 978-1-940283-54-8 (Large Print Version)

ISBN 978-1-940283-53-1 (eBook Version)

To Steven

"Love your neighbor as yourself."

~*Romans 13:9*

CHAPTER 1

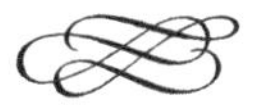

Sugarcreek, Ohio
January

Ten-year-old Calvin Brook's stomach growled with hunger. On the days that he walked home from school, he often smelled the aroma of fresh-baked pies wafting from a small building behind the Sugar Haus Inn. The scent, a combination of spices, fruit, and pie crust baking, was intoxicating. Especially for a growing boy who was almost always hungry.

The small, one-story building behind the inn was painted white, which matched the bigger house where he had noticed that three old Amish ladies lived. The big house had a sign that said, "Sugar Haus Inn." The little building behind the inn had a sign over it that said, "Sugar Haus Pies."

He rarely got to taste pie anymore. At least not since his grandma died. He had never experienced hunger when she was alive, but life was a lot different now.

A small schoolhouse, which was only a short walk from the inn, drew his attention. Sometimes he saw those weird Amish kids playing outside when he walked past. Sometimes he caught a glimpse of a few older Amish girls walking the short distance from their school to the pie building in the afternoon.

Lunchtime felt far in the past as he stood there, sniffing the air like a hungry pup. He could barely remember having eaten lunch; it was so long ago. As usual, there had been no breakfast for him this morning.

Well, actually, Alex, *had* poured him a bowl of cold cereal and called it breakfast, but it wasn't a *real* breakfast, not like his grandma used to make. Grandma always said cold cereal was not a meal, it was a snack. Calvin wholeheartedly agreed. Especially when he thought about the buckwheat pancakes she used to make. Store brand cereal did not come close to satisfying hunger like Grandma's breakfasts.

The January cold stung his gloveless hands, but he wore a new, warm, coat which was a Christmas gift from a local church. They had also given him and several other children a sock hat and gloves. He still wore the sock hat, but he'd lost the gloves. This he regretted as he dug his raw hands deeper into the coat's pockets.

That aroma! He stood on the side of the road wishing for pie and having no idea how to go about getting any. His mouth filled with saliva, just thinking about the possibility of all the baking going on in that small building. He had loved his grandma's apple pie and was reasonably sure he could consume one all by himself. Or cherry! Or peach! It didn't matter what kind of filling it had. Any kind would do. He loved them all.

As he stood there, a horse pulling a buggy clip-clopped down the road and pulled into the Sugar Haus Inn's graveled driveway. An Amish man got out and went into the pie house. The man came out a few moments later with three Amish girls who all piled into the buggy. They wore black, high-top tennis shoes with their light-colored dresses, which struck even Calvin as odd, but they still sounded and acted like the girls at his school. They were giggling and talking and seemed to be having an awfully good time together.

After their buggy trotted back down the road, Calvin saw a thin, elderly Amish woman in a dark purple dress and a black coat walk from the pie house back into the inn and close the door. It looked like the pie house was abandoned for the time being, but that enticing aroma kept tickling his nose.

Perhaps it wouldn't hurt to investigate just a little. Alex probably wouldn't even notice if he didn't come home right away. For all he knew, Alex was still in bed or staring at some stupid TV show. After moving them from Chicago to this weird little town with the giant cuckoo clock, Alex hadn't even bothered to get Wi-Fi set up at the stupid house they were renting. He rarely even carried a phone anymore.

In Calvin's opinion, Alex spent way too much time sitting around doing nothing, but Alex was not Calvin's immediate concern. At the moment, it was his stomach that begged for attention.

He sauntered across the yard, cold hands in his pockets, trying not to look suspicious. Nobody stopped him.

So far, so good.

After making it to the pie house without getting apprehended, he peered through one of the windows. At least twenty golden pies sat cooling on a long, wooden counter in the middle of the room. He was staggered by such culinary wealth.

With his nose pressed against the window, he found himself craving a closer look. He didn't intend to touch anything, but he thought it would be so nice just to be in the same room as all those pies. Plus, he was freezing and it looked warm in there. Gingerly, he tried the doorknob fully expecting it to be locked. It should have been locked, but it was not.

The door opened smoothly and silently. Calvin stepped inside and was hit with a wall of warmth and the thick, delicious aroma of fresh baking. The long counter, filled with cooling pies, beckoned to him. Steam still wafted out of the little slits on top of their perfectly golden crusts. He put his hands behind his back, determined not to yield to temptation.

A cherry pie with a lovely lattice-work crust caught his attention. He couldn't imagine how those girls or that old woman had made such an intricately-woven topping, but it looked delicious. Grandma had made cherry pie, too, but her crusts had never been that elaborate.

Carefully glancing around to make sure no one was watching, he pinched off a bit of crust. Just a little pinch. He didn't think anyone would even notice it was gone. He placed the tiny taste of crust in his mouth and closed his eyes to savor it as it melted onto his tongue with a delicious buttery flavor. After that, there was simply nothing to be done but to risk yet another pinch.

The pie filling, a shimmering red with fat cherries poking up all over, made the intricate crust look even more enticing, but perhaps the filling wasn't all that good. Grandma had forgotten to put the sugar into one of her cherry pies once, and it had tasted awful. Perhaps he should check.

Carefully, he stuck his pinky finger into one of the open squares in the golden lattice-work. The filling was still hot, but not hot enough to burn his tongue. He lifted his finger to his mouth and closed his eyes again as the rich, sweet, cherry flavor filled his senses. Nope, nothing wrong with that filling. It was sweet and just tangy enough to be interesting...and he was so very, very hungry.

At that point, he knew he would probably be getting into a whole lot of trouble very soon, but he couldn't help himself. He dug into that pie with both hands and began to eat one fist full after another as fast as he could, hoping to fill his belly before anyone could stop him.

CHAPTER 2

Alex Lane glanced out the kitchen window, wondering why Calvin was taking so long to walk home from school. The wisdom of accepting guardianship of the child and moving him to this town was still a decision he doubted, but he could not have abandoned the boy and continued to consider himself human.

Unfortunately, Aunt Beatrice could not have died at a worse time, nor could she have asked a less capable person to care for her grandson.

Alex went back to the task at hand--attempting to make soup. His head ached from the effort. Concentrating on any task these days felt like he was moving in slow motion. All he wanted to do was go back to bed.

After the gargantuan effort it had taken to pack up, move to Sugarcreek, and enroll Calvin in school, his bed had become his sanctuary. That and the oblivion a bottle of pills his doctor had prescribed to "get him over the hump."

Ah, Aunt Beatrice. If only you had realized the mess you were putting us in, leaving him to me. How I wish there had been anyone else who could have taken him!

He glanced down at the cutting board where an onion lay half chopped. The knife he held was dull. There had been a time in his life when he would have sharpened it without giving it a thought, but these days even a small task like that simply seemed like too much effort.

The cut-up onion stung his eyes and made them water as he dumped it into the boiling water. As he set the knob to simmer, he had to wipe tears off his face with the tail of his t-shirt. Whether the tears were brought on because of the onions, or for an entirely different reason, he did not know and he didn't care.

He picked up the prescription bottle sitting on the window sill. It was becoming harder and harder to limit himself to the two pills a day the doctor had prescribed. Some days he took more. Sleep was the only thing that kept the memories of his failure at bay.

He sat the bottle back down. The very least he could do was try to be awake each day when the kid got home.

CHAPTER 3

Officer Rachel Troyer Mattias lay in bed, one arm encircling her three-week-old baby girl. Both were fresh from their bath and wore cozy new bathrobes. Baby Holly's was pink with lace accents and matching booties, which her Great Aunt Lydia had crocheted for her. Rachel's robe was plain white, a recent Christmas gift from her Aunt Bertha.

They both smelled of lavender from the drops of essential oil Rachel's husband, Joe, shook into the water when he drew their bath. Joe was thoughtful like that, and Rachel was wise enough to appreciate it.

She was due at work soon. In a few minutes, she would need to dress and go to work. But for now, she savored this intimate moment with her family. Life felt so simple and rich when she was at home with Joe and her children.

She gazed down at the baby—this precious and unexpected gift from God. Could she possibly love her more if she were her flesh and blood? Not possible. Her gratitude to Holly's biological father, Dane, who had sacrificially given up his rights to his baby daughter, was boundless.

"Have you made up your mind yet?" Joe sat down on the bed beside her.

"It's hard, Joe." Rachel caressed her daughter's silky hair. The short, blonde strands curled around her finger while Holly happily gurgled and kicked her tiny legs. A pink booty worked its way off her minuscule feet. Joe nestled her little foot back inside the bootie and securely tied the small pink ribbon.

"I'll support whatever you choose to do," Joe said. "But the restaurant is making a decent profit. If we're careful, we can live on what we take in."

"I'm grateful the restaurant is doing well," Rachel said. "But, I love my job."

Joe was a great father and husband. He spent as much time caring for their two children as she did. Besides that, he was good at it. If there was ever a man who adored his family and wanted to help take care of his children, it was Joe. The problem was her shifting work schedule and the sudden, middle-of-the-night calls to their small police station which sometimes necessitated her response. She was the only cop on the five-person Sugarcreek police force fluent in Pennsylvania Deutsch.

For Joe, running a successful restaurant wasn't exactly a nine-to-five workweek either. Balancing two more than full-time jobs while building a business and raising a family was taking a toll on them both.

Rachel felt so divided. How could one choose between two great loves? She was needed and valued by the Sugarcreek police team. She felt passionate about protecting this small town that, except for the few years she had worked in Cleveland, had been her home since birth.

"And then there are your aunts." Joe brought up one more valid point. "They are not getting any younger. I'm afraid our responsibilities to them will become heavier in the near future."

Joe picked up Holly and cuddled her against his chest. He was wearing the new Levi's she had gotten him for Christmas and they fit him well. Joe was smart, kind, and handsome—a rare find. She gave thanks daily for him and Bobby, his six-year-old son, who had walked into her life two years earlier.

"How blessed are we that Dane chose us to raise his little girl!" Joe's cheek was pressed against their tiny daughter's silky hair.

"I still can't get over it." Rachel said. "But I feel sorry for him. That was a terribly stiff sentence he received for doing no more than defend himself."

"We don't know for certain that's true," Joe said. "We weren't there, and neither was the jury."

"But you weren't there the night Dane chose to give Holly to me," Rachel said. "He could have run, but he made certain his little daughter was legally ours first. He wanted to make sure that she was safe with someone he trusted. The look I saw on his face that night as the lawyer drew up the papers--the love and willingness to sacrifice I saw there! He's had a hard life, and he's had to do terrible things, but at heart, I know he is a good man."

"I'm sure you're right, but mainly I'm just grateful that we have her. Our family is growing, sweetheart! Before long, we'll need to buy a mini-van. I'll start working on getting a pot-belly, and you can wear mom-jeans," he teased. "I can't wait to see you in mom jeans."

Rachel laughed but watching Joe hold that baby continued to melt her heart. Not all that long ago, he had been an elite athlete. His pitching prowess had put him in the ranks of some of the greatest pitchers in the world. His skill had made a good living for him until shoulder injuries, and the trauma of his first wife's murder permanently took him off the baseball field.

Now that Joe's baseball-themed sports restaurant was catching on and becoming a popular tourist haunt, life was becoming particularly complicated. They recently added a breakfast menu, which was flourishing, but it also created a sort of tight-wire act with Joe's business partner, his brother Darren.

Living so frantically could be maintained for a while, but it wasn't good for the long run. Rachel knew how delicate the balance was in their lives. It wouldn't take a lot to tip them over the edge into chaos. Bobby's grades were already slipping a little.

At that moment, Bobby came running in from school and bounced onto the bed with them.

She wasn't sure with whom she had fallen in love with first, Joe or Bobby, but Joe liked to tease her that she had only married him so she could be Bobby's mother. She always told him that this wasn't far from the truth.

Bobby was such a tender-hearted little boy, and so brave. She would never forget the image burned into her mind the night she found her sturdy little son standing with his back against a tree, a butter knife in his hand for protection against the kidnappers whom he had just escaped. Tears had been streaming down his face as he stared into the dark woods, but he was ready to fight with nothing but a butter knife. Her heart had ached with love for him. It still did.

Bobby had been through enough trauma in his short life. Having a baby sister suddenly appear had been a welcome surprise, but little Holly had most definitely disrupted their family's schedule. Rachel agreed with Joe, they needed to find a way to give both children more stability, and yet…

"I can't give up my job to just anyone, Joe. I love this town too much. I'll have to help Ed find someone who is a good fit before I can leave."

"I'm sure quite a few locals would jump at the chance," Joe said.

"We can't simply pin a badge on one of our substitute deputies," Rachel said. "I don't think any of them have the maturity or the experience yet."

Bobby wasn't paying attention to their discussion. He was too fascinated with the fact that his baby sister had curled her tiny fist around his pinky finger.

"Aw." Bobby was entranced. "Look! She's already holding my hand. She knows I'm going to take good care of her."

That, Rachel knew, was the absolute truth. Holly was one lucky little girl to have Bobby for a big brother.

"Sugarcreek's crime rate is one of the lowest in the state," Joe said. "Maybe one of the lowest in the nation. You don't think any of the substitute deputies can handle it?"

"It's getting harder and harder to hold onto that low crime rate. We need someone with real-world experience. Someone who is seasoned and yet has enough sense not to point a gun at every Amish kid who gets tipsy during Rumspringa." Rachel shook her head. "Trust me on this—the chief is *not* going to be happy about me leaving, but I agree with you. For our children's sake, I need to take a break from police work for a while."

"Your aunts are going to be thrilled," Joe said.

"Bertha will be convinced that her prayers have finally been answered." Rachel went to the closet and pulled out her black Sugarcreek police uniform.

"Who knows?" Joe said. "Perhaps her prayers have been answered. If I were the Lord, I would definitely pay attention to whatever Bertha instructed me to do."

She smiled at the image of God obeying Bertha. Her aunt was, indeed, a formidable woman.

"If you don't mind packing Holly's formula and diapers while I get dressed, I'll drop her off with Bertha on my way to work."

"Am I going with Daddy?" Bobby asked.

"If you want to earn a paycheck, you are," Joe said. "Besides, Uncle Darren and I need the help."

"Yay!" Bobby jumped off the bed and ran to his room to get ready He seemed to enjoy feeling like he was part of the team that kept Joe's Home Plate working smoothly. He was also saving up for a pony.

Dressed and ready for work, Rachel secured Holly in her car carrier, kissed Joe and Bobby good-bye and strode out to the squad car thinking how much nicer it would be if she could be working with her family at their cozy restaurant tonight instead of driving around in the snow wondering how many fender benders she would have to tend to before her shift was over.

CHAPTER 4

Bertha Troyer tidied up the teacher's desk in the one-room schoolhouse which had been built next door to her home. She and her sisters had donated the land for the building only last year. In her late seventies, she had impressed even herself today by having enough stamina to teach thirty-two children from the ages of six to fourteen.

She was not surprised when Amos Mast, head of the parochial school board, stopped by while bicycling home from work.

"Were the scholars well-behaved?" he asked.

"They were very well-behaved," Bertha said. "The children made allowances for me, and I made allowances for them, and we got along well. There is even the chance that one or two of us learned something along the way."

"I'm so sorry I had to ask you to come this morning," he said. "But I couldn't find anyone else when Naomi took ill so suddenly. You were the only one I could think of who lived close enough to get here before the children started showing up."

"I am grateful to be of help," Bertha said. "Will you need me tomorrow?"

"No, Lily Weaver says she can take over until Naomi recuperates."

"That will be good." Bertha was relieved. Lily was eighteen-years-old, bright, and energetic. She would do well. "I hope Naomi recuperates soon."

"As do I. Let me finish up here," Amos said. "I'll take care of straightening the desks and banking the fire. "You go on home. You've done enough, and I thank you."

Wearily—it had been quite a long day—she donned her coat, scarf, and gloves, and walked against the frigid January wind toward the Sugar Haus Inn where she and her two younger sisters lived.

Bertha was hungry and exhausted. She found some leftover fried chicken in their propane refrigerator, pulled out a drumstick, and as she ate it standing over the sink to catch the crumbs, her heart smiled at the memory of the noon meal she had eaten earlier.

The frantic call from Amos to substitute teach had left her with only a few minutes to dress before rushing over to the school. There was no time to pack anything for her midday meal. Normally, her sister, Lydia, would have noticed and brought her something, but Lydia and Anna had left for a quilting that morning.

After their silent prayer, the children tore into their food containers. Bertha watched as they unwrapped carefully prepared meals. It was quite an array. Amish mothers took their family's nutrition seriously. To Bertha's knowledge, no child in their settlement—or adult for that matter—ever went hungry.

As she had sat there, watching the children enjoy their food, Francine, one of the older girls, realized the teacher had no lunch. She approached the desk holding a sandwich in a zip-locked bag.

"I had a big breakfast, and my *maam* packed way too much," the girl said, placing the package on Bertha's desk. "It's Trail bologna, cheese, and tomato. You are welcome to it if you want."

The sandwich had been made with thick slices of homemade bread and looked delicious.

"Thank you," Bertha said. "Your mother is a wonderful good bread baker. I hope you are learning from her."

"I am." Francine smiled and went back to her desk in the back of the room.

This set off a similar reaction with the rest of the children.

"I have a pickle you can have."

"My *maam* made extra cookies and told me to share them."

"Do you want my apple? We have plenty back home in the cellar."

So typical of her people, Bertha thought. Amish children were very deliberately taught to share. It came as no surprise that a makeshift lunch was being created for her, and she was touched.

She loved these children—all of whom she had known since babyhood. She loved them just like she had loved the children in the Mennonite orphanage while serving in Haiti a lifetime ago. One thing she learned during her years there was that children were pretty much the same regardless of race, country, or language.

The biggest difference between the children who inhabited her classroom today, and those she had taught in Haiti so many years ago, was a matter of nutrition. Ohio Amish children were usually well-fed and well-loved. Their cheeks were ruddy from outdoor play and sparkling good health. The children from Haiti haunted her to this day.

She comforted herself with the knowledge that she had done the very best she could for them.

After washing the chicken down with a glass of cold milk, she felt a little better as she climbed the steps to her bedroom.

She closed the door, lifted off her black bonnet, unpinned her dress, and replaced it with a clean one from her closet. Two of the children had runny noses today, and she would prefer not to get sick. She would also prefer not to pass anything on to Rachel's new baby girl whom she would be babysitting shortly.

The slam of the back door downstairs told her that her sister was home. Lydia and her three helpers must have made quick work of pie baking today.

While pinning the front of her fresh dress closed, from the vantage point of her window at the back of the house, she saw a young boy sneaking around the pie house.

Unsupervised little boys and pies were not a good combination. Rachel's husband, Joe, needed those pies for his restaurant, and this boy—an *Englisch* boy at that—could not be up to anything good.

The sight of the boy carefully opening the door to Lydia's little pie factory drove all thoughts of weariness away. She hurried downstairs to thwart whatever sort of mischief the child had in mind.

Lydia came out of the downstairs bathroom just as Bertha was heading—full tilt—out the back door.

"You'll need a shawl if you are going to the barn," Lydia called. "It is cold out."

"I am not going to the barn," Bertha said. "A child just went into the pie house, and I want to see what he is up to."

Lydia grabbed her coat off the peg on the wall and followed Bertha outside. It was only a few steps from the back door of the inn to the pie house. Lydia was buttoning her coat when Bertha entered and stopped dead in her tracks. She felt Lydia bump against her with a soft "oof!"

The boy, a little carrot-top with big, blue eyes, glanced up, startled. He had no eating utensils but was digging into one of the pies with his fingers and scooping the dripping contents into his mouth. He had chosen to focus his attention on a cherry pie, and it was all over his face.

She glanced at the other pies and took a breath of relief. They were intact. She had gotten here in time. They could afford to lose one pie.

Except for his new, blue coat, the boy looked like he was not particularly well-cared-for. He wore dirty tennis shoes, wet with snow, one with a broken shoelace and a hole developing in the toe. Why did the boy not have decent boots to wear in this weather? His faded jeans ended a full three inches above his ankles, and there was a rip in one knee.

His red hair stuck out from beneath his black sock hat. Freckles covered his face—or at least as much of his face that wasn't hidden beneath cherry pie filling.

She felt her heart soften. Growing children could often be overwhelmed by hunger. Still, they needed to be taught.

"You do not have permission to be here," Bertha said, sternly. "And you certainly do not have permission to steal food that does not belong to you. Where do you live? Who are your parents?"

His eyes darted wildly around the room, looking for an escape, but she and Lydia were standing directly in front of the only viable exit.

A familiar voice behind them spoke up. "What's going on?"

Bertha turned. It was their niece, Rachel, dressed in her Sugarcreek police uniform. The heavy, black, police coat Rachel wore against the January cold, plus the bullet-proof vest she donned when on duty, made her look larger than she really was. She was also wearing her black police boots and hat, both of which added to her height.

Bertha knew Rachel, in full uniform, must look very official and intimidating to the boy. The pink baby carrier dangling from Rachel's left hand only somewhat spoiled the effect.

"We seem to have attracted a new guest." Lydia's voice was kind.

Lydia had such a soft spot for children, even when they were misbehaving. Bertha preferred a more disciplined approach.

Rachel carefully sat the baby carrier on a nearby table. Whether it was for effect or merely a habit, she had her hand on the butt of her holstered gun as she approached the boy. He trembled at her approach.

"What is your name?" Rachel's voice was matter-of-fact.

The boy, obviously terrified, backed away from her.

Lydia, so tenderhearted she could not bear to see anyone frightened, or even uncomfortable, began to reassure him. "You are not in trouble, child..."

Rachel held a finger in the air to stop Lydia from saying anything more.

"I just need to know who you are," Rachel said, kindly. "Tell me your name."

The boy nervously wiped the red pie filling from his hands off onto his jeans. Fear filled his eyes.

"It's okay." Rachel squatted down, putting her face at the same level as his. "I'm not here to hurt you, I just need to know your name."

He would not meet her eyes.

"You know it's wrong to steal, right?" Rachel said.

He squirmed, dug the toe of one sodden shoe into the wooden floor, and nodded.

"Were you hungry?" Rachel asked.

He nodded again, vigorously.

"You did not have to steal. These ladies would have been happy to feed you if you had just asked."

He glanced up at Bertha and Lydia. His eyes were such a deep blue, they were startling in his pale face.

"She's right," Lydia said, softly. "All you had to do was ask. We would never turn away a hungry child."

A look of suspicion crossed his face. As though weighing and discarding their words.

Lydia went to the sink, ran a washcloth beneath the faucet, and squeezed it out. She approached the boy to wipe his face with the wet cloth, but he jerked his head back when she tried to touch him with it.

"You have pie on your face." Lydia handed the washcloth to him. "I'm sure it is very sticky. It might feel good to clean yourself up before you go home."

Carefully keeping his eyes on the three of them, the boy wiped off his mouth, his hands, and took a swipe at his pants leg.

A mewling sound came from the baby carrier. Rachel stood

up to reach for it, Lydia turned to go to it, and Bertha, who was standing right beside it began to remove the covering that Rachel had zipped over the carrier to protect the baby from the cold.

With all three women momentarily distracted, the boy dropped the washcloth on the floor and was out the door before anyone could catch him.

"It was only a pie," Lydia said. "Poor child. From the looks of things, I have a feeling he doesn't have the best home life."

"Probably not," Rachel said. "I wish he had given me a name. I could have checked up on his situation. He's not a kid I've ever seen before. I'll see what I can find out."

With the boy gone, all three women surrounded the three-week-old baby girl who peered out from within the depths of the carrier with bright eyes while furiously sucking a pink pacifier.

"Well, hello there!" Lydia said. "Aren't you just the most precious thing?"

Bertha glanced at Rachel. "I thought you were against the use of pacifiers."

"I am," Rachel said. "Or at least I was. It's great in theory, but the problem is that they work. It helps keeps her happy. I can't bear to hear her cry."

Rachel unbuckled the carrier straps and lifted out her infant daughter. The baby was dressed in stretchy, one-piece white pajamas. Her wispy, nearly transparent hair stood out from her head with static electricity like dandelion fluff. She was so new, her little legs were still folded up against her body as Rachel put her on her shoulder and patted her tiny bottom, which was decorated with a pink heart sewn onto the pajamas.

Lydia and Bertha sighed in unison. There was just something about a baby, and this one was especially precious to them.

"Lord willing, your sweet *bobli* will never have to experience real hunger," Bertha said.

"I can't imagine the pain of not being able to feed my child," Rachel said. "I don't think I could bear it."

"Many mothers have no choice," Bertha said. "But by the grace of God, I don't think you will ever have to experience it. Shall we get her settled inside the house so you can go to work?"

"I'll just straighten up in here a bit before I come in." Lydia picked up the pie plate the boy had attacked and held it so everyone could see. "The child was hungry. Most grown men couldn't polish off a whole pie in one sitting."

"Darren will be here soon to get the pies before the dinner crowd starts arriving," Rachel said. "You might want to lock the door just in case the boy decides to come back. We wouldn't want him to bring some of his friends with him."

"Do you think he'd do that?" Lydia asked, concerned.

"Who knows?" Rachel deposited the baby back into the carrier, covered her with a blanket, and zipped the black covering shut against the frigid wind. "The boy is *Englisch*. Who knows *what* he might choose to do. Some Englisch children are very poorly taught."

"True." Bertha held the door open for Rachel. "If the boy was one of ours, I would deal with him much differently. His parents would already have been called."

"If the child was Amish," Rachel said, "It would never have happened. He would already have plenty of good things to eat. A pie wouldn't be much of a temptation. His mother would have had included a piece or two when she packed his lunch."

"*Ja,*" Bertha said, nodding, remembering. "Our ways are better. Children should never have to go hungry."

CHAPTER 5

Sugarcreek
1959

Bertha was nineteen and reading aloud from The Budget, a Sugarcreek-based newspaper with news from Amish and Mennonite communities from around the world. Her seventeen-year-old sister, Lydia, was piecing together a quilt from carefully chosen squares of lovely fabric as she listened.

It was Saturday night, and they both had washed their hair earlier to give it time to dry overnight before church in the morning. The back of Bertha's nightgown was damp from her freshly shampooed hair. She had one other nightgown that was still dry, into which she intended to change right before going to bed. Her hair was thick, blonde, and it fell past her waist. Many of her friends admired Bertha's hair, but they were not envious of how long it took to dry.

Both she and Lydia sat near the fireplace to help hasten the drying process. She shrugged her shoulders against the uncomfortable feeling of her damp nightgown clinging to her back as she read a letter from the wife of a Mennonite missionary doctor in Haiti that had recently been printed in The Budget.

"Many of the mothers here in Haiti are so poor," Bertha read. "They are forced to make dirt cookies in a desperate attempt to fill their children's hungry bellies."

Lydia's hand, busily pushing a needle through a dark blue quilt block of fabric, paused and looked up. "You are not serious!"

"I'm afraid so," Bertha said. "The doctor's wife, Charlotte, even included the recipe."

"There is a recipe for such a vile thing?" Lydia shook her head.

"Listen to this," Bertha said. "' Mothers knead one part salt into one part fat. Then they mix that with five parts water and ten parts of dirt. When it is smooth, they measure out flat dollops to bake in the sun. When the mixture has hardened, they give the cookies to their children to eat. It is the only way some of them have to keep their children from crying from hunger.'"

Quilt block forgotten Lydia's hands dropped to her lap as she tried to comprehend what Bertha was reading. "Can such a terrible thing be true?"

Bertha quickly scanned the next paragraph. "Charlotte says she didn't believe it at first either, but yes, it is true."

"A mother so desperate to fill the ache in her child's belly that she has to resort to dirt?" Tears filled gentle Lydia's eyes. "The very thought breaks my heart!"

"Charlotte says the mothers also eat the cookies, especially the pregnant ones who get so hungry."

They stared at one another, aghast.

"Is there anything we can do?" Lydia asked.

"I don't know," Bertha said. "Let me keep reading."

"Although we cannot feed the whole nation, at our Mennonite-run children's home, the food is simple, but they usually do not have to go hungry. If there is anything left at the end of the day, we feed any street children who are around. They have learned to look for this, and when we walk outside, we are often swarmed by hungry children."

"I wish we had money of our own to send to them," Lydia said.

"Money is an issue, but it doesn't seem to be their biggest problem." Bertha stared at the pages in her hand, transfixed.

"What do you mean?"

"Although money is welcome," Bertha read again from the letter. "It is volunteers we need the most. People who are willing to help. Trained nurses are especially in short supply."

"Well, there's nothing we can do about that," Lydia said. "It isn't as though either of us are nurses or could ever become one—that takes more education than we are allowed. But maybe I could sell some of my quilts and send them the money. It might help. It is not much, but it is better than nothing."

Bertha nodded, but she was barely listening. She felt such a stirring in her soul about the plight of the Haitian mothers and children that she found herself longing to go there immediately to help in any way she could. But that was impossible. Riding in an airplane, even for something as crucial as helping feed and care for hungry children, was strictly forbidden by their Ordnung. She would never get permission.

"I'm sure any quilt you made would bring a good price." Bertha, distracted by her thoughts, tried to focus on what her sister was saying. "In fact, I think the one you're making right now would be perfect."

"This is for our cousin, Eli's wife. She picked out the colors and bought the material, but as soon as it is finished, I'll start making one to sell for the Haitian children."

"I'll ask our Daett if he will allow me to use a portion of my pay from working at the grocery store to help you purchase quilting material."

"I doubt he will agree to do that," Lydia said. "He is depending on your salary to purchase that new strain of field corn he wants to try this spring."

Bertha, her chin resting on her fist, gave it some thought. As a single daughter still living beneath her parent's roof, she was expected to turn her salary over to her parents, just like all other Amish sons and daughters were expected to do. Her parents, in return, gave a small portion back for pocket money, but it wasn't much. This was not something she ever questioned, nor did Lydia, nor did any of their friends. Their parents had provided for them during their early years, and it was an accepted custom for Amish children to give their parents whatever pay they received after they graduated from the eighth grade and found a job.

On the other hand, if a son or daughter were willing to do extra work in the evenings after their other work was completed, or if they worked a second job on Saturdays, sometimes the parents would allow them to keep that money for their own.

Bertha had an idea.

"Yesterday," she told Lydia, "as I was walking to work, the Englisch woman who just moved in down the road was getting her mail. She asked if I knew any girls willing to clean house for her once a week. I told her I would ask around. If I took on that extra job, maybe Daett would allow me to use that money to purchase material for your quilts."

"Oh!" Lydia said. "That would be wonderful. Then we could have quilting frolics with our friends every time I finished a quilt top. Everyone would pitch in. We would be able to donate all we make from the sale to Charlotte and her husband to use for the children's home!"

"I'll help with the quilting, too!" Bertha said.

"That's all right," Lydia said, a little too quickly. "Purchasing the material is enough. I'll take care of the rest. A quilt has more value if the stitches are uniform and yours are sometimes...well..."

"I understand." Bertha was not hurt by Lydia's evaluation of her sewing ability. She rarely had the patience required for the intricate work of piecing and quilting. She tended to work better on a larger scale.

As Lydia happily chatted on about what kind of pattern she would use for the quilt, Bertha's mind kept churning. Working a second job to purchase fabric and thread was not a sacrifice. She was strong and healthy and had more than enough energy for whatever she wanted or needed to do. Shopping for the fabric would be enjoyable. Even though they were required to dress in plain clothing, they were not forbidden to use patterned material in their quilts. It would be so much fun spending a day fingering and choosing pretty fabric from the dry goods shop in Sugarcreek.

But Bertha could not get the nagging feeling out of her mind that it was not enough. Not nearly enough. Earning money for quilt material was one thing, but she kept wishing she could do more.

Dirt cookies, of all things! How could she look the other way and enjoy her relatively easy life when desperate mothers were forced to feed their children dirt! How could anyone? She wanted to experience the satisfaction of helping those women and children first-hand.

But how?

Hidden deep in her heart was another wish she could never fulfill. She wished to become a nurse and have the knowledge to make people well. That desire had taken root when her little brother, Frank, got ill, and the doctor taught her how to care for him. When Frank got better, the doctor had praised her for being a "good nurse." The desire to become a real nurse had secretly burned inside her heart ever since although she tried to ignore it. Lydia was right. More formal schooling than the prescribed eight years of elementary school that Amish children were allowed, was strictly forbidden.

The lack of further education didn't seem to bother Lydia, but it constantly niggled at Bertha. How wonderful to possess the knowledge and skill to save a life or help alleviate someone's pain!

But this, alas, was not something she would ever get to experience—not if she were to remain Amish, and she would stay Amish. It was all she had ever known. It was the narrow path she would need to walk to get to heaven.

CHAPTER 6

Calvin ran as fast as he could for as long as he could after he escaped from the woman cop and the two old Amish ladies. By the time he got to the rented house where he lived, he was out of breath and had a stitch in his side. During his flight, he had also managed to lose the warm hat the church people had given him.

After hiding behind the house, panting, and peering around the corner to see if the cop was chasing him, he thought he might have calmed down enough to go inside without raising suspicion. He tried to act nonchalant as he sauntered into the house he shared with Alex.

His heart sank when he saw his guardian in the kitchen, stirring something in a big pot on the stove. Life was better when Alex didn't try to cook. Calvin hoped he would give up and order pizza or go pick up chicken nuggets from the McDonald's up the road. It didn't happen all the time, but it happened often enough that he was forever hopeful

"Hey there, buddy," Alex said, as Calvin sneaked inside. "Something happen today? You're kind of late."

"I met up with some kids," Calvin lied. "We played kickball."

"So you're making friends? That's good." Alex's words didn't match the tone of his voice.

Calvin wandered over to see if he could figure out what Alex was trying to make. He was grateful his cousin and guardian had been willing to take him in. The alternative would probably have been the foster care system, so he was grateful Alex had agreed to the arrangement.

Still, Alex wasn't Grandma, and he never would be.

"What are you making?" Calvin asked, without much hope.

"Beef vegetable soup," Alex said. "I found an old recipe left behind in a drawer. I figure it's time we ate something healthy for a change."

Calvin did not reply. In the past three months, since his grandma died, every time Alex attempted to cook something "healthy," it had turned out especially badly.

The soup smelled pretty good, but it was hard for Calvin to work up any enthusiasm for it, what with the biggest part of a cherry pie residing in his stomach.

"Let's give this a try," Alex said, with forced cheerfulness. "I tried to follow the recipe exactly, but we'll have to see if it worked."

There were two soup bowls already laid out on the small, bare kitchen table. One spoon sat beside each bowl. A glass of water as well.

Somehow, those two bowls looked so much lonelier and less appetizing than when he'd been living alone with Grandma. She would have used a fresh tablecloth and maybe even decorated the table with flowers. If she made soup, there would be bread and butter or crackers and peanut butter to go with it. And there would be the knowledge that some sort of dessert lay in wait in the refrigerator.

Dessert was always a surprise. Grandma wouldn't let Calvin even peek in the refrigerator until he'd eaten enough of his dinner to warrant something sweet.

A boy's need for dessert never seemed to enter Alex's head. As far as he could tell, his guardian considered any form of sugar to be next-door to poison. So, sweets were entirely off the table. It made life hard.

Alex ladled the healthy-looking soup into mismatched bowls, sat down and, without another word, dipped his spoon into the soup and started to bring it to his mouth. Calvin sat with his hands in his lap.

"What's wrong?" Alex asked, spoon suspended in the air. He nodded toward Calvin's bowl. "Go ahead and eat."

Calvin couldn't talk around the lump in his throat. Grandma always wanted a prayer said before every meal. Sometimes she would say it. Sometimes she'd ask Calvin to bless the food for both of them. Come to think of it, if Grandma was still alive, not only would there be a good meal on the table, he wouldn't be in trouble right now with the police for having stolen a pie. Really. He wouldn't.

Unable to verbalize the sadness and turmoil going on inside his heart, he didn't answer. He just sipped a spoonful of soup.

It was so salty, he nearly spit it out.

He watched as Alex came to the same realization, sat his spoon down, and pushed back from the table. "Pizza?"

Calvin nodded.

Alex sighed and stood up. "Okay. Go get your coat."

Calvin obeyed, but his stomach felt funny, and it wasn't all from a stolen pie. He was worried. What would happen if they accidentally ran into that woman cop while they were out getting pizza? For all he knew, she would arrest him and put him in jail!

If that happened, Alex might decide not to keep him anymore. He might not be as nice to live with as Grandma, but he was a whole lot better than nothing—even if he did act sad all the time.

Calvin was pretty certain that the reason Alex acted sad was because he had been saddled with a ten-year-old boy who had nowhere else to go.

CHAPTER 7

Sugarcreek
1959

Bertha approached her father with her plan early the next morning over breakfast.

"Lydia and I are hoping to make and sell quilts so we can donate the proceeds to a mission work in Haiti," she said. "I will continue to bring you my salary for working at the grocery store, but if I take on extra work, may I use that money for our project?"

"You are planning on making quilts to sell?" Her father's bushy eyebrows lifted. "This is a surprise. I was not aware that you had mastered that craft, Bertha."

His voice was gentle, but Bertha knew he was gently poking fun at her, and she blushed. It was a well-known fact in her family that she was no seamstress. Lydia had been born with a gift for it. Bertha had not.

"I will provide the extra money to purchase material and quilting thread," Bertha glanced at her sister. "Lydia and her friends will be the ones making the quilts."

Lydia, sitting beside her, nodded in agreement.

"Will this extra work prevent you from helping with gathering in the hay?"

"No, Daett."

Her father gave it some thought, then he turned to her mother.

"Do you see any problem with it?" he asked.

Her mother finished slicing a fresh loaf of bread onto a plate, and then passed it around the table before answering. Bertha noted that Frank took three slices before passing the plate on. He was growing so fast!

"If the girls are willing to work extra for such a good cause," her mother said. "I see nothing wrong with allowing them to do so."

"Then that is your answer, daughter," he said.

"Thank you, Daett."

Her father was not a hard man, but it was not an easy task to make a living as a farmer. He needed all the help he could get. It was merely a fact that the person most capable of farm chores was his oldest daughter. He had worked her hard over the years, but she was not resentful. The endurance and heart to work hard was a valuable thing. It always paid off, and she expected it to pay off now. Not for her, of course, but for the children who were forced to eat dirt cookies. To keep that from happening, she was willing to do whatever she must.

Her father would have preferred God give him a son for his first-born, but that didn't keep him from using Bertha and Lydia in the fields during plowing and harvesting season. The work was hard on Lydia, she tended to wilt if she spent too much time in the fields, so as Bertha grew stronger, he allowed Lydia to stay inside and help their mother with domestic chores. Sometimes that included taking in occasional boarders for extra income. He relied more and more on Bertha to take on the work of a son.

Bertha's little brother, Frank, tried to help, but he was still too young to do much besides get in the way. She kept him with her from an early age, though, because it was vital for him to learn how to work the land as well. She spent a large part of her time in the field keeping an eye on him, making certain he didn't get hurt.

Lydia was apologetic about being the one who helped their mother indoors, but Bertha assured her she would rather work outdoors than be cooped up in the kitchen. Lydia accepted her reassurances with relief. At seventeen, Lydia was already a better cook and baker than their mother.

Taking on the once-a-week cleaning job for the Englisch neighbor would not be a hardship. She had plenty of energy. Sometimes on the alternate no-church Sundays, when they stayed at home and rested, she felt like she might burst if she didn't find something to do.

She intended to talk to their neighbor soon and find out how much housework the woman had to give her. It would be such a blessing knowing that her extra labor would go to help feed hungry children.

CHAPTER 8

"Are you sure you are feeling up to caring for Holly this evening?" Rachel asked as they entered the inn's kitchen. "From what I hear, you had a pretty long day teaching school."

"Of course, I'm feeling up to caring for the baby," Bertha said. "But how did you know about me teaching school?"

"Have you forgotten the power of the Amish grapevine?"

"I am painfully aware of my people's ability to gossip," Bertha said. "Who told you?"

"Amos passed by on his way home from work just as I was loading Holly into the squad car. He told me what happened and said he hoped it hadn't been too much for you," Rachel said. "Look, if you are too tired to do this..."

Bertha waved away Rachel's concern. "A healthy and contented newborn is no trouble. All she needs is a diaper change, some food, and to be rocked. Lydia and I are happy to provide that."

"I am going to be making other arrangements," Rachel apologized. "But for now, I need your help. Joe can't watch her tonight. There's some big football game on. He and Darren mounted a second large-screen TV at the restaurant, and they are planning on live streaming it. There will be a crowd."

"I don't even understand what that means," Bertha said. "And I don't care to know, but what about Bobby?"

"Bobby would be devastated if he didn't get to be at the restaurant with his dad on game night."

Bertha lifted the baby from the carrier, sat down in the rocking chair that they kept in the kitchen, and began to rock little Holly.

"I can take care of one baby. No trouble. But at my age, I don't think I would be up to caring for dozens anymore."

"Do you ever miss it?" Rachel began taking baby paraphernalia out of the diaper bag, laying it in neat piles on the kitchen table. Extra diapers. Extra baby bottles. Extra wipes. Two changes of clothing.

In Bertha's opinion, Rachel was overdoing it, but that was a young mother for you. She stopped evaluating the contents of the diaper bag and considered Rachel's question for a moment.

"Yes. I miss the children I had under my care," she said. "I often wonder how their lives turned out. On the other hand, I do not miss the poverty or the desperation I battled there."

The youngest of Rachel's three aunts came down the stairs, rubbing her eyes.

"Hello, Anna," Rachel said. "Were you asleep?"

"Uh-huh." Anna noticed that Bertha was holding the new baby, and she reached out her arms. "Ooh! Can I hold her?"

Bertha glanced at Rachel inquiringly. They both knew Anna meant well, but she wasn't always as steady as they would like. It had become a worry. She'd fallen twice in the past month.

"It's your decision, Rachel," Bertha said.

"Let's go into the living room where you can sit on the couch, Anna," Rachel said. "And we'll bring her to you."

They watched Anna lumber into the living room, where she plumped down on the couch. Bertha had always been concerned about Anna, but she was growing more so these days. Anna had Down syndrome and now that she was nearing sixty, she had developed some heart issues that worried them all a great deal. Her doctor stressed that Anna needed to rest more, which had been hard to get her to do at first, but now it was getting hard to get her to stop. She was sleeping more and more these days. Plus, without moving around as much as she once had, she was beginning to have weight issues that also took a toll on her weakened heart.

Once Anna was obediently seated on the couch, Rachel placed cushions all around her just in case she might accidentally lose her hold on the baby. Then Bertha nestled Holly in Anna's outstretched arms.

Both Rachel and Bertha stood poised, ready to catch the infant in case Anna was not able to hold onto her, but it was not needed. Anna cuddled the baby girl and began to hum a little tune to her while Holly solemnly regarded Anna while sucking on her pink pacifier.

"We have kitties," Anna whispered to the baby girl. "They are out in the barn. They are too little to play with yet, but I will take you to see them when they're older."

She glanced up at Rachel. "Is that all right?"

"Yes, dear heart," Rachel said. "And I will go with you. We will show Holly the kittens together. Would you like that?"

"Oh, yes!" Anna said. "Like when you were little and we played together."

Bertha scooted an ottoman over for Anna to prop her feet on so she could be more comfortable. Anna's comment about how she and Rachel had played together stabbed at Bertha's heart.

Children loved Anna. For a long time after Rachel's parents' death, Anna had been ten-year-old Rachel's preferred confidante. Then, like all the other children in Anna's life, Rachel had eventually outgrown her. There was still a great love between them, but Rachel began to function in the adult work world, and Anna was not able to follow.

Now it was Anna and Bobby who were pals. He was a kind little boy, but he would also grow up. Bertha just hoped that Anna could live long enough and with enough health that she could be a playmate for Holly when she got a little older. Anna was magical with children.

That was the thing about life. It seemed there was always something clutching at her heart. More so every year. When she was younger, she had been stronger. She would weep at some heartbreak, and then she would square her shoulders and go on. Now, not so much. Bertha had endured a lot, but the one thing she did not think she could stand was watching Anna's health deteriorate. She could not bear to lose her. None of them could.

"I should be back about eleven." Rachel smoothed a finger over Holly's cheek.

"I know," Bertha said. "We'll be fine."

"Next week, I'll have the morning shift, and Joe will be able to babysit. It is nights that are hard for him. That's when they have the biggest crowds."

"Having so many people wanting to eat at Joe's restaurant is a gift from God," Bertha said. "That is what we prayed for."

"Do you think we might have prayed too hard?" Rachel gave a soft chuckle. "It takes everything Joe and his brother can do to keep up with it all."

Bertha smiled at Rachel's joke, but she kept a close eye on Anna. Her younger sister seemed to be already tiring.

"I need to go." Rachel said. "Thanks again. For everything."

Bertha noticed that her niece thumbed tears from the corner of her eyes as she walked out the door.

Selfishly, she was pleased that leaving the baby was hard on Rachel. Her most fervent prayer was that Joe's restaurant would do so well that Rachel would quit her job as a cop.

She had never approved of Rachel's choice of work. It hurt to see her only niece walking around wearing a gun.

Unfortunately, Rachel had taken after her father, Frank, Bertha's younger brother. Instead of becoming Amish, he married an *Englisch* girl and then astonished everyone by entering the police academy.

She continued to mourn this action of her brother's. Had he not chosen that profession, he might still be alive. Being a cop in Sugarcreek wasn't as dangerous as working in a larger city, but things still happened.

Preferring not to think about the death of her younger brother, she concentrated on this beautiful infant with which the Lord had chosen to gift their family. Holly was perfection.

It wasn't that Bertha particularly valued beauty, although Holly was undoubtedly lovely. What she still craved, even after all these years, was the sight of a well-nourished, healthy baby. It did her heart good to see little rolls of fat on a babies' legs and arms.

She also loved seeing their little round bellies well-filled with nourishing warm milk. Last Sunday, one of the young mothers left worship to nurse her baby in an upper room of the home where they were meeting, and when she came back down the stairs, the child was so charmingly milk-drunk, Bertha completely lost track of the minister's sermon.

Lydia came inside after cleaning up the mess that the Englisch boy had left in the pie house. Her face softened when she saw Anna holding baby Holly.

"We are so blessed," Lydia said.

"We are," Bertha agreed.

It occurred to Bertha that Lydia had always been the happier of the two of them. If there was even a hint of a silver lining in a situation, Lydia would find it. If she couldn't find one, she had a remedy. She would bake to excess.

Some people drank or took drugs or went to see counselors when they were sad. Lydia chose to make heavenly works of edible art instead. She would go into the kitchen, and soon, four or five dozen cookies would be packed up ready to take over to the Amish school as a surprise for the children. When she returned from delivering them, Lydia's mood would be sunny again.

Lydia also noticed that Anna was starting to tire. Quickly, she sat down close to her and asked if she could hold little Holly now.

"Uh-huh." Anna's face showed relief as she handed the baby over. "You can have a turn."

"Can I get you something?" Bertha asked Anna. "A snack? Something to drink?"

"No." Anna shook her head.

"Are you feeling okay?" Bertha asked.

"I'm just sleepy." Anna shoved the ottoman away, stood up slowly, and struggled a moment for her balance. "I think I'll go to bed now.

As she plodded up the stairs, Lydia and Bertha exchanged looks.

"She's not getting any better," Lydia stated the obvious. "It might be time to take her to the doctor again."

"I'm thinking the same thing," Bertha said. "Although I dread what he might have to say."

"Don't expect trouble before you know it exists. Maybe the doctor will just increase her medicine."

"I think the medicine might be part of her sleepiness."

"Oh." Lydia pondered this for a while. Then, just like Bertha knew she would, Lydia said, "*Gellasenheit.*"

"God's will?" Bertha said. "Of course, we will accept God's will, but I still want to discuss her medication with the doctor."

"Of course," Lydia said. "But we must prepare ourselves to accept whatever God sends."

It was the way of the Amish to accept all things, both good and bad, as *Gellasenheit,* or God's will. It was a fatalistic mentality that had served them well. Lydia often accepted unquestioningly whatever she perceived as the will of God, even if it was heart-breaking.

Bertha, not so much. This was yet another struggle in a long list of spiritual failures throughout her life. In her opinion, if it was God's will to take Anna, she was not going to accept His decision easily.

CHAPTER 9

Sugarcreek
1959

It was late summer and windy as Bertha walked home from work. Brightly colored leaves swirled about in the air. Her steps were light because her dad had said yes to her and Lydia's request. She had been looking forward to talking with their new neighbor, Sophie Young, all day. Her only fear was that Sophie might have already filled the position. Bertha chastised herself for not having jumped at it the minute Sophie mentioned it.

As she came around a corner, Bertha saw that Sophie was struggling against the wind to peg her family's clothes onto the clothesline. She was dressed in baggy purple shorts and a white t-shirt. Her hair was all up in pink plastic curlers.

The first thing that struck Bertha was that if she ever put her thick hair up in pink plastic curlers, it wouldn't dry for a week. The second thought was surprise that any self-respecting woman would hang clothes out this late in the afternoon. Every Amish woman she knew would be embarrassed if they didn't have their laundry hung out long before eight o'clock on a Monday morning. Earlier, if at all possible.

But that was the way of the Englisch. One never knew what those people might take it in their heads to do or when. There didn't seem to be a lot of order in their lives.

As she walked toward her new neighbor, she hoped the wind would dry the clothes before nightfall, although she'd seen a few non-Amish allow their wet clothing to hang out all night long. Such a thing would have humiliated her mother beyond bearing.

"Hello!" Sophie saw Bertha and happily waved her over. She didn't seem embarrassed in the slightest that Bertha had caught her hanging out her laundry at four o'clock in the afternoon...in shorts and pink curlers. "Have you found anyone to help me clean house?"

She pulled a wet sheet out of her laundry basket and snapped it open, ready to peg it to the clothesline. Sheets were a little tricky to hang without accidentally dragging them in the dirt. Especially on a windy day.

"Yes." Bertha caught one edge of the sheet and held it off the ground while Sophie anchored it with a clothespin. "I'll do it."

"You?" Sophie reached for a washcloth and hung it on the line beside the sheet. "I thought you already had a job."

"I do, but the store where I work closes early on Saturdays, and I can stop by on my way home."

Sophie pulled a bath towel out of the basket, and Bertha cringed. Didn't the woman know that she was supposed to hang her laundry longest to shortest? Sheets came first—all of them—then bath towels, then hand towels, then dish towels, and then washcloths! The symmetry was pleasing to the eye and served to let any passerby know with one glance that the woman running the household knew what she was doing!

"That should work." Sophie seemed utterly nonplussed by the fact that her laundry line looked like it had been hung up by an unsupervised three-year-old. "They've just put me on full-time at the hospital, and I could really use the help."

"You work at the hospital?" Bertha felt her throat tighten with interest. She hadn't really known much about their new neighbor except she was

Englisch, had no children, was unmarried, and yet thought she needed help with keeping her house clean.

"Yes," Sophie said. "I'm a registered nurse. I work in the emergency room."

Bertha's heart swelled with envy. What would it feel like to be able to say that? What would it be like to have this Englisch *woman's skill and training?*

Her mind overflowed with questions. How did one become a nurse? Where did one go? How much schooling? How long would it take? Was it even possible for someone like her, with only an eighth-grade education, to become one?

She dare not ask. Asking would be as great a sin as doing. If she asked anything about what it took to become a nurse, and if her father found out about it...

Actually, she didn't know what he would do, but she was sure it wouldn't be good. First of all, he would forbid it. No doubt about that. Dreaming of becoming a nurse was about as ridiculous as thinking she could fly to Mars. Amish girls did not become RN's. Everyone knew that.

"Then it's settled." The Englisch woman took the last item of laundry out of the basket, a white pillowcase, and hung it beside another washcloth before glancing at her watch. "I'd love to chat, but I need to be leaving soon. I'm working the night shift this month."

Bertha couldn't help it. She blurted out the question burning in her mind before she could stop. "How did you become a nurse?"

Sophie cocked her head to one side. "I went to the Massillon Community Hospital School of Nursing."

"Is it far from here?"

"About forty-five minutes by car. Why do you ask?"

Bertha's thoughts were too muddled to share. She couldn't entertain the idea of more schooling, let alone getting a nursing degree. It was out of the question. A silly fantasy.

"Oh, nothing," Bertha said. "I was just curious."

"I'll see you tomorrow afternoon, then." The Englisch woman picked up her empty laundry basket and went back inside.

Bertha felt like crying from frustration. She might not be a great maker of quilts like Lydia, but she knew she had the strength, stamina, and heart for nursing. She had known she had a gift for it ever since she was a child.

In addition to knowing she had a gift for it, the thing that kept gnawing at her mind was the fact that she did have a choice. She was not yet truly Amish. Not officially. She had taken the classes required for becoming Amish, and a baptism ceremony was scheduled for next month. That baptism would represent the line of demarcation for her from being raised Amish to actually becoming Amish. Until that moment, she had a choice. Once she crossed that line, though, all options would be closed. Once she formally became Amish, she could be shunned for going against the church rules. If she decided to go to nursing school after baptism, her mother, father, sister, and brother would no longer be allowed to speak to her or even share a meal with her.

Choosing not to become Amish was not quite as harsh as leaving the church after one was baptized, but it would still bring about relational hardships. She would never again enjoy the close friendship and companionship she had now with those of her church. Her people might be polite and even kind—although she'd heard some terrible stories about those who chose to leave—she would be considered Englisch from the day she made her decision.

Charlotte's letter, with its pitiful recipe for dirt cookies, tugged at her heart, but it could not help her decide which way she should go. If only she knew for sure God's will for her life.

One thing she did know. The image of children eating dirt cookies would never leave her. She also knew deep within her heart that with the proper training, she could make a small difference in that unfortunate country.

Life would be so much easier if God would just send her a letter telling her what He wanted her to do. She would gladly obey whatever He said. No matter what the sacrifice.

She was almost at her doorstep when a new thought struck so powerfully that she stumbled from the impact of it. Perhaps God had already sent her a letter—the one from Charlotte about dirt cookies. Maybe the reason she couldn't stop thinking about it was that the message had been from Him all along. It had just taken her a while to recognize it.

CHAPTER 10

Calvin had lived with his grandmother in a small suburb of Chicago most of his short life. He did not remember his mother or his father. From what he had been told, a bad guy had broken into their home and taken their lives. Calvin was only a few months old, asleep in his bed, and left unharmed.

When Grandma got sick, there weren't any other close relatives to take Calvin in. They did not have a large family. A few months before she died, she had asked his cousin, Alex, to promise he would look after Calvin when the time came. Alex had given his word.

Calvin remembered Grandma being so relieved.

"He's a good man, Calvin," she said. "You will be safe with him."

Calvin wasn't worried about being safe. He was upset that his Grandma was sick, and then after she died, he was upset that her cozy house and contents had to be sold, and then after her house sold, he was upset that he had to go live in Alex's downtown apartment.

There was no yard where Alex lived. Calvin didn't like that. He was used to having a yard to play in. Grandma had owned a cherry tree in her back yard with branches so low that Calvin could climb them. When the cherries were ripe, there was nothing he loved more than climbing up into the tree and eating his fill. He would come back into the house with his face, hands, and mouth stained with cherry juice, and Grandma would laugh and tell him to save a couple of cherries for the birds.

Then at night, Grandma would sing him to sleep with one of her story-songs. In cherry season, it was usually the one about a little boy who didn't want to share his cherries with a little bird named Robin Redbreast.

He choked up just thinking about how good it had always made him feel having Grandma tuck him in at night and hear his prayers and sing him to sleep. He hoped he hadn't done anything to make her die.

It had been a simple relationship. Calvin loved his grandma, and she loved him back. Alex was okay, and he was trying to do his duty, but Calvin could tell that he didn't love him. In fact, he was pretty sure no one loved him now that Grandma was gone.

He'd only lived with Alex for three months. During those three months, an awful lot had happened. The biggest thing was something bad had happened in Alex's life. Calvin didn't know exactly what it was. All he knew was that suddenly Alex quit working and they moved to this place called Sugarcreek.

Calvin had a yard to play in now, but the house was old and ugly, and it smelled funny. Alex said it was what they could afford for now. When Calvin asked why they had to move to this town, Alex said it was because the crime rate was so low. He didn't want Calvin to get into trouble, and he thought living in this town might help.

It worried Calvin that he was already in trouble.

Starting school in a strange place in the middle of the winter while he was still grieving and disoriented from his grandmother's death made him feel empty inside. His grades weren't very good right now. He hadn't made any friends. Christmas had been dismal.

Calvin had many issues, but the biggest one bothering him right now was the big kids who had started picking on him on the school bus. Grandma had always driven him to school. He'd never had to fend for himself before. He didn't know how. These days it felt easier just to walk the mile home, even if it was really cold.

Of course, if he hadn't been walking instead of taking the bus, he wouldn't have smelled the pies, wouldn't have been tempted to sneak a taste, and wouldn't have gotten into trouble.

Oh, how he regretted eating that pie! He wasn't sure what Alex might do if he discovered that he was harboring a thief. Would he turn him over to children's services? Would he put Calvin in the foster system? Calvin had known a couple of foster kids at his old school, and they didn't seem very happy about their situation.

Alex was a terrible cook, but he tried to be kind whenever he came out of his fog long enough to notice he had a small boy living with him. If Alex ever decided he didn't want him around anymore, Calvin didn't know what would become of him.

"You aren't eating your pizza," Alex pointed out after they'd ordered and been served at the Park Street Pizza, not far from their house. "It's pretty good. Are you sure you're feeling okay?"

"Sure." Calvin took a big bite of pizza that he didn't want. "I'm fine."

He hoped Alex wouldn't suspect that he'd spoiled his dinner with a stolen pie. He feigned enjoyment. "This is really good pizza!"

Alex looked at him quizzically, as though he knew Calvin might be fibbing.

Calvin continued to chew with enthusiasm and forced himself to swallow. With any luck, he wouldn't throw up. With any luck, Alex would never find out what he had done.

He hoped they would go home soon. Bedtime couldn't come soon enough when a boy was ten and burdened with a guilty conscience.

CHAPTER 11

Sugarcreek
1959

"What's a GED?" Bertha said.

"GED stands for General Educational Development." Sophie sat at the kitchen table folding clean dish towels while Bertha ironed. The iron was electric and had a cord, which felt awkward to Bertha, but she was gradually getting used to it.

"Never heard of it." Bertha finished pressing one of Sophie's white nursing uniforms and carefully hung it on a wire hanger. She held it up and admired it. What would it feel like to have the right to wear one of these?

"It was originally used for soldiers who quit school so they could fight in World War II. The government didn't think it right for those men to have to go sit in a high school classroom before they could be admitted to college." Sophie finished folding the dish towels, then rose and placed them in a kitchen drawer.

Bertha pulled another uniform out of the laundry basket and sprinkled water on it from a metal sprinkler with a cork that Sophie stuck in the end of a water-filled pop bottle. It worked well. Bertha was learning quite a lot from her new employer.

"But I'm not a soldier."

"No," Sophie said. "You are an Amish woman with only eight grades of schooling. You have no idea if you can do college-level work until you take and pass that test, and neither will the Massillon School of Nursing."

That seemed sensible.

"But what if I can't pass it?"

"Then, I don't think you can become a nurse."

"Is the GED hard?" Bertha unplugged the iron, sat it on a cold stove burner to cool, folded up the ironing board and put it in a narrow closet in Sophie's kitchen.

"I have no idea," Sophie said. "I never had to take it, but I'll find out what you have to do."

"My father will be really angry if he finds out."

"Then, don't tell him. You are nineteen years old," Sophie said, patiently. "You are not a child. We are talking about a test. A piece of paper. There is nothing wrong with finding out if you are capable of passing it. You can worry about college and your dad later."

"If my bishop hears..."

"Who is going to tell him?" Sophie said. "Not me."

"Let me think about it," Bertha said.

"Of course," Sophie said. "Take your time. But if you decide you want to become a nurse badly enough to do this, I'll help you study for it."

Bertha filled the sink with soapy water and began washing the dishes that had piled up during the week. She thought about it until the dishes were washed, dried, and put away. She thought about it while she wiped off the counters and mopped the floor. She thought about it while she scrubbed Sophie's bathroom until it gleamed.

Even taking the GED test would cause talk and gossip among her people if they found out what she was doing. And they would find out. Sophie had no idea how enmeshed and nosy her people could be about one another.

Somehow, someway, they would see something and begin to wonder what she was up to.

As Sophie said, she was nineteen. What that meant among her people was that it was time for her to start getting serious about some young Amish man and begin to plan a life with him. Studying for a high school equivalency test pointed at aspirations an Amish girl had no business having.

It wasn't just her who would be affected. If it got out among her people that she was considering becoming a nurse, her mother and father would have to deal with gossip and questions. If she spoke aloud her wish to become a registered nurse, it would bring about a flood of comments—all negative. Her parents would immediately fear that their daughter was contemplating the worst action imaginable—becoming Englisch.

The Amish had no prejudice against knowledge. They were well-read people. It was the getting of it in a high school and college setting that set off alarms. Those places were seen as filled with much dangerous knowledge as well as good.

Her people admired and appreciated the doctors and nurses who treated them. Still, such was their fear for their own children's adherence to their faith, the possibility of further formal education was forbidden.

Bertha wasn't sure she could withstand the pressure that would be brought to bear on her decision, but oh, how she wanted to try!

CHAPTER 12

Snow had not been predicted, but snow they got. Rachel kept the squad car running as she called the wrecker to come for a gray Toyota Camry that had slid off the road and hit a telephone pole. There had been some damage to the front bumper, and the airbags had deployed, but the four college students inside were unharmed. The license tags were from Akron, and the students were carpooling back to a university she had never heard of in Arkansas.

She suspected alcohol to be a factor and was pleasantly surprised when it wasn't. The kids were respectful and polite. The only problem was that the driver hadn't been skilled enough driving on slick roads.

As the windshield wipers marked time, it reminded Rachel of the metronome her mother had kept on the top of the piano long ago, where every day she was expected to practice during the longest fifteen minutes in her short life. She had been four, which was the same year her mother had died. She barely remembered her, and she suspected that the memories she did have were mainly drawn from a faded photo album that Bertha had held onto for her.

Considering the Amish dislike for photographs, the fact that Bertha had retained the photo album spoke volumes about her aunt.

There were times when Bertha seemed to be more Amish than anyone Rachel knew—like her aunt's continued disapproval for Rachel's job. Her aunt's pacifism went so deep, she seldom missed a chance to voice her opinion about the fact that Rachel's work required her to carry a gun.

On the other hand, Rachel knew that there had been a time in Bertha's youth when she had rebelled against her Amish church to the point of leaving it so that she could obtain the nursing degree she wanted.

Years later, she came home and made the kneeling confession that would allow her to return and be accepted into her parents' Amish church. Rachel knew It made it easier to care for her aging parents without censor, but still, it must have taken a great deal of humility.

Sometimes it felt as though she knew Bertha better than anyone. Then Bertha would say or do something that would surprise her. There was much about Bertha's life that remained a mystery.

For instance, the fact that Bertha had never married. It certainly hadn't been for lack of interest on the part of the local Amish men. Rachel remembered the strained irritation Bertha had shown in the presence of any man who presumed to try to court her.

Yes, Bertha was a puzzle, but she was also a rock in Rachel's life. No matter what happened, as long as Bertha was living, Rachel knew she could count on her for help.

Bertha and Lydia had raised her, loved her, disciplined her, taught her, and nursed her back to health after the beating she'd endured breaking up a domestic dispute while working as a cop in Cleveland.

There had been bandages to change, broken bones to heal, and a depression so deep she could hardly speak for weeks. Lydia made nourishing broth and tempted her with easy-to-eat meals, Bertha had bossed and bullied her out of her self-pity, ultimately making her so angry she ended up fighting her way back to normalcy—just to show Bertha she could!

Which was, of course, Bertha's intention.

Now, Bertha was caring for little Holly way past her own bedtime. It wasn't fair.

It made Rachel feel even more determined to have that talk with Ed about finding someone to replace her on the force. It was her place to raise her daughter, not Bertha's. Her aunt had done enough. She deserved to rest.

Her thoughts were interrupted by a call from the dispatcher. A possible break-in at a private residence. Rachel did a U-turn in the middle of route 93 and headed toward the address she was given.

Her aunts would have to care for little Holly awhile longer, and Rachel was not happy about it.

CHAPTER 13

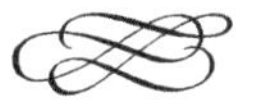

Sugarcreek
1959

"You'll get no money from me for this!" Her father's face was red with anger. "Don't expect me to support you."

Bertha thought of the hard labor she had done for him over the years, as well as handing him every dime she made from her job at the store.

"I never expected anything from you, Daett." She wondered if he realized how true that was.

"The members of our church will say that I do not have control over my daughter."

"I'm nineteen, Daett," she said, wearily, hoping this conversation would be over soon. She had already seen her high score on the GED dismissed as nothing by him. Worse than nothing. Sophie, however, had been impressed, as had the college counselor.

"You were supposed to be baptized next week," Daett said. "Do you want to go to hell?"

"No, Daett," she said. "I just want to go to Haiti."

"Haiti!" he thundered. "Why?"

"Because that country is already hell for many who live there."

His voice turned deadly. "Do not blaspheme in this house."

"I am not blaspheming. I'm speaking the truth!"

Out of the corner of her eye, she saw Lydia and her mother standing just inside the door, their mouths agape. She didn't blame them. Theirs was not the kind of family who shouted.

"You will obey me in this, daughter," he said. "You will give up the notion of becoming a nurse. That is not a proper choice for a daughter of mine."

"And if I disagree?"

"If you continue on this path..." Her father hesitated.

Bertha could tell that he was carefully weighing the impact of his next words. She held her breath, praying he would not say what she feared, he would say.

"You will no longer be welcome in my home."

Lydia gasped in disbelief, and Maam cried out as though in pain.

Her father shot a stern look at her mother, daring her to say a word against his decree.

"From the time I was born..." Bertha also hesitated, choosing her words carefully, "I have been taught to be obedient. I learned to obey Maam, and you. I learned obedience to the bishop and the Ordnung of the church. But I have also been taught that above all else, I am to be obedient to God. In choosing to get my nursing license and go to Haiti, I am obeying God. I believe He set it in my heart to do this hard thing and I cannot do otherwise. I believe it would be a sin to disobey."

Her father, unable to answer such an argument, broke her heart by turning his back on her. She waited for a kind word of reconciliation or at least acknowledgment, but instead, he stared out the window with his back rigid with anger or disappointment. She wasn't sure which.

That night she lay beneath sheets she had previously washed and ironed and tucked onto the twin bed in Sophie's second bedroom. Her cheeks felt itchy from the tears drying on her face.

Her heart felt strangely light, though. The moment she had dreaded had come and gone. It had been even worse than she had anticipated, but it was over now. She would continue to honor and love her father and mother, but she would also embrace what the nursing school had to teach her. When she was finished, she would use that knowledge to help sick and starving children.

Gellasenheit was the last word she thought of before she fell into an exhausted sleep

CHAPTER 14

Bertha walked the floor with baby Holly, glancing out the front window at the darkness every few minutes hoping Rachel would come soon. Apparently, she had been forced to work longer than she expected.

The wind had picked up, and the snow started shortly after Rachel left. That could mean slick roads and wrecks. Bertha tried not to worry as she walked the floor, hoping to get the baby back to sleep. Newborns were sweet, but they could be cranky. Especially at night.

Sometimes it seemed like she had struggled against worry her whole life despite believing worry was a sin. In fact, she had long ago concluded that worry was sometimes a manifestation of superstition. Instead of praying, or problem-solving, people subconsciously attempted to keep bad things from happening by worrying about them. Such was human nature.

Try as she might, she could never entirely lose that weakness.

Still, she had used up the formula Rachel left for Holly, and she had no idea what to do if the baby got hungry again before her mother came home.

Was that a car she heard? It was hard to tell with snow on the ground. It often cushioned the sound of tires. She checked out the window and saw that it was, indeed, her hard-working niece. She opened the door, and Rachel blew in with the wind and snow, apologizing.

"I'm so sorry, Bertha." Rachel glanced at the clock just as it began to strike midnight. "I received a call about a possible break-in, and I had to go investigate. It took longer than I expected."

"Is everyone okay?"

"Yes."

Rachel stomped the snow off her boots onto the braided rug Lydia kept in front of the door for that very purpose. Then she gently lifted a drowsy Holly from Bertha's arms. As she did so, it was all Bertha could do not to sigh with relief. It had been a terribly long day.

"It was an elderly couple," Rachel said. "I don't think you know them. The wife was already sound asleep when her husband decided to go outside to check the thermometer to see how cold it was. The screen door had one of those old-fashioned hook fasteners. When it closed behind him, it accidentally locked him out. He was only wearing his pajamas."

"That is dangerous," Bertha said. "It's below freezing outside! Is he okay?"

"When I got there, he was already inside, but he'd given his wife quite a scare. When he couldn't wake her up by pounding on the door, he went around to the bedroom window and started knocking on it. The blinds were pulled. She couldn't see that it was him, and it just about scared her to death."

"They were *Englisch*?" Bertha asked.

"Yes."

"It is a wonder she didn't shoot him," Bertha said. "*Englisch* people are sometimes too quick to shoot."

"True, but she called the police instead," Rachel said. "I'm the one who got the call. That's why I'm late. I had to get both of them calmed down and make sure he wasn't going into hypothermia. He'd been out there on the porch longer than was healthy for a man his age."

Bertha was distracted as the baby started to fuss again.

"We are out of formula," Bertha said. "I think she's hungry. You'll need to hurry and get her home."

"Of course," Rachel said. "I'm still figuring things out about how much formula to pack. Were there any other problems?"

"I will admit it took Lydia and me awhile to figure out how to put those disposable diapers on her. Holly was patient with us two old women as we fumbled around. The last time I took care of an infant, it was with cloth diapers." Bertha laughed at herself. "But Lydia and I are quite up-to-date now!"

"But are you okay?" Rachel asked, concerned. "Has this tired you out too much?"

"I am fine," Bertha scoffed. "Don't worry about me. I am pleased to be able to help. It has been a joy caring for this sweet child."

"Well, okay." Rachel sounded doubtful. "But thanks so much. I'll let you go to bed now."

Bertha stood at the door until Rachel got Holly securely strapped in. She waved as Rachel pulled out, not wanting her niece to know how drained she felt.

That was one of the most annoying things of all about growing older. One had so much less stamina.

There had been a time when she could toil all day in a shelter covered with nothing but a corrugated tin roof upon which the hot Haitian sun broiled down. Many days she could have cooked a steak on that roof had she wanted to, and if she'd had a steak. Which she didn't. Meat of any kind was hard to find, and much of what was available she didn't trust. There had been outbreaks of anthrax. Owners were often so poor and desperate, they sold diseased animals.

Tonight, being a full three hours past her usual bedtime, she fully expected to drop off to sleep the moment her head touched the pillow, but it didn't work out that way. Sometimes, if she got overly tired, her mind would refuse to turn off, and her thoughts would skitter about like Anna's chickens trying to catch an influx of buzzing June bugs. Too much had happened today, and her mind kept turning things over and over.

The combination of the Amish children sharing their lunch with her, that ragamuffin Englisch boy who had eaten one of Lydia's pies, and then having run out of formula for Holly with no easy way to get more until Rachel returned home--had left her lying in bed, staring at the dark ceiling, remembering the precious, dark-skinned, emaciated babies she had held in her arms and tried to save. It wasn't something one got over in a day...or a lifetime.

It had bothered her more deeply than she had allowed Rachel to know that she had run out of formula for Holly. She didn't like dealing with a hungry baby.

Food made such a difference. Food was everything. There had been times in Haiti when she would have gladly traded her hard-won nursing knowledge just for enough to feed all the hungry children for a day.

It took her well past midnight to settle herself enough to finally go to sleep.

CHAPTER 15

Massillon, Ohio
1959

"Do you know how to make soup?" Miss Ella Cummings, a former head nursing instructor at Massillon School of Nursing, now in her mid-eighties and confined to a wheelchair, was cranky and rude, and Bertha wondered if she had made a terrible mistake applying for a position working for this woman.

The problem was—without a job and an inexpensive place to stay, there was no way she could afford to go to school. Period. Ella Cummings, with no one to help care for her, was offering room, board, and a small salary—but only to a nursing student. It had sounded like the perfect solution until Bertha met her.

"Yes," Bertha said. "I can make soup."

"I doubt it." Ella shook her head. "The last girl they sent me barely knew her rear end from a hole in the ground, let alone how to make a good potato soup."

"I can make good potato soup," Bertha replied.

It was true. Bertha wasn't the cook that her sister was. Lydia had a special gift in the kitchen, but Bertha was more than competent.

The woman made a rude sound of derision. "Betcha you don't."

Bertha put her hands on her hips. This was going to be interesting. "Betcha I do."

Ella blinked. "Then don't stand there like some big ninny. Prove it. Potatoes are under the sink. Celery, butter, onion in the refrigerator. Milk, too. You got one-half hour to bring me a bowl of soup, or I'll ask them to send me another fresh young thing who thinks she knows something."

With a huff, the old woman wheeled herself into the living room, where she turned on the TV too loudly.

Thirty minutes. Not much time to turn raw potatoes into soup, but Bertha was reasonably sure she could do it. First, she turned the hot water faucet on, as well as an electric burner to heat up while she hunted for a pot. She found one with a lid in an upper cabinet. She filled it with hot water and put it on the burner. The sooner it boiled the better chance of getting the potatoes cooked through.

While the already hot water quickly came to a boil, she peeled and diced the potatoes into the boiling water. While the potatoes boiled, she heated a cast iron skillet, threw a stick of butter in, chopped up a couple of stalks of celery with half an onion, and threw everything into the butter to fry.

While she waited for everything to cook, she saw a half-bag of flour on the counter and got an idea. If there was an egg or two in the refrigerator, she would make egg noodles. Once rolled out and cut, they cooked in boiling water in seconds.

There were two eggs. By the time Bertha whipped together the eggs, flour, and salt into a stiff dough, she noticed the celery and onion had turned translucent. She scraped them, along with the butter in which she had sautéed them, into the water.

The kitchen was beginning to steam up from the rapidly boiling water, and the aroma of onions, celery, and butter was in the air. While they cooked, she rolled out the egg noodle dough and cut it into thin ribbons, which she lifted with a knife into the boiling water. Twenty minutes in, she watched the noodles puff up as they cooked.

Freshly made egg noodles were much tenderer than store-bought ones. It was the way she preferred to have her potato soup, but perhaps Ella didn't like noodles. Some people said they didn't, although Bertha thought that was foolish talk. How could anyone not enjoy homemade noodles?

The combination of well-cooked, falling-apart diced potatoes and the excess flour that had fallen off the noodles, thickened the soup liquid. Bertha turned off the burner and poured in just enough whole milk to make the consistency of the soup perfect. Some salt and pepper. She tasted it. More salt and pepper. Something was missing.

She went back to the refrigerator and found a small jug of cream. She poured in a half of a cup, stirred and then tasted it again. Yes, that was it. The soup was delicious now, and she would dare anyone to say it wasn't.

A decorative tray was sitting on the counter. She ladled soup into a big bowl, laid out a soup spoon and cloth napkin, filled a glass with water from a pitcher in the fridge, and carried it into the living room.

"Where would you like me to set this?" she asked.

Ella looked at the clock on the wall, as did Bertha. They both saw the same thing. Bertha had brought the tray in with five minutes to spare.

"Put it on the table here beside me," Ella said, picking up a spoon. "You're fast, I'll give you that much, but speed doesn't necessarily mean it'll be any good."

Bertha said nothing. She stood with her arms folded and waited.

Ella dipped her spoon in.

"You made noodles?" she asked, surprised.

"That's how I prefer it," Bertha said. "I thought you might like it that way, too."

Ella studied Bertha over her glasses. "You have an accent. I can't place it."

"I was raised Amish."

The old woman took another spoonful of potato-noodle soup.

"Of course. That would explain it, then."

"Explain what?"

"The noodles." Ella pointed at the bowl of soup. "You got any objection to using electric?"

"None."

"You engaged?"

"No."

"Got a boyfriend?"

"No."

"Why do you want to be a nurse?

"Because there aren't enough good ones to go around, are there?" Bertha said. "Especially in a country like Haiti."

"That's what you have your sights on?" Ella asked.

"It is."

Two more bites of soup before Ella spoke again. "Haiti and her people will break your heart."

"I'm counting on it," Bertha said.

It was then that Ella's demeanor changed right before Bertha's eyes. Even the tone of her voice changed. Bertha got the impression that she was seeing the head nursing instructor Ella had been before age and infirmities had soured her.

"I had one other Amish-raised girl come to school who wanted to train to become a nurse," Ella said. "She was a hard worker, but some of the classes were nearly impossible for her to pass because she didn't have the science and math background most of the other girls did."

This was not good news. Could Bertha have gone through all she had just to find out that passing the GED wasn't enough? That she didn't have enough educational foundation to make it through?

"Did she have to drop out?" Bertha asked.

"No. The girl was a worker. She graduated with honors, just like you are going to do." Ella scraped the bottom of her bowl. "You want to know why?"

"Yes."

"Because I'm going to be here to help you. Chemistry will probably be one of the hardest hurdles for you, and I've always been deadly with that."

"Mrs. Cummings?"

"Call me, Ella, please."

"Does this mean I have the job?"

The old woman nearly choked on the last spoonful of soup.

"Of course you have the job. This is the best potato soup I've ever eaten. The bedroom at the top of the stairs is yours. Actually, the whole upstairs is yours since I can't go up there anymore. You'll pick up groceries for me, do some housekeeping, help me get ready for bed and then dressed again in the morning, plus probably keep me thoroughly entertained with your ignorance. For that, I will give you enough pocket money to take care of your personal needs, and foot the bill for your classes."

That was way more than Bertha had expected. She had been told she would only get room and board and would have to take on a second job to pay for her tuition. She felt her eyes start with tears and tried to force them back. "Are you sure?"

"Of course, I'm sure. Just don't start bawling about it." Ella looked at her with what Bertha came to think of as Ella's teacher stare. "I turned out top-notched nurses for more years than I can count. I still do. Only now, I do it one at a time."

CHAPTER 16

Calvin glanced around the elementary school cafeteria, undecided while holding his food tray and wondering where to sit. None of the tables looked particularly inviting. Everyone had friends except him. Of course, he'd only been living here a few weeks, but nothing was getting any better. The other kids all seemed to have known each other forever, and no one seemed inclined to get to know him.

Well then, he didn't want to know them, either.

He finally opted for one of the long tables in the far corner. Only two seats were taken, and those were occupied by a couple of the little kids. First graders. He sat down at the far end and looked at what the cafeteria ladies had put on his tray. It wasn't very inspiring. Mashed potatoes. Canned peas. A small brick of fish. An apple. A carton of chocolate milk.

He didn't like fish or canned peas. The mashed potatoes were okay, so he ate them, but when he was finished, he was still hungry, so he drank all the chocolate milk and took a bite out of the apple. It wasn't very sweet, so he swallowed the one mouthful and laid the apple back on his tray. He ate one pea. It was as tasteless as it looked. The fish—

well, he would have to be starving first. There was no way he was going to eat any of that fish.

It was going to be a long, hungry afternoon. Again. He hated this school.

All of this was new to him. When Grandma was alive, he didn't hate school at all. He liked it. She packed him a lunch, and she only put things in it that Calvin liked. He had friends there, too, and so did Grandma. She knew his teacher and attended every parent-teacher conference. She told him it was a joy to go to the meetings because his teachers always had good things to say about him and that made her even more proud of him.

"Hello."

Calvin glanced up. One of the first graders from the other end of the table was standing in front of him.

"My name is Bobby," the first-grader said. "What's yours?"

"Calvin," he said.

"Do you want this?" Bobby held up a small zip-lock baggie with a yummy-looking thick, chocolate square in it. "Daddy made brownies last night, and he put an extra one in my lunch."

"Don't you want it?" Calvin asked.

"Sure." Bobby shrugged. "But I've already had one, and Mommy says I need to learn to share because I got a new baby sister at home, so I'm practicing up."

A lump appeared in Calvin's throat at the first-grader's kindness. He managed to mumble out, "Thanks."

Don't be a baby, he told himself. Don't start crying.

He hoped the little kid would go away until he could get his voice under control.

That didn't happen. Bobby pulled out the chair across from him, sat down, crossed his arms on the table, and smiled. "What grade are you in?"

"Fourth."

"You're new."

"Yeah."

"Do you want to be friends?"

Be friends with a first grader?

"Yes." The word came out before he could even think.

"Good, 'cause my daddy says a man can never have too many friends,"

Calvin pulled the brownie out of the bag Bobby gave him and took a bite.

"Good, huh?" Bobby said.

Calvin, his mouth filled with brownie, nodded.

"My daddy is a good cook. He owns a restaurant in town."

Calvin thought longingly of what it might be like to have a dad who owned a restaurant.

"My mommy is a cop," Bobby continued to make conversation. "She's not my first mommy. My first mommy died, and then we came here, and then we met Rachel. She's my new mommy now."

On nothing more than the strength of a brownie and a first grader with a kind heart, Calvin made his first friend in Sugarcreek. It felt good until Bobby left to rejoin the other first-grader at his table, and Calvin remembered what Bobby had just said. His mom was a cop? Calvin's chewing slowed down. Didn't he just say he had a baby sister at home?

He did not want to see that woman cop who had caught him eating a stolen pie ever again. It might not be such a good idea to become friends with that little kid. In fact, maybe he didn't even need any friends. At least not in this stupid school.

He knew what he would do. The solution appeared to him like a revelation from God. He would become so tough inside he wouldn't care about anybody or anything. That's what he'd do from now on. Not care. Maybe then the loneliness wouldn't hurt so bad.

CHAPTER 17

Lydia cracked a fresh brown egg on the edge of the cast-iron skillet and dropped it into the hot melted butter where it sizzled. They had chosen to have a breakfast-for-lunch meal. This was something they often did when the inn had no guests. Today it was just the three of them.

"That's the last of the eggs," Lydia said. "Do you mind running out to the chicken coop and seeing if the hens laid any this morning, Anna?"

Anna, who was stroking her gray cat while seated in the kitchen rocker, didn't move. This was odd. She usually loved gathering eggs.

"Aren't you feeling well?" Bertha, who had been setting the table, stopped and studied her.

"I'm tired," Anna said.

"You just woke up from another long nap." Bertha's worry made her sound annoyed. "How can you be tired?"

Anna's lip started to quiver at this mild observation. Her baby sister was the sweetest, most loving person Bertha had ever known, but it was hard for Anna to deal with anything even remotely sounding like a reproach.

"That's okay, Anna." Lydia saw the quivering lip. She gave Bertha a quick look of concern, then pushed the skillet to the back of the wood stove where it was cooler. "I'll go gather the eggs. Anna, maybe you should go back to bed and rest until you feel stronger. I'll bring lunch up to you."

"Okay." Anna rose from the armchair and lumbered toward the living room.

"She's getting worse," Bertha said, as they watched their sister plod up the stairs.

"I know," Lydia said. "It's breaking my heart, but I don't know what to do about it."

"Her next regular doctor's appointment is in two months, but I think I'd better call and see if I can get something sooner."

Lydia pulled on her choring coat and tied her woolen scarf snuggly beneath her chin. "I'm starting to think it might be something more than her heart."

"Oh?" Although Bertha was the one with the medical background, there were times when Lydia could be quite insightful. "What do you think it is?"

"Do you remember the way I acted after my first miscarriage?"

Lydia had suffered several miscarriages during her marriage. She rarely mentioned that time in her life, although Bertha knew it had to have been devastating.

"I wasn't living here then," Bertha reminded her. "I was still in school."

"That's true," Lydia said. "And I didn't want to worry you, so I didn't say anything in my letters, but I got to where I didn't want to get out of bed. It wasn't physical, I just felt very tired and sleepy. I've read since that sad people sometimes tend to sleep a lot."

"You mean, you think Anna might be depressed?"

"Maybe. It's just a thought." Lydia shrugged as she went out the door. "But it's not her nature to act like this. Anna has always loved life, but now it's like all the joy has drained out of her."

Lydia was right. Anna's recent behavior was unusual for her. Of course, the cold winter days that kept them all cooped up inside the house was not helpful to anyone's psyche. Bertha was feeling a little down herself, but now that Christmas had passed, and there was nothing new to look forward to, it was like Anna had utterly lost her sparkle.

While Lydia gathered eggs, Bertha looked up the number of Anna's heart doctor in the telephone book, wrote the number on the back of a used envelope, then she donned her coat and boots and headed outside to the phone shanty at the end of their driveway.

It was time for her to call her niece and discuss her fears about Anna. It annoyed her when Rachel did not answer her phone. Bertha did not like leaving a message and kept it as short as possible.

"When you get a chance, I need to talk to you, Rachel. It's not an emergency, but…" Bertha hesitated. Then she hung up. There was so much more she wanted to say, trying to leave a message felt overwhelming.

With Rachel not available, Bertha called Anna's doctor's office and asked for the soonest date possible. However, the secretary answering the phone gave her the disturbing information that Anna's doctor had retired, and a new doctor was taking over his practice. This was not good news. She liked Anna's doctor. He was in his seventies, which made it easier for her to trust him. These new doctors coming into the area just kept looking younger and younger. Bertha wasn't at all sure that they actually knew anything. She preferred her doctors to have at least a few strands of gray hair.

CHAPTER 18

Massillon, Ohio
1963

Bertha Troyer sat stiffly on stage as the Dean of Nursing called the names of women awaiting graduation from the Massillon Community Hospital School of Nursing.

As she listened for her name, she scanned the crowd, hoping for a friendly face and knowing there would be none. Her cocky new nurses' cap, tilted at just the right angle, felt odd after having worn an Amish bonnet most of her life. She had to fight the desire to adjust it.

Her starchy white nurse's uniform felt odd, too, even though it fit her well. Maybe a little too well. Ever since she had begun wearing non-Amish clothes, she had attracted more attention than she wanted. There was something about her 5'11' body and natural white-blonde hair that made most men look twice. She didn't like the extra attention, but there wasn't much she could do about it. She hadn't been the one to choose the standard nurse's uniform.

The white stockings and garter belt had been a trial to get used to. One of the things about her former life that she missed was not being expected to wear any stockings. The long dresses did not require such a thing.

The nursing shoes, however, were very comfortable. They were not as comfortable as going barefoot, of course, which she had done most of her life, but they were necessary.

Her graduating class of twenty young women had drawn quite a crowd. The college auditorium was full of smiling faces, but not one person from her family had shown up. She did not really expect any of them to come, but she couldn't help hoping there would be someone in the crowd who would be proud of her and proud of what she had accomplished.

It had often struck her as ironic that she was basically considered the black sheep of the family now. Such a rebel she had been for wanting an education! Such a rebel she had been to follow her dream to become a nurse!

But it had been worth it.

If all went well, she would be stepping onto an airplane next week. Although she had not formally joined the Mennonite church, she had been in contact with Charlotte, the woman who had written the letter about the dirt cookies. Charlotte's husband had pulled strings with some of the leaders of the Mennonite group who supported the work done in Haiti. They had paid her and two other nurses' passage to Haiti.

The time had finally come. This was precisely what Bertha had fought for —a bigger life than what was expected of her back home. Marriage was all well and good, and she wanted all of that someday, but it was not the focus of her existence like it was with most of her childhood friends.

It wasn't until after she and all the other graduating nurses had walked across the stage to receive their diplomas, that she saw a black bonnet bobbing about in the crowd that was milling about. Her heart nearly stopped—could it be? Had someone from her church or family come to see her? She had sent a letter to her family, inviting them to her graduation, but she knew none of them would come. Lydia and her mother would want to, but would not be brave enough to go against Daett's wishes. Or at least that's what she had thought.

She felt like she was swimming upstream as she made her way through the crowd with people congratulating her all along the way. Then she saw her younger sister, Lydia, looking very small and lost standing there in her favorite dark purple dress, craning her neck to try to see.

Although they were not usually a demonstrative family, Bertha ran and hugged her. After four long years, it was so good to see a member of her family again.

"I had to come," Lydia said, as the crowd jostled around them.

"I'm so glad you did!" Bertha said. "I wish you had come long before."

"You know how it is," Lydia shrugged. "We are supposed to ignore you so you will come back to the church, to God."

For the first time, Bertha noticed how foreign Lydia sounded. For the first time, she realized that living among the Englisch during her years in college had changed even the way she heard her sister's voice. She had never noticed that Germanic lilt in her family's voices before. It had merely sounded normal.

"I do not need to be brought back to God," Bertha said, carefully. "I never left Him. In fact, I plan to serve Him even more in the coming months. I just heard yesterday, I've been selected to work at the hospital in Haiti, along with two other nurses I graduated with. I leave next week!"

Lydia's face registered shock. "I thought you would come back to us when you finished your nursing training. Everyone thought you would. I never dreamed you would go through with your plan to go to Haiti. It is so very far away from us. What if something happens to you? How will we get to you?"

"I've worked too hard for this," Bertha said. "I can't move back home now. I know this is what God wants me to do. I can feel it."

"That's hochmut," Lydia chastised. "You have become prideful, my sister."

"I am not proud." Bertha felt hurt. She and Lydia had always been close. Lydia knew how strongly she felt about helping heal others. How could that be hochmut?

"I do not want you to go." Lydia looked like she might start crying.

"Let's not argue, Sister," Bertha said. "Come back with me to my room. Let me show you where I've been staying. I'll introduce you to my friend, Ella, who has been so good to me. Have you eaten? I'll make sandwiches. It

will be like old times again. We'll be together. I want to hear everything. All the details about what has been going on back home!"

Bertha had not realized how desperately she wanted to see her sister until Lydia stood before her. Oh, how she had missed her!

"I am sorry." Lydia shook her head. "I must get back. My Joseph will be finished with his auction at Mt. Hope soon and wanting his dinner."

"How did you get here?"

"Joseph is such a kind man. He understood my need to see my sister. He said that I could come to the auction with him. Then when we got there, he hired an Englisch driver from Mt. Hope to bring me to your college. None of our people know that I came. I told them that I was going to the auction with Joseph—and I did. I did not lie. But I did not tell them that I would also be coming here." Lydia looked around the auditorium. "This school you chose is a big place. I did not know where to go. I almost missed the graduation. I got lost twice and had to ask directions. Now I must go."

Bertha saw something akin to fear in Lydia's eyes. Her hopes of having a long talk together before she flew to Haiti wilted.

"I will walk you back to the parking lot so you won't get lost again," Bertha said, gently. "Will your driver still be there?"

"I told him that I would not be long," Lydia said. "He will be waiting."

Bertha had long legs that could eat up a mile in fifteen minutes but she took small steps now, trying to have as much time with her sister as possible.

"Tell me about home," Bertha asked. "Is everyone well?"

"Yes," Lydia said. "Everyone is well. Maam sometimes cries from missing you, but she tries to hide it. Our little brother still asks about you. He keeps thinking you will come back. Daett does not mention you."

"I will write from Haiti," Bertha said. "Do you think Daett will let Maam and little Frank read my letters?"

"I think Daett will pretend not to care that you have written, that is the way he acts about the ones you have sent so far, but I think he misses you most of all."

"Only because I am as good as a man behind a plow," Bertha's voice sounded tinged with bitterness. "He misses his 'big girl's' muscles."

"That is not true. Daett cares for you and misses you terribly," Lydia said. "I've seen him secretly reading your letters, but he worries about your soul."

"Tell our father that my soul is just fine. I have the training and heart to help sick people feel better. It would be wrong for me to ignore it. God does not intend for us to bury the talents he has given us. That is scripture, Lydia."

"Such talk confuses me," Lydia said. "I like things to be simple. It is easier just to do what others say. I am not as brave as you."

"You are brave in your own way. How is our mother? Is it not almost time for her to deliver?"

"Oh! That's something I wanted to tell you about! She had the baby last week. A little girl named Anna. I did not write because I wanted to tell you myself."

"And all is well with the baby?"

"We aren't sure," Lydia said.

Bertha's heart sank. Her mother was thirty-seven. Not old, but not young either when it came to child-bearing.

"What's wrong with the bobli?"

"We think little Anna might be a...special baby."

Bertha's heart sank further. Her people often referred to children with various genetic issues as "God's special children."

"What is the problem?"

"She appears to be mongoloid," Lydia said. "But she is still too young for us to be certain."

"But she is loved?" Bertha said, hoping she knew the answer. With Daett, it was not always easy to predict.

"Of course," Lydia said. "Very much so."

Bertha noticed that Lydia did not look as well as she could. There was a pallor about her, and dark circles beneath her eyes.

"You are not well," Bertha said. "What is wrong?"

"It is nothing," Lydia said.

"You are not speaking the truth."

"I had another miscarriage last week," Lydia said. "It was early, but still..."

Bertha's heart dropped at this news. The one thing in the world that Lydia wanted was a child.

"Another miscarriage?" Bertha said. "How many have you had?"

"Two," Lydia began to cry. "I wish you were not leaving. I wish you would come home and join the church. Haiti is so far away. I'm afraid something will happen, and I will never see you again."

"It will be all right," Bertha tried to comfort her sister. "I will write often."

"Bad things happen in places like Haiti," Lydia said. "I've read that there are people who practice something called Vodou. You will be in danger."

"I will be fine," Bertha reassured her. "I'm healthy and strong, and the people there will value a trained nurse. Even the people who do not believe in the same God as we do will respect someone who can help them feel better."

"Will you come home before you leave?" Lydia said. "To say good-bye?"

"I might end up in an argument with our father, which would not be respectful. It is better that I stay here until time to go."

"Not even to see baby Anna?" Lydia said. "She is so sweet."

Ah, their little sister. Bertha wanted to examine the infant herself and see if she was, in truth, a mongoloid baby.

Lydia was sobbing quietly as she climbed into the driver's car that Joseph had hired. It broke Bertha's heart.

Bertha waved to her, biting her lip to keep from crying also, as the car pulled away. It had been so kind of Joseph to allow her this moment with her sister to say good-bye. It had also been brave of Lydia to try to come. Her heart swelled with love for her family, but as the car drove out of sight, her mind moved to practical matters, and she began to enumerate the things she needed to pack before she left next week. It was no small thing to leave for what would be at least a two-year stay, especially when she did not know for sure what would be available to her on the island.

Ella had offered to purchase whatever she needed to take with her. It was a small bonus for her four years of excellent care, Ella had said. Now that Bertha knew Ella had family money behind her and wasn't paying her out of a small pension, she agreed with thanks.

Bertha tried to always be honest with herself. As she watched her sister's car drive out of sight, she realized Lydia's comment about being hochmut still stung. Perhaps it was because it was the truth. Deep in her heart, she felt like what she was doing was of much greater importance than what her mother and all the other Amish women she knew chose to do with their lives. That was wrong of her. Perhaps, she acknowledged to herself, she was a little hochmut after all.

CHAPTER 19

Sugarcreek
1963

In the end, Bertha could not bear to leave for such a long time without trying to see her family once more. She was not sure how she would be received. She didn't know if anyone would even speak to her, but that didn't matter. She needed to at least try.

As her hired driver drove her up the long driveway, her heart swelled at the sight of her beloved home. It was nothing more than a large, plain, farmhouse that her grandfather had built when he first came to Tuscarawas County, Ohio. But except for the time she had spent living with Ella, it had been the only real home she had ever known.

Within those walls, Lydia, Frank, and she had been born, had learned to walk, had been cuddled, and taught right from wrong. She loved that old house, and she loved the people within. If her father threw her out, then that was his decision. At least she would know she had tried.

All these thoughts raced through her mind as she climbed out of the driver's car pulling her two heavy suitcases behind her.

Those who did not formally embrace the Amish faith through baptism were often allowed some contact with their families. It was not exactly forbidden for her to make this journey back home, but having watched her church's treatment of a handful of others who chose not to become Amish, her expectations were not high.

Her family was sitting at the table, eating when she came through the door. Her mother's face lit up when she saw her, and then she saw her mother glance at her father to gauge whether or not she was allowed to show her joy. Her father was not a difficult man, he wasn't even a particularly stern man, but he was and had been very disturbed by his oldest daughter's rebellion.

She knew in some of the other men's minds at his church, it spoke of his lack of leadership. A father, they would think—and probably say—who was indeed the head of his family would not have raised a daughter who disobeyed by running off to nursing school.

"So, you have come home, daughter?" her father said, as she came through the door.

"For a short visit, only," she said. "My plane leaves tomorrow."

"Ah," he nodded. "So, you will be flying high in the sky where God never intended a man or a woman to be."

"That's what I am told."

Even though it had been four years since she had come home, her father did nothing more than shake his head with regret and continue to eat. Still, she was grateful he didn't immediately tell her to leave.

Four years had made a lot of changes in the family. Her brother, Frank, shoved his seat back and came to hug her. They had always been close when he was a little boy, but now he was no longer small. He came up to her shoulder, and he had been only about to her waist when she left. Such a fine-looking young man!

"So," Frank said, his voice cracking with either emotion or immature vocal cords—she wasn't sure which. "You have not come home to stay?"

"No." She smoothed Frank's hair back from his forehead. "But I would be grateful if my family could give me a bed for the night. I will leave early tomorrow."

The question hung in the air, unanswered by her father. The rest of the family waited tensely for his answer.

"You may stay if you wish," her father finally said. "I will not turn my daughter away from her home. Not when other Englischers come and go beneath my roof who are not so dear to me."

She felt her heart leap with gratitude! Not only was she allowed to spend the night, but he had also used loving words!

"Thank you, Daett," she said, humbled and grateful. "I will tell my driver it is all right to go."

Bertha went to the door to motion her driver to leave. The man acknowledged her with a wave as he drove away.

Her mother glanced at her father's face, questioningly. He nodded, giving her permission to rise and greet their daughter. She jumped to her feet, ran around the table, and grabbed Bertha's hand.

"Have you eaten?" she asked.

Bertha shook her head. "No."

"Come, come! Sit down. We have plenty. It will be so good to have my daughter's knees beneath my table again!"

Her mother grabbed a plate and cutlery from a cupboard.

"We have a baby sister!" Frank said. "Her name is Anna."

"How wonderful!"

"She's asleep," Frank said. "But I'll go get her!"

Bertha deliberately pretended to be surprised by the news about the baby. She did not want to have to explain about Lydia coming to her graduation and their conversation there. She wasn't sure how her father would react, and Lydia was so much more sensitive to criticism than she.

"I will make up your old bed that you shared with Lydia," her mother said. "It is where Lydia and her husband stay when they come for overnight visits."

Frank returned two-week-old Anna in his arms. He was obviously proud of his baby sister as he gently placed her in Bertha's arms.

Anna was tiny and precious, wrapped in a fluffy, white blanket. Her wisp of baby-fine hair was nearly non-existent as Bertha caressed the short strands.

"We have been wondering..." Her mother hesitated, as though needing to gather her courage before plunging on. "...if she might be one of God's special children."

Bertha had spent enough time in the nursery ward of her teaching hospital to know that Anna had what Dr. John Langdon Down had named Mongolism back in the 1800s. Sweet Anna was indeed what the Amish called one of God's very special children.

She opened her eyes now, looked up at Bertha, blinked, and Bertha lost her heart to her new baby sister. This one would need protection from the world as she grew older. Fortunately, little Anna had been born into a culture that would value and protect her. She would be loved and have a good life.

"Yes," Bertha said. "I would say that she is one of God's very special children."

Her mother accepted this diagnosis from her medically-trained daughter by merely lifting her chin and squaring her shoulders.

"Well then," her mother said. "That is that. God's will."

Frank resumed his seat. His plate was heaped with food, which she knew was part of growing so fast. Young boys had hollow legs, her grandmother had always said.

Bertha knew that the food had already been blessed, but the gratitude in her heart was so great that she bowed her head in silent prayer as well. She prayed for each member of her family, including her little sister.

"And where exactly will you go tomorrow when you get on the airplane and leave us again," her father asked, once she had finished her prayer and raised her head.

"Two other nurses and I will be landing in Port o' Prince tomorrow. After that, we will go wherever we are told we are needed."

"Haiti is severely impoverished," her father said. "Your work will not be easy."

"I am not afraid of hard work," she said. "You know that, Daett."

"True," he said, sadly. "I have missed your help."

"How long will you be?" Frank asked.

"I have agreed to stay for two years," she said. "Then I will be allowed a sabbatical for a month. I will determine then if I'm going back."

"I will be out of school by that time," Frank said.

"You will be a great help to our father," Bertha said. "I know he will welcome your full-time help with the farm."

She saw a cloud pass over Frank's face, and she wondered if her rebelliousness against church rules would hurt him. She hoped not. She admired and respected her family's culture. She would have remained happily Amish for the rest of her life, were it not for the nagging knowledge that she was meant to do what she was doing.

She and her family talked long into the night about what she knew about the small, beleaguered, Caribbean country. It was as though now that her father had accepted the fact that there was nothing he could say that would keep her from her path, he relaxed his vigil over her soul and simply enjoyed their visit together.

With Frank sitting next to her on the couch, as though to soak up closeness with his big sister while he could, and while cuddling little Anna on her lap—wanting to absorb as much of her baby-sweetness as possible before leaving—Bertha told her family about her job with Ella, and how good the woman had been to her. They were also interested in the difficulty of some of the classes and about the types of things she had learned.

They listened raptly, which was the way of her people. They were good at giving one another the space to talk and share one's story.

When at last her father declared it time for bed and began to extinguish the lamps, she made her way to the bedroom where she and Lydia had spent so many nights together and fell into the comfort and cocoon of that old bed. The fresh linens on it smelled of the sunshine and fresh air in which they had been dried. That was, and always had been, the scent of home.

It was so good to be with her family again! It would be hard to leave tomorrow, but go she must. The country of Haiti beckoned to her.

CHAPTER 20

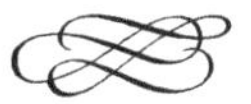

"It's going to be tough finding someone to replace you," Ed said. "Cops who speak Pennsylvania Deutsch are pretty much nonexistent. You know that. We've had much better relationships with the local Amish population ever since you came on the force."

"I know. I'm sorry," Rachel said.

The language issue was one of the many reasons Rachel hated leaving. She knew how hard it was going to be to find someone to replace her.

It wasn't that the Amish needed someone who spoke their language to communicate. They were, as a culture, essentially trilingual. Pennsylvania Deutsch was the language they spoke among themselves and to their small children. When the children entered school at age six, they were taught English as their second language, and usually quickly became proficient in it.

The third language—formal German—was as different from Pennsylvania Deutsch as Old English from modern-day English. It was the language into which Martin Luther had translated the Bible that many Amish still used. It was also the language spoken by the martyrs five hundred years earlier, who wrote the songs in the Ausbund, the hymnal from which their people still sang. Many of the sermons were preached in this third language, so it was taught to school children, as well.

The Amish were, as a whole, suspicious of the police and avoided any contact with them. Instead, they preferred to deal with issues privately within the church. They were usually quite reticent when it came to answering questions or giving information. That is—except with Rachel. The minute she began to speak to them in their mother tongue, she could see them visibly relax. Discovering that she spoke their language created an almost immediate trust.

Regrettably, there had been the few times that Amish children needed to be taken out of a home. Speaking no English, they were bewildered and terrified—until Rachel began to comfort and reassure them in their own, familiar language.

"If a situation comes up where I am truly needed," Rachel said. "You know I'll come. It's just the day-to-day police work that I have to pull away from."

"You could hire a babysitter," Ed said, hopefully. "My kids had babysitters, and they turned out okay. That baby of yours probably doesn't even care who is giving her a bottle or changing her diapers."

Ed, who had known and worked with her father, was an excellent chief of police. Fair, hardworking, genuinely compassionate, but his lack of understanding in this case rankled, and the mama bear in her came to the surface.

"Holly might not care, but I care," Rachel said, sharply. "Unless you've forgotten, you were on a fishing trip when my Bobby was kidnapped. I went after him despite my pregnancy. I saved my son, but I lost that baby. I don't know if I'll ever be able to carry a child full-term, Ed. This might be my last chance to experience caring for a baby, and I don't want to miss a second of it. I want to snuggle with her and help her take her first steps. I want to be there if she gets an earache and not be waving bye-bye while someone else comforts her."

When she stopped her tirade, she realized that she was standing, hands-on Ed's desk, leaning toward him and trembling with emotion. Until this moment, even she had not realized how passionately she felt about taking over the care of her daughter, whom she had only had for a couple of weeks.

"I'm sorry," Ed said. "I didn't mean to upset you."

"We've been through a lot together, Ed." Rachel dropped back into her seat. "I won't leave you in the lurch, but you need to understand that I'm giving notice as of today."

"A month?" Ed asked. "Two months?"

"Two weeks." The memory of the fatigue she saw in Bertha's face last night came to mind. "And I won't be working the night shift again. I need mornings so Joe can care for Holly."

"That's asking a lot." He sounded frustrated.

"I've never asked you for any special treatment over the years, Ed, and you know it."

"I know," Ed said. "I'll take the night shift rotation until we find someone."

CHAPTER 21

After she met with Ed, Rachel drove over to the entrance of Garraway Elementary School and waited for Bobby to come out. She didn't always pick him up. Sometimes he rode the bus to her aunts if neither she nor Joe was going to be home. But when she could, she liked to give him the treat of having her parked outside—especially if she was in her squad car. He thought having a mom who drove a police car was cool. As a stepmother, Rachel was especially happy when Bobby thought something she did was cool.

She stood beside the car while she waited. She loved watching for the moment he caught sight of her and came running. He was still young enough that he wasn't embarrassed when she knelt to hug him. That first hug from him after a day of being apart was sweet indeed. Especially since she knew that hugs in public probably wouldn't last much longer.

And then there he was. Her son. The most beautiful and precious boy in the world.

"Mommy!" he screeched and sprinted toward her.

She crouched to catch him, but just as she hugged him, she glanced over his shoulder and recognized a red-headed boy a few years older than her son. He was wearing the same coat she'd seen in the pie shop. He scuffled along with his head down, wearing the same ragged tennis shoes. His red hair was no longer covered with a sock hat.

Keeping her eyes on the boy, she told Bobby, "Wait here by the car. Don't move. I need to talk to that child."

She strode over to where he was getting ready to cross the street and laid a hand on his shoulder. He jerked in surprise, glanced up, saw her, tried to run, and found himself held in a firm grip.

"I'm not going to hurt you," she said. "What is your name?"

"Johnny?" he said.

The question mark at the end of his answer led her to believe he had given her the first name that came into his head.

"Tell me your real name, please."

"His name is Calvin," Bobby said, materializing beside her.

"Thank you, Bobby," she said. "Now, go stand beside the squad car like I asked you to."

"Calvin is new," Bobby offered, before obeying her. "He doesn't have any friends yet 'cept me."

She waiting for Bobby to be out of earshot before saying, "Is that true?"

Calvin squirmed. "I got friends."

"Of course you do," she said. "I mean the fact that you're new. How long have you been living here?"

He shrugged.

"You're cold," she said, noticing his chapped hands. "Would you like me to take you home?"

She saw a spark of fear, and he tried to run again.

"Honestly, Calvin." She grabbed him by his coat collar before he could get away. "I just want to help you."

"Are you going to put me in jail?"

"No," she said. "I would never put a child in jail. I just want to take you home."

"Alex told me never to ride with strangers." There was a sort of longing in his voice that made her think maybe he had been dreading the long, cold walk home.

"And who is Alex?"

"My cousin."

A cousin? No parents? This did not sound good.

"He's my guardian."

That made a little more sense.

"Alex is absolutely right. You should never accept a ride from a stranger." She loosened her grip on his coat. "My name is Rachel Troyer Matthias. I've been a cop here for a long time. My son's name is Bobby—you already know him. I have a new little daughter named Holly. You've met her too. My husband runs a restaurant in town called Joe's Home Plate. He used to be a famous baseball player, but he mainly flips hamburgers these days. Now, there. I'm not a stranger anymore. May I drive you home?"

"I am really cold," Calvin said, longingly.

"I know," she said. "My car is warm."

"Is Bobby really your son?"

"He's my stepson. His mother died when he was little, and I married his dad."

"My Grandma died."

"When did your Grandma die?" Rachel offered him her hand. He stared at it for a moment, and then he took it. His hand was freezing.

"Before Christmas. I live with Alex now."

"I want to meet this Alex," Rachel said.

"Are you going to tell on me?" His small face was pinched with worry.

"That depends," Rachel said.

"On what?"

"On what I think of Alex," she said.

"Oh." He thought this over as they walked. "Alex is a good guy."

"I'm glad to hear that."

She dug a second booster seat out of the trunk. Calvin was at the upper limit of needing one, but she didn't want to take a chance. She always kept a sturdy baby carrier and a couple of booster seats in her trunk for emergencies. In this town, she never knew when she might need them. The local Amish population, so used to carrying their children on their laps in their buggies, often could not provide one.

"You'll have to tell me how to get to your house," she said after everyone had been belted and buckled in.

There was only a slight hesitation from the back of the squad car before Calvin pointed left out of the school parking lot and said, "Go that way."

CHAPTER 22

The house where Calvin lived wasn't far. Less than a quarter-mile down the road from her aunts' place.

"That's it," Calvin said, as soon as it came into view.

Rachel knew the house well. An old Amish man had lived there when Rachel was a girl. Sometimes her aunts sent her up the road to deliver food to him.

A non-Amish distant relative had inherited the house and ignored it. For years it had stood empty, but apparently, it had been sold, and the new owner was renting it out. She hoped the owner had put in electricity and a bathroom. The home had neither when she was a child.

In an area that boasted pristine houses and yards, the place stood out as looking run-down and uncared-for. It looked like what it was—a cheap rental for someone without a lot of money.

She and Calvin got out of the car and walked to the front door. A sodden grocery circular lay on the top step, looking like it had been there awhile. She knocked, intending this to feel like nothing more than a friendly visit. If she got a bad vibe from the man, she would check up on him in more depth later. Calvin was beside her, fidgeting from one foot to another.

"You know," she said, while they waited. "You really could have just asked Lydia for some pie. She's a very kind person, and she loves children. You should stop in and get to know her."

Calvin glanced up at her. There was something like hope that flared in his eyes, but then it extinguished itself.

"She won't like me now," he said. "Not after what I did."

"You are wrong about that," Rachel said. "If you stop by and apologize, I guarantee the two of you could become great friends."

Footsteps sounded inside the house.

"Hello?" A man she assumed was Alex answered the door. "Can I help you?"

He looked to be in his mid-thirties. Maybe five feet ten inches. Barefoot. Brown hair that looked like he had just gotten out of bed, and hadn't been inside a barbershop for a couple of months. A good bit of beard stubble. Gray flannel pajama bottoms. A faded black t-shirt that was stained and torn.

Not a bad-looking fellow. No tattoos or piercings, but he looked rough around the edges. Of course, so did Joe when he first climbed out of bed. The big difference was that Joe got up around five a.m.

Alex didn't act startled when he saw her uniform, but Rachel did catch a quick, quizzical glance at Calvin.

"Are you Alex?" she asked.

"I am," he said. "Has Calvin done something wrong?"

"No." She weighed her words carefully. A parent, guardian, or foster parent could sometimes take things out on a kid if they thought they had brought police to their door.

"My name is Rachel Matthias. I was picking my son up at school and found out his new friend, Calvin, lived close by my aunts. They own the Sugar Haus Inn down the road." She gestured in the general direction. "We were on our way to visit them, and I offered to bring

Calvin home. I'm afraid my aunts and I didn't realize you had moved in. We are usually better neighbors than that."

"Thank you," he said. "I'm not sure why Calvin is so dead set against riding the bus, but I figure the exercise won't hurt him. The town seems safe enough."

"Right." She thought the exercise wouldn't hurt the child if he had decent boots and gloves and if he wasn't abducted on his way home. She'd been through one kidnapping and was no longer under the illusion that Sugarcreek was entirely safe for a child. Safer than most, of course, but no place was utterly immune to people with evil on their minds.

Since this was nothing more than a short investigatory visit to make certain that Calvin was in no immediate danger, she didn't point any of that out.

Tiring of the adults, and seeing that she wasn't going to tell on him after all, Calvin ducked into the house, leaving her and Alex standing at the open door. Dressed as he was, Alex had to be cold, but he didn't show it as he patiently waited for her to either say something or leave.

"Calvin says you are his cousin and guardian?"

"I am," Alex said.

"I haven't seen you around," she said. "Do you have family in Sugarcreek?"

"No." His relaxed demeanor didn't change. This was a man who was not uncomfortable with silence, nor was he going to offer any more information than she'd already gotten…which was zilch.

"Well, good meeting you," she said. "Welcome to the town. Let me know if the two of you ever need anything."

"Thank you, Officer," he said, closing the door. "I appreciate that."

She walked back to the squad car, musing about the meeting. She didn't get the impression that something was wrong. Nothing was setting off the bells of what she called "cop's intuition," and Joe called her "spidey sense."

But there was a troubled expression behind Alex's eyes. Something was wrong, and whatever it was could have been the reason he had ended up in a run-down rental on the outskirts of Sugarcreek.

"Is Calvin okay?" Bobby asked when she got back.

"I think so." Rachel slid into the front seat of the squad car.

"The big kids pick on him," Bobby said. "That's why he doesn't want to ride the bus."

"Calvin's a good bit older than you," she said. "How do you know that?"

"The boy who picks on him is Eddie's big brother."

"And who is Eddie?" She turned to back out of the driveway and saw that Bobby was looking out the window at the forlorn house.

"Eddie's my friend. His big brother picks on him, too."

"Thank you for telling me that," she said. "It helps."

Before heading home, she glanced at her cell phone. Somehow she had missed a call from Bertha. Hitting the speaker icon, she listened to Bertha's voice as she drove the short distance to her and Joe's home. It was something about wanting to talk with her. It didn't sound urgent, so she went home to take over Holly's care so Joe could go help Darren prep for the evening at the restaurant. The suppertime crowd would be coming in soon.

"She's been fed, burped, bathed, and has fresh diapers. Should be getting ready for a nap any time now," Joe said as he grabbed his keys.

Rachel took their fresh-smelling daughter from him and gave him a quick kiss as he headed out the door. It was hot dog night at the restaurant, and they had already decided that Bobby would go with his father for supper.

"I'll pick you up later," she told her son, interrupting him as he chattered to his father about how many hot dogs he planned to eat.

As soon as they left, she went to the kitchen. She was tired already, and her second shift had just begun. Protein. She needed protein. With the baby in one arm, Rachel headed for the refrigerator where she grabbed two cheese sticks to eat on the way to her aunts. If her aunts' phone was inside, she could have just called, but it wasn't inside and probably never would be. She did not want her call to be the one that caused one of them to fall outside trying to answer it.

The other reason she needed protein was because Lydia always had food ready—but too much of it tended to be sugar-laden. It seemed to Rachel like she was constantly battling the desire to please Lydia by happily eating whatever treat she'd recently made while attempting to keep from putting on weight.

"Your great-aunt Lydia is trying to kill me with sugar," Rachel kissed Holly. "But in a couple of years, you are going to love her cookies!"

Thanking God that Holly was such a good-natured baby, she tore the plastic off a cheese stick with her teeth, took a bite, chewed, and swallowed while she put Holly in a tiny snowsuit. The cheese stuck in her throat. She grabbed a bottle of water out of the fridge and downed half of it before putting the baby in the car seat carrier and then headed back out the door to see what Bertha wanted to talk to her about.

Rachel loved her two children desperately. She loved her life with Joe. She loved her job and her aunts and this community. She was grateful for the unexpected success of their restaurant. But, as Joe had recently pointed out, it was beginning to feel as though their lives had turned into passing Holly back and forth like a little football before one of them started running down the field with her. The problem was—they seemed never to reach the goal. They just kept running.

CHAPTER 23

Bertha enjoyed reading The Budget. It was a remarkable newspaper and there was always a copy lying around the inn. Their occasional Englisch guests who read it for the first time sometimes expressed surprise when they saw how far-flung all the Amish and Mennonite settlements were.

She usually took the time to explain that moving to new places was one of the earmarks of the Amish and the Mennonites. They moved for so many reasons. More fertile land, or cheaper. Sometimes they moved to escape a bishop in their church who might be more conservative or less conservative than they wanted.

They moved when a church outgrew the two-hundred member number that was conducive to meeting in one another's homes. At that point, there would often be a discussion about which families would leave and start a new church somewhere else. Sometimes no one wanted to leave and they would have to draw lots.

And sometimes they moved simply out of curiosity about what it would be like to live in a new place. The grass, even for the Amish and Mennonites, often looked greener in another state or county.

Because of this willingness to move, The Budget served a great purpose. Each settlement had a "scribe" who would write letters to the newspaper about the goings-on in their community. Everything from reports about the weather and crops to the sad news of tragedies and deaths. Visits from relatives from other churches were often reported.

The only problem with The Budget, in Bertha's opinion, was that there was so much of it. She seldom had the time to read everything in it before the next one arrived.

"Anything interesting?" Lydia asked as she cut out quilt pieces at the kitchen table.

Bertha scanned the pages for news from the settlements where various relatives had settled. "Looks like Cousin Bert got in a new batch of baby chicks down in the Gallipolis settlement. He's planning to go into the organic free-range egg business."

"Free-range is all we've ever known," Lydia said.

"Apparently a lot of people are wanting to buy those kinds of eggs. Maybe we should go into the organic egg business, too."

Lydia looked at her over her glasses. "You're joking."

"I am."

"Anything else?" Lydia went back to her quilt pieces.

Bertha turned the page. "Cousin Ada up in the Evert, Michigan settlement broke her leg."

"Poor Ada," Lydia clucked her tongue. "Does it say how it happened?"

"It says here that she fell off the wagon during a hayride."

"Oh, poor woman!" Lydia gasped. "What was she doing going on a hayride? She's no spring chicken. She's only two years younger than me."

"It says here some of the youngies had teased her into riding along, and Ada did. The youngies are very sorry. They are asking for a card shower for her."

Bertha gave the rest of the paper only a cursory glance, ready to fold it up and place it in the pile that Lydia used to get the cookstove fire started in the mornings. Then her eyes snagged on a missive she had not noticed. It was news from a Mennonite church in Sarasota, Florida. She was surprised to see that she knew the scribe.

"I will temporarily be taking over writing reports for the Budget from our sister, Mary Miller, who is having eye issues. Cataract surgery has been scheduled, and she asks for your prayers. The temperatures have been holding well here in Sarasota, which makes the orange farmers happy. It looks like a good crop this year. We had visitors at church this morning from a new settlement in New York State, the Timothy Hochstetlers. Jenny Yoder had her baby, a little boy. The mother and child are doing fine. Jenny's husband, Mark, reports that the baby has a healthy set of lungs. On a personal note: This week is the first anniversary of the death of my dear wife, Charlotte. She continues to be greatly missed by her family and all who knew her. Respectfully, Dr. Anthony Lawrence--scribe.

Charlotte Lawrence--the woman whose letter to The Budget about dirt cookies--was gone?

"What's wrong?" Lydia asked. "Are you all right?"

Bertha could not answer. At her age, so many friends and relatives had died that she thought she had almost developed immunity to grief. She was wrong.

She hadn't even known that Charlotte and Anthony were living back in Sarasota. The last she had heard, they were involved in a work in Honduras. Had they moved to Florida because of Charlotte's illness?

It was, of course, none of her business. She and Charlotte had not spoken in years. Still, there had been a time when she felt as though they were as close as sisters. The knowledge that Charlotte was gone hit her harder than she could ever have predicted.

She heard Rachel's car pulling into the graveled driveway.

Bertha did not want to cry in front of Rachel or Lydia, but she feared she would if she stayed in the kitchen one moment longer.

She grabbed her coat, shoved her feet into her galoshes, and hurriedly filled a pail with warm, soapy water.

"Chores." She mumbled to Lydia as she headed out the back door.

By the time Bertha got to the barn, she was trembling and her knees felt so weak that she nearly collapsed before she could sit down on a bale of hay. She leaned her head back against the rough-hewn wall and gulped great breaths of air, grateful she had made it to the barn without falling apart.

There was much she had not told her family about those first months in Haiti. There was much she never intended to tell them--things she had kept hidden in her heart for over fifty years.

CHAPTER 24

Haiti
1963

The man waiting to greet the three nurses as they got off the military transport at Bowen Airport was tall, dark, and not particularly handsome. At least he wasn't to Bertha's eyes. She was used to Amish farmers and carpenters—men who were ruddy and muscular. This man was tall, gangly, and ever-so-slightly hunched as though he had spent too much time sitting at a desk.

"Good day!" he shouted in a British accent over the sound of a prop airplane ready to take off. "You girls are a sight for sore eyes!"

Bertha and her friends clung to the handrail as they climbed down the mobile steps an airport worker had shoved up to the airplane. The weather had been iffy, and the flight—the first any of them had ever experienced—had been frighteningly bumpy. Even Bertha, the strongest of the three, felt her knees wobble as she made her way down toward the tarmac.

She swayed slightly as she stepped onto firm ground. It felt like she had walked into a blast furnace. The heat waves shimmered, and the smell of hot asphalt rising to greet her was nearly overwhelming. Nothing she had ever experienced in Ohio could have prepared her for this.

Their greeter, unperturbed by the heat, saw her sway and flew to her side to steady her. The shock of feeling this stranger's arm gripped tightly around her waist brought her back to her senses. Surprised and ashamed by her unexpected weakness, she shook off his help.

"I'm fine now," she said. "Thank you."

"You're sure?" He studied her face for a moment. "It sometimes takes a bit of time to get used to the heat."

"No. Really. I'm fine." She felt her cheeks grow pink. It was the first time she had ever been held so closely by a grown man. Especially one who towered over her. It was rare for her to even stand next to a man taller than she.

"Dr. Anthony Lawrence, here." He dropped his arm from around her waist and shook hands with the three nurses. "I'm the Assistant Director of the Schweitzer Albert Hospital in Desjardins. It appears that we will all be working together. Welcome to the country of Haiti!"

"I'm Bertha Troyer." She willed herself to regain some dignity. "This is Darlene Johnson and Jane Porter."

She was a little worried about Darlene. The woman had been airsick on the ride here and was still a bit green. She looked even worse than Bertha felt.

Dr. Lawrence noticed Darlene's discomfort.

"Don't worry, Miss Johnson," he said. "My wife is at home getting your beds ready and fixing a light supper. You'll all be able to lie down soon and rest."

The idea of lying down seemed wonderfully attractive. It had been an extraordinarily long day for all three women.

The ride to the Lawrence's home took place in a dusty jeep into which he crammed Jane, Darlene, Bertha, and all their luggage. They hung on for dear life while he swerved this way and that, avoiding giant potholes in the primitive, rutted roads.

From the backseat of the jeep, she got a bird's eye view of the countryside, which was even bleaker than she expected. It was a dusty, dirty, impoverished country in which she and her friends had arrived.

The Lawrence's house was on a street near the hospital. Half-naked children ran about laughing and playing some sort of kickball. One child carried a live chicken—apparently a pet—beneath his arm. Or perhaps it was his family's dinner. She had no way of knowing. Her knowledge of the culture was shallow at best. Even though she had tried to read up on the country, there simply wasn't that much written about it that she could find.

The house was peeling stucco with a rusted tin roof. When they entered, she saw that it was not much more than one living area with two smaller rooms jutting out on each side. The middle room contained a small sink and stove and some rough shelves. Two crates with loose boards laid on top served as a table.

Dr. Lawrence led them into another room where there were three pallets laid upon concrete blocks.

"You may stack your luggage in the corner," he said. "This is where you will spend the night. Our boys will sleep with Charlotte and I. You will take their beds."

"Thank you," Bertha said.

Jane nodded her thanks. Darlene stood in the middle of the room with her mouth screwed up in disapproval, as though appalled at the conditions under which they would be sleeping.

"I'm sure you are used to better lodgings," Dr. Lawrence said, "but we've only been in this house a short time and are still waiting for the furniture to arrive my wife's family is sending. We were blessed to find a house, especially one that has a bathroom and running water. After living in one room at the hospital for four years, this feels like a mansion. Charlotte! Our guests are here!"

A woman hurried out of what Bertha assumed was the master bedroom.

"Hello." Charlotte smiled and opened her arms wide. "Welcome to our home!"

She was a small woman, wearing a faded blue dress sprinkled with small white flowers. The gauzy kapp of a Mennonite woman was fastened over light brown hair falling out of a bun.

"Please take a seat, and we can get to know one another before the children get home," Dr. Lawrence hopped up to sit on the table.

Bertha could see no other place to sit except for a few cushions piled against the wall. She sat down upon one of them, tucked her legs beneath her, and covered them modestly with her skirt. The other two nurses did the same while Charlotte and her husband beamed down on them.

"Dinner is almost ready," Charlotte said. "I hope you like beans and rice. It is a staple here. You will be eating a lot of it."

"Beans and rice sound fine," Bertha said.

Charlotte busied herself with a pot on the two-burner stove while Dr. Lawrence sat on the table, swinging his legs.

"So how do you like it here so far?" he asked.

Jane, Darlene, and Bertha looked at each other. All three were exhausted, and Bertha guessed that they were all verging on a sort of culture shock.

"It is very different than Ohio," Darlene said in a small voice.

Dr. Lawrence barked out a laugh. "I'll wager it is!"

"Did you mention a—a bathroom?" Jane asked. "It has been a long trip and..."

Charlotte pointed toward their bedroom. "Right through there. I should have thought. Of course, you need to freshen up."

As Jane rose to her feet, Bertha and Darlene got up and followed her into where Charlotte had pointed. The Lawrence's bed was made up with a brightly-colored sheet, and a few clothes hung from nails that lined the wall. There was no closet, nor was there so much as an extra chair.

The bathroom was a sorry affair with a small lavatory, a primitive shower, and a commode so stained with rusty water that Bertha guessed Charlotte had probably given up on scrubbing it clean.

Darlene looked inside with distaste.

"You use it first," she said to Bertha. "You're braver than me. If you don't die, I'll go in."

Jane and Darlene waited outside while Bertha used the commode and flushed. It shuddered for a moment, but it worked. Then she washed her hands and face from the trickle of water that came out of the lavatory faucet. It was a pitiful little stream, and she wondered if it was at all possible to coax a shower out of the one she saw in the corner. Thankfully, the water felt cool, and after drying her hands and face on the thin towel hanging nearby, she felt a little better.

"Your turn," she said, as she came out of the bathroom.

"I think we've made a mistake," Darlene said. She seemed genuinely distraught, nearly in tears. "This is a terrible place."

"It isn't so bad," Jane said. "At least they have running water. That's more than I grew up with back home."

"I need a bath," Darlene said. "I feel dirty and disgusting just from being here. They made us sit on the floor!"

"Be quiet," Bertha warned. "You can deal with it until we get to where we are going. Perhaps there will be better facilities for you when we get to the hospital."

"But we're almost sleeping on the floor," Darlene gave a delicate shudder. "Who knows what kind of thing might crawl over or bite us tonight?"

Bertha had not known Darlene well before they came, but she was already starting to form a dislike for her. Apparently the girl had not realized the state of poverty she was getting ready to enter when she came to this country.

Of course, Bertha wasn't sure she had entirely realized it either.

"We'll be fine," Bertha said. "Now, finish up so we can go have dinner with the Lawrence's. I like them."

As she entered the main room, Dr. Lawrence was helping his wife set out plates and food on the table. From a corner, he brought folding chairs. There were not enough to go around, but that was no surprise.

"I always eat standing up anyway," he said when he noticed Bertha mentally counting the place settings.

"It is nice of you to take us in," she said. "Where will we be staying tomorrow?"

"That's something we need to talk about," he said. "It turns out, I am going to have to share you with another facility that needs help."

"Another facility?"

"One of our Mennonite children's homes is nearby. The woman who managed it had a medical issue that forced her to return to the states. We were hoping one of you might be willing to take over."

"Can the hospital spare one of us?" Jane asked.

"I've been training some nationals to help. They do not have your education, but they are competent with basic things. My question is, do any of you feel like you can take on the project."

"What is involved?" Bertha asked as she settled herself at the table.

"It's a combination of being a teacher and nurse to approximately thirty children. All of them are of different ages and levels of education. It would be a lot like teaching at an old-fashioned one-room schoolhouse. Erma was quite competent at it, but not everyone would or could do it."

"I think I would rather work at the hospital," Jane said. "Unless you have no one else."

"I like children," Darlene said, "but I don't know if I could keep track of that many."

Dr. Lawrence addressed his next comments to Bertha, as though he was hoping she would accept the job.

"The side-benefit is that the children are very loving. It is a job for a kind person who loves children, who doesn't mind helping care for them, and who has a great deal of energy. The church pays a small stipend, but it takes some people a great deal of time and energy to raise funds for it, so the stipend isn't much. Whoever takes the position will only have enough to get by. A nurse would be ideal because there are many diseases in Haiti, and the children are not immune."

Bertha didn't even have to give it any thought. It sounded exactly like what she had come here to do. Help the children.

"I'll do it," she said. "Gladly."

"Even though it goes way beyond your nursing skills?"

"Of course."

"Do you like children, Bertha?" Dr. Lawrence asked.

"Very much. I was raised Amish. In an Amish community, there are always small children around. From the time I was five, I almost always had one in my arms or on my hip. If not my younger sister and brother, there were plenty of little cousins to help care for."

"Charlotte?" he said. "What do you think?"

His wife was leaning over, stirring to fluff up a pot of rice she had just brought to the table. The steam clouded her round glasses.

"I think Bertha is a gift from God," she said. "The children will be blessed to have her."

Three little boys came crowding through the door. The oldest was maybe ten, the youngest about six. They wore matching blue uniforms with knee socks. Each had a small stack of books under their arm. It was evident that they had just come from school.

"Say hello to our friends," Dr. Lawrence said. "This is Miss Porter, Miss Troyer, and Miss Johnson." He nodded toward each woman in turn. "And these are our sons," he said, proudly. "Mathew, Mark, and Luke."

The little boys were well-taught. They solemnly shook each of the three women's hands—then excused themselves and went to the other room, presumably to shed uniforms and books.

"Anthony is hoping for a John someday," Charlotte said. "But I think Gwen is a nice name. It was my mother's. Dinner is ready, by the way. Anthony, would you say the blessing?"

As Bertha bowed her head, a feeling of extreme peace flooded her heart. For the first time in her life, she felt like she was doing the right thing at the right time in the right place. She'd worked hard for this moment, and she savored it. At last, she was in Haiti. Exactly where God wanted.

Her life's work had finally begun!

CHAPTER 25

Rachel stopped by the Sugar Haus Inn and found a cozy scene in her aunts' kitchen. Lydia was cutting quilting squares and Anna was sitting at a side table sorting and counting her collection of seashells.

"How many do you have now?" Rachel asked Anna.

"One hundred and three," Anna said, proudly.

"Former guests sent her cockle shells from Australia," Lydia said. "It was very thoughtful of them."

"See?" Anna held up four tiny white shells. "Pretty!"

"Very pretty." Rachel duly admired them before lifting Holly from her carrier.

"May I hold the *bobli*?" Lydia pushed back from the table and held out her arms, into which Rachel placed her little daughter. Holly studied Lydia with solemn, blue eyes.

"Look at that," Lydia said, fondly. "Everything is so new to her, she's even interested in an old lady in a prayer kapp."

Lydia cooed over the infant as she rocked back and forth on her straight-backed kitchen chair. She glanced up at Rachel with the glow of happiness in her face, sharing the great gift of snuggling a newborn.

There was only one thing that had ever trumped cooking and quilting for Lydia, and that was getting to hold a baby. A series of miscarriages had left her childless but with a never-ending love for children. Rachel had lost count of the baby blankets Lydia had knitted for the new mothers at church over the years.

"You have a good *maam*," Lydia untied the baby's warm, fuzzy cap, pulled it off, and laid it on the table. Holly's silky, nearly-white hair stood straight up from her head from the static electricity, which gave her a startled look. She was in the process of sucking her thumb and took it out of her mouth just long enough to give Rachel a look that seemed to say, "Do you see what's happening here, mommy?"

Rachel and Lydia laughed at the expression on Holly's face.

"Is your sweater keeping you warm, our sweet *bobli*?" Lydia said as she unbuttoned the soft wool outer garment.

"It's her favorite." Rachel grinned. "She knows her Aunt Lydia knitted it. That moss green is so lovely."

"Pink can be overdone," Lydia said. "That's what I was thinking at your baby shower. Of course, Holly was already here, so everyone knew she was a girl. I was afraid there would be too much pink."

"Where is Bertha?" Rachel asked.

Anna was so absorbed in arranging her collection of seashells, she seemed to be in her own world, but Lydia glanced up from adoring the baby. "Bertha went to the barn. I think she was upset."

"Why was she upset?" Rachel asked.

"I'm not sure. She was reading interesting pieces from The Budget to me. Then she suddenly looked like she was about to cry, and left."

Rachel reached for the paper and scanned the various pages. To her eyes, there was nothing that could have made Bertha cry. News about weather and crops, births and deaths, chickens, and out-of-town visitors.

"I do not see anything in here," Rachel said.

Lydia kissed Holly on top of her fluffy head. "It's best not to ask.

Sometimes when Bertha gets upset over something, she'll be quiet and cranky for days before she'll break down and talk about it."

"And sometimes Bertha gets cranky for no reason at all," Rachel said.

"There's always a reason," Lydia said. "Sometimes, it seems to me it often happens whenever she thinks about Haiti."

"She's never talked about it to me all that much," Rachel said. "I've always thought that odd."

"As close as we've been, and as long as we've lived together, she does tend to change the subject whenever it comes up," Lydia said. "I think it is painful for her, so I leave it alone. It's strange, though. She was there for so long, you would think stories about it would constantly be on her lips."

"It reminds me of some war veterans who will talk about anything except the war," Rachel said. "I can't imagine Haiti having been an easy place to work."

"There are wars that don't involve guns," Lydia said. "But they still leave scars. I have long suspected that our Bertha may have fought many battles while she was there."

"I have often suspected the same," Rachel said. "I'll leave her alone for now, but do you know what she wanted to talk with me about? She left a message on my answering machine. That's why I came over."

"Oh! We've made an appointment with a new doctor for Anna," Lydia glanced at her younger sister, who seemed absorbed in arranging her seashells.

"What's wrong?" Rachel was instantly alarmed.

"She just seems to be especially tired these days," Lydia said. "Bertha and I have become concerned. It's too cold and too far to take the buggy. The appointment is at two in the afternoon, the day after tomorrow. Is it possible for you to take them?"

"I'll make it possible," Rachel said. "I want to hear what the doctor has to say, as well."

Anna was humming to herself as she continued to rearrange her shells.

Lydia and Rachel exchanged glances that held many unspoken worries.

"When I was ten, after dad's death, Anna was my best friend," Rachel said. "She always had a hug or some small gift to give me whenever I was struggling. She helped heal my heart after Dad died. I don't know what I would have done without her."

"We used to play together." Anna glanced up at Rachel and smiled. "I liked that."

"I did, too." Rachel realized Anna was paying more attention than she'd known. "And you are still my best friend."

"I know," Anna said, simply, going back to sorting her shells. "But, now I play with Bobby."

CHAPTER 26

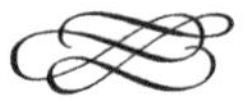

Bertha didn't need a mirror to know that her face was blotchy and her eyes badly swollen from crying. It was a relief Rachel did not come out to the barn to find her. The last thing she wanted was to go back inside and have to explain why she'd been sitting out in the barn bawling.

To give herself time to recover, she began to do her evening chores. She fed their horse and scattered some chicken feed outside the barn. Then she opened the door of the chicken pen and let the hens out to give them a chance to dig in some fresh earth. She watched as they flapped and scrambled their way out onto the barn lot and began scratching and pecking at the dirt.

She was grateful that it was almost milking time. It would give her an excuse to stay outside in the barn a bit longer before she went back into the house. Perhaps if she stayed out here long enough, Lydia would think it was being outside in the cold weather that had caused her red nose and eyes.

She grabbed the soapy water bucket, squatted down on her milk stool, washed off their Jersey cow's udder, and positioned the milk bucket beneath the cow. Leaning her head against Marigold's stomach, she began the task of squirting streams of milk into the sparkling stainless steel milk bucket.

Until recently, their cousin, Eli, who owned the farm next to theirs, provided them with plenty of milk. He kept a few head of cows and sold to one of the cheese-making plants in the area. But Eli was having some trouble with arthritis and no longer wanted to keep up with all that milking. He'd sold his dairy herd to his oldest son.

One cow was special, though, and he didn't want to part with her. Marigold was a gentle beast to whom he'd gotten attached. When Bertha offered to take Marigold off his hands, he'd jumped at the opportunity. Sometimes, when Bertha came out to milk, Eli would already be there ready to do the chore for her.

She didn't blame him. There was something about being in a barn that always felt healing to her. She thought it was the scent, which was partially a mixture of earth, manure, hay, and the feed they gave their livestock.

Or perhaps it was the company of Marigold, herself. Bertha had read in a farmer's magazine recently that the latest health craze was something called "cow cuddling." Some people were paying up to three hundred dollars an hour to spend time with a cow. A photo in the magazine showed two cows lying in a meadow, each patiently allowing a woman to lounge against them.

Despite all of Bertha's years of dealing with cows, this was not a behavior with which she was even vaguely familiar. Unless it was getting ready to rain, when most cows automatically laid down in a field, it would be hard work to get a cow to simply lie down and stay there. Cows needed to eat. They wanted to be up grazing.

She also wondered if there were flies in that meadow, and if—as was the nature of cows—it ever needed to swat a fly with its tail. Bertha had been smacked in the face many times by a cow's tail. Kicked, too. Even now, there was always the possibility of the cow sticking its back hoof in the pail of milk and knocking it over.

It would take someone better with animals than her to train a cow to lollygag around in a meadow with some city woman reclining against it. In Bertha's opinion, women who had enough time and money to hire a cow to hug, needed to—what was the phrase the young people used these days? Oh yes. They needed to get a life.

But she did understand the desire. The article said that the cow's body temperature was higher than a human's, and its heart rate lower, which automatically caused a person's heart to begin to slow down as well. The article said cuddling a cow was a great stress relief.

She didn't know about that. She rarely thought of herself as being stressed—that was city talk. But she did know that she had always felt refreshed and invigorated after milking. Buying milk at the grocery store would be easier, maybe, but that would involve hitching up the buggy and driving into town. If she did that, what would become of her mornings and evenings in the barn?

With the milk bucket full and Marigold's udder sufficiently drained, she stood up from the milk stool, slowly. It was getting harder to rise from such a low position, but she was determined to keep moving. Getting up and down from the milking stool a couple of times a day was good exercise. She had always been a strong woman and intended to continue to be so as long as possible.

Her eyes scanned the sky as she walked to the house. Those were snow clouds again. She would gladly welcome spring when it came. Snow tended to get old soon after Christmas had come and gone.

Rachel and the baby had already left by the time Bertha came back into the house. That was just as well.

Lydia looked up from her quilting. "Are you okay?"

"I am," Bertha said.

One of the things she appreciated about her sister was that Lydia seldom pried. She seemed to know that if Bertha wanted to tell her anything she would.

"Rachel was here," Lydia said. "She couldn't stay long, but she had gotten your message and said she would be able to take Anna to the doctor."

“That’s good, then.” Bertha removed her heavy winter outer clothing. “That’s very good.”

CHAPTER 27

Haiti
1963

Charlotte's kitchen was sparse in the extreme. The family-owned exactly five bowls, five forks, and five tin cups. Just enough to feed their family. For the children to eat, the nurses hurried to finish their meal, and then Charlotte washed the bowls, filled them again, and handed one to each of the boys who took them outside to sit on the front steps while they ate.

As Charlotte tended to the children, Dr. Lawrence continued to question the nurses.

"So, tell me why you're here?" he said. "How did you women conclude that your heart's desire was to end up working for a pittance in one of the most impoverished nations in the world?"

No one volunteered an answer. He glanced around the room. "What about you, Jane?"

"Me?"

"You are the only Jane I know," Dr. Lawrence said.

Jane, a lovely brunette with dark eyes, had spoken only a few words since they left that morning. Now, to Bertha's surprise, Jane opened up and quite a lot to share.

"My father was a medical missionary to India," she said. "Until his health got worse and he had to come home. He never ceased to talk about the days he had spent caring for people there. He had me late in life. My mother was a lot younger. I helped her nurse him through his final illness. Now...I figure it's my turn to do mission work. I guess it's kind of a way to carry on his work. I loved my father very much."

"Why Haiti instead of India?" Dr. Lawrence asked.

"It was where my church wanted me to go. They are helping to support me. The church isn't large. The treasurer pointed out to the leaders that it is a lot cheaper to fly to Haiti than India, and the need is as great here as it is there."

"Does that bother you?" he asked.

"Not really," she said. "I just want to serve. My church is making that possible. How can I complain?"

Bertha had liked Jane before. Now, she liked her even more.

"And you, Darlene?" he asked.

"I'm not sure what to say." Darlene's eyes were downcast. "I got my nursing degree partially so that I could help put my fiancé through medical school. We planned to set him up in his own private practice. Then we would get married and I would work with him. At least that was the plan. I found out a few months ago that he had changed his mind. He dropped out of school and said he didn't want to be a doctor after all. He said that was what his parents had wanted for him."

"What did he want to be?" Dr. Lawrence asked, gently.

"An actor," Darlene said. "He'd gotten into the theater in a big way before we met."

"And where is he now?"

"Los Angeles," Darlene's voice was quiet. "I told him we could still get married. I would get a job as a nurse out there in California and support him while he found work. He said no. Then he broke up with me. I found out later that he took a friend out there with him instead of me."

"A girlfriend?" Dr. Lawrence asked.

"No." Darlene's voice got even smaller. She looked at the floor as she answered. "His friend wasn't a girl."

"Ah," Dr. Lawrence said. "I see."

Bertha didn't.

"I know it doesn't feel like it now," Dr. Lawrence said. "But your fiancé was kind to break up with you. The marriage could never have been a good one."

"I know," Darlene said. "But it is still hard. I feel so naïve and stupid."

Naïve. His friend wasn't a girl. Wait a minute. Bertha got it now. Poor Darlene!

"But why did that make you choose Haiti?"

"I come from a small town. Everyone knew what had happened. I just wanted to get as far away from home as possible. My preacher suggested coming to Haiti, and I figured, why not?"

"I think you did a brave thing," Dr. Lawrence said. "Haiti will be good for you, and you for it."

"I hope so."

When Dr. Lawrence asked Bertha her story, she explained the impact the recipe for dirt cookies in Charlotte's letter had on her. She told of having to choose to leave her church.

"You left the Amish to come here?" Dr. Lawrence said.

"I never joined," she said. "There is a difference."

"Do you regret it?"

"Not yet. I believe I'm where God wants me to be."

She was seated closest to Dr. Lawrence, and as he listened to what she had to say, she noticed that unlike so many people she had known, he listened with his whole body. She had never had anyone focus so intently on her when she spoke. When he nodded in agreement with the choice she had made, she felt like a child the teacher had just praised in front of the class.

"My family pretty much disowned me for my decision as well," he said.

"Your family did not want you to become a doctor?" Darlene asked.

"No," he said. "They were fine with me becoming a doctor. My family was appalled when I embraced Christianity."

"I don't understand," Jane said.

"I come from a long, proud line of people who worshiped human intelligence instead of God." He said. "My great-grandfather was a professor of mathematics. My grandfather was a chemist with scores of adoring students. And my father was a brilliant inventor. They were so very smart; they seemed to think that there was no need for God in their universe."

"Then what drew you to faith?" Bertha asked, intrigued.

"The study of medicine. The more I learned about the intricacies of the human body, the less I could cobble together a belief that there could ever be enough billions of years for any of that to happen except by design. Call it what you will, but I am utterly convinced there is great Genius behind the creation of this world."

Bertha found herself leaning on one elbow with her chin in her hand, listening to Dr. Lawrence tell of his conversion. She knew many men whom she respected and loved. Her father and grandfather, cousins, many of the older men in her church. She knew them well, she had conversations with many. But never had she heard a man talk about his faith like Dr. Lawrence. She was entranced.

"And that is why my family doesn't know what to do with me." Dr. Lawrence chuckled. "I tend to make everyone very uncomfortable when I go home for holidays and insist on saying a prayer of thanks for the food to a God that they do not believe exists." He toyed with a salt shaker. "I'm a bit of an embarrassment to them, I suppose. They rather dislike having to introduce me to new people. I can almost feel them wanting to say, 'This is our son, the one who lost his mind, discarded every rational thing we ever taught him and is now a medical missionary in Haiti.' But they are way too civilized to say such a thing out loud."

When he stopped telling his story, it felt to Bertha as though she had come out from under a spell. She had been listening so intently, she hadn't realized that it had grown dark as they chatted.

"I'm afraid it is time for the children to go to sleep," Charlotte said. "And

all of you must be very tired after your trip. Perhaps it would be wise for all of us to go to bed soon. The children have to get up early, and so do we."

"I will take you nurses to the hospital with me tomorrow," he said. "After I get Darlene and Jane settled, I'll take Bertha to our children's home. There is much work to do there and not nearly enough hands to do it. You'll be assisted by some of the native women. They're quite eager to learn, and they can take an enormous amount of the burden off of you if you take the time to teach them. And don't worry. You will find yourself doing plenty of nursing. I will be surprised if there isn't a line of patients outside your door every morning when you get up, once it gets out that a nurse from America is in residence. I'll make sure you have some supplies."

Bertha had a lot to think about as she tried to sleep on one of the boys' small beds. In addition to being a nurse, she was going to have a whole new challenge. Fortunately, she had yet to find a challenge she could not meet and she was determined that she would succeed in this endeavor as well.

Her last thought before she fell asleep was that Charlotte was a lucky woman to be married to a man as wonderful as Dr. Lawrence.

CHAPTER 28

Amish women often shopped in groups, sharing the expense of hiring one of the multi-passenger vans that dotted the landscape of Amish country.

Rachel's aunts enjoyed these shopping frolics, as they were sometimes called, but for their doctor and dental appointments, they preferred Rachel to drive them. She readily agreed because she wanted to stay abreast of what the various medical professionals told them.

The presence of Holly now made taking them to their medical appointments a little more complicated than in the past. Rachel's personal vehicle was a classic two-door Mustang. She loved driving it, and the aunts didn't seem to mind climbing in and out of the back seat, but getting Holly's car seat in and out was more difficult than she'd bargained for. As much as it pained her, she had to admit that it would be a good idea to trade it in. She needed something a little more appropriate for a mother with two children and three Amish aunts to drive around.

Today, Baby Holly and Bertha were sharing the backseat. They'd only gone a couple of miles after Anna's doctor visit when Holly started chewing on her fist. Rachel knew her daughter was doing this because Bertha kept telling her.

"This child is hungry," Bertha said, disapprovingly.

"I fed her at the doctor's office," Rachel said.

"I didn't see you," Bertha said.

"You didn't see me because I gave her a bottle while you were in the room with Anna."

"I don't care when you fed her," Bertha said. "I know a hungry baby when I see one, and this baby is hungry."

"I will feed her as soon as I drop you and Anna off," Rachel said.

"Good," Bertha said.

Rachel usually didn't mind taking her aunts to doctor's appointments, but having a new baby to carry along with her was proving to be more difficult than she had expected. Especially since Bertha was convinced that she knew more about caring for an infant than Rachel.

Bertha probably *did* know more about babies, but it was still annoying having her handing out unsolicited advice every five minutes. Rachel knew she should be grateful for Bertha's expertise, but she felt ignorant enough as a mother without having it pointed out to her so often.

Anna quietly sat beside her in the passenger seat with her purse open upon her lap as she peered into it.

"Fifteen. Sixteen. Seventeen..."

"What are you counting, Anna?" Rachel asked.

"My shells."

Of course, she was. Arranging and rearranging her shell collection and counting them every few days was something that gave Anna a great deal of comfort. Still, it seemed to Rachel like Anna was becoming a little more obsessed with it than usual. Was she feeling that bad?

"How many are there?" Rachel asked gently.

Deep silence while Anna pondered the question.

"I don't know," Anna said. "I lost my place. I have to start over."

"One. Two. Three. Four. Five…"

Rachel didn't interrupt Anna again.

"So tell me what the doctor said," Rachel asked Bertha. She could see in her rearview mirror that Bertha was busy tucking the blanket in more firmly around Holly, who continued to make suckling noises as she chewed on her fist.

"Her old doctor has retired," Bertha said. "Today, we saw a new one."

Bertha fell silent, watching out the window. Rachel hoped Anna hadn't gotten bad news.

"And?"

"He seems to think quite the opposite of what Anna should do than her old doctor," Bertha said. "He believes that Anna might be a little too inactive. He wants her to start taking a walk every day. Outside. He said mild exercise would be good for her."

The snow was getting heavier. Rachel turned on her windshield wipers and watched for black ice.

"Has he noticed that it is January in northern Ohio?" Rachel said. "Not the safest time for Anna to go walking outdoors."

Anna seemed unaware of their conversation as she concentrated on counting her shells. The problem was, she kept getting distracted. She had to inspect each one as she took it out of her purse and laid it in her lap. There was a growing mound. Rachel wondered if there was anything at all in Anna's purse besides seashells.

"He knows perfectly well what the season is and where we live," Bertha said. "He's young, but I think he might be rather good at his job. He said the heart is a muscle that needs a certain amount of exercise and a certain amount of rest. He said that too much of either at Anna's age is not a good thing."

"Do you agree with him?"

"Yes. I'm thinking maybe Anna's previous doctor, the one who told us to make sure that Anna got lots of rest, was getting a little tired himself."

"Did this new one have any ideas about how we are supposed to get her the exercise she needs?"

"I asked him that. He suggested Anna start spending the winter months in Florida. He is aware that a great many of our people go to Sarasota in the winter."

"He didn't change her medication?" Rachel asked. "He just told you to take her to Florida for the rest of the winter?"

"He didn't change her medication, but he was very deliberate about taking the time to talk with her instead of only me," Bertha said. "He's the first one to do that."

"How interesting."

"I thought so," Bertha said. "She showed him some of the shells she'd brought with her. He asked her if she would like to go to the seashore again, and she got all excited and said, 'yes.' He seems to think her health would improve if she spent time walking the shore and collecting shells instead of staying here in the winter."

"Do you want to go to Florida, Anna?" Rachel asked.

"Uh-huh," Anna said, still concentrating on examining her shells.

"And what do you think, Bertha?" Rachel asked. "You're the medical professional in the family."

Bertha mulled it over. Rachel thought she seemed unusually pensive and irritable today.

"I think we need to take her to Florida," Bertha said. "But I do not look forward to the trip. I no longer enjoy traveling."

As Rachel pulled into her aunts' driveway, she intended to help them in. The roads had been slick with ice, and she knew the walk to the door could be treacherous. She left Holly in her car seat. With any luck, the baby wouldn't start crying while Rachel made certain the aunts got into the house safely.

"You don't have to help us," Bertha said. "We are quite capable of walking on our pathway and steps."

"I know," Rachel said. "But I'd feel better if you let me assist you."

Bertha made a disgruntled noise before pulling herself out of the car. Rachel leaned into the back seat on the other side and stuck a pacifier into Holly's mouth. Then she helped Anna out. Carefully, the three of them started toward the house.

Anna was on one side of her and Bertha was on the other. Rachel was holding onto their arms, ready to catch and steady them if they slipped.

"This isn't necessary," Bertha protested.

"I know," Rachel soothed. "I just want to be sure you get to the house in one piece. It's so very slick out."

"I go outside all the time without you hanging onto me," Bertha protested.

"But..." It was at that moment Rachel felt her feet fly out from under her and she landed flat on her back.

As she lay there dazed, she found herself staring up at Bertha and Anna, who were looking down at her with concern.

"Are you okay?" Bertha asked.

Rachel didn't answer. The blow to the back of her head had made her see stars, and she felt no immediate desire to get up. She lay there a few seconds longer gathering her wits, and while doing so, noticed that both Bertha and Anna were wearing their no-nonsense, black, rubber-soled shoes. The shoes were ugly, but they were much better on ice than the more stylish footwear she had chosen for the day. Depend on the Amish to be practical rather than fashionable. The irony of having nearly taken Bertha and Anna down with her was not lost on any of them.

Carefully she got to her feet, measured with her eyes the length she would have to walk to get to the porch and the much shorter distance back to her car. Rachel made a decision.

"You two go on ahead," she said. "I'll just take Holly home."

"Well, okay. If you are sure you can leave us on our own," Bertha's voice held a touch of sarcasm.

As Rachel pulled away, she didn't blame Bertha for being annoyed with her. She would probably be the same when she was Bertha's age if Holly or Bobby grew too solicitous.

On the way home, she worried about the trip to Florida. It was probably going to be up to her to drive them there. With the baby—well—she wasn't looking forward to the trip, either.

CHAPTER 29

After Rachel dropped them off, Bertha and Anna went into the kitchen without mishap. Bertha helped Anna with her coat, untied her scarf, knelt, and helped her take off her shoes. Until this winter, Anna had insisted on taking care of these small tasks, herself. She was a little clumsy, but she could do it. Now, she stood resigned, like an obedient child.

Bertha also noticed that Anna's coat was getting a little snug. They did not have a bathroom scale, but it was starting to become evident that Anna had put on weight.

"Can I go lay down?" Anna complained. "I'm tired."

"Of course you can," Bertha said.

"What did the doctor say?" Lydia asked after Anna left. Bertha noticed that Lydia was in the middle of supper preparations, which included making a special treat for Anna.

"Do you suppose we could cut down a little on some of Anna's food?" Bertha asked.

Lydia looked up, surprised. She was putting pats of butter on top of rolled out pastry crust to make Anna's favorite dessert, a combination of pie dough, sugar, butter, and pecans.

"But Anna loves this dish." Lydia protested. "I make it special for her."

"And she won't stop eating it until it is all gone," Bertha said.

Lydia sprinkled sugar and pecans on the raw pie crust dough and rolled it into a sort of pastry log. She sliced the top diagonally several times, laid it on a cookie sheet lined with baking parchment, and shoved it into the woodstove.

"I know I shouldn't," Lydia said, miserably, wiping her hands on her apron and dropping into one of the kitchen chairs. "But I'm just so anxious about her."

"And when you worry, you bake," Bertha said. "In this case, it might not be such a good idea."

Lydia repeated her unanswered question. "What did the doctor say?"

Bertha told her.

"What are we going to do?" Lydia asked.

"I guess one of us is going to have to go with her to Florida," Bertha said, "Or someplace else where it is warm and she can get out more. He mentioned the Pinecraft community as a possibility."

"Doesn't Cousin Rosa live there?"

"Our cousin who married that Beachy Amish man? The one who drove a big car? I thought she still lived in Illinois. When did she move?"

"A couple of years ago, I think," Lydia said. "Her husband was sick, and they went there for his health. The other day when Cousin Eli stopped by, he mentioned that her husband had passed away last year, but she'd decided to stay in Florida."

"Do you remember Rosa as a little girl?" Bertha said. "We used to babysit her, although she wasn't that much younger than us."

"She was a lot of fun," Lydia agreed. "Always laughing."

"Maybe a little too much fun," Bertha said. "It's a pretty big step from Old Order Amish to Beachy. I always liked Rosa, but I dread making such a long trip. Maybe we could just take Anna to a store or shopping mall every day. Someplace where she can walk inside until things warm up outside."

"No." Anna stood in the doorway between the living room and the kitchen listening to their conversation. "I want to go to the beach."

"It's a very long trip," Bertha was surprised to find Anna so adamant. She'd barely shown any interest at the doctor's office or the trip home.

"I want to go to the beach."

"It will take a lot of arrangements," Bertha said.

"I can find seashells." Anna paused a moment to gather her words. "I don't want to sleep all the time anymore."

Lydia and Bertha shot a look at each other. This was a long sentence for Anna to utter. Apparently, she had understood more about what was going on with her health than they had realized.

"I don't think I can leave Joe without any pies," Lydia said. "The girls who help me are good, but I don't want to leave them completely unsupervised. It will have to be you who goes, Bertha. I'm sorry."

Bertha sighed. "Of course it will."

"Just think," Lydia said, encouragingly. "It will be warm and sunny. You can go barefoot. You might enjoy it more than you think."

"I won't enjoy it," Bertha was emphatic. "But I will do what has to be done."

"You always do what has to be done," Lydia said, with sympathy. "You always have."

Bertha sighed. It was true. She had always done what had to be done, but Lydia's words made her sound like an old plow horse. Plodding along. Doing her duty.

Well, it was too late to change things now. She was headed to Florida whether she wanted to go or not.

CHAPTER 30

Their first night in Haiti was uneventful, and Bertha slept well despite the heat and unfamiliar surroundings. She almost always slept well and awoke refreshed. This morning was no exception.

They had not been awakened by screams during the night, so apparently, nothing had slid or crawled across Darlene. Although judging by the dark circles beneath Darlene's eyes when Bertha awoke, she doubted the other nurse had slept at all during the night.

Remembering the young woman's revelation the evening before, Bertha gave her the benefit of the doubt about whether or not she would stick it out. Like most people who found themselves in uncomfortable situations, Darlene was probably doing the best she could.

The breakfast Charlotte made them of oatmeal porridge was bland and tasteless, much like her lackluster attitude as she served it. The moment they were finished, Dr. Lawrence loaded the three nurses into his jeep and drove to the hospital.

"Is your wife all right?" Bertha asked. "It seemed like she didn't feel well this morning."

"Charlotte has migraines," Dr. Lawrence said. "Often, like last night, if she overdoes, she'll awaken with one."

"I'm sorry to hear that," Bertha said.

"I've done all I know to do to help her," he said. "I wish the Lord would take this pain from her—it can be very inconvenient—but so far, our prayers have gone unanswered."

Bertha was sorry Charlotte dealt with migraines. She knew they were painful, but she could not fully relate. There had been so little pain in her own life. She'd had a headache only once that she could remember, and then it was quickly dispatched with a couple of aspirin.

Schweitzer Albert Hospital in Desjardins was primitive compared to the hospital in the states where they had trained, but it was a great deal better than nothing—which was what the Haitians had before its inception.

At the hospital, she quickly embraced Jane and Darlene and wished them Godspeed before climbing back into the jeep.

As they left the hospital, it was disturbing to see the line of patients lined up outside, stolidly waiting to be seen. She hated the fact that Dr. Lawrence had to take time away from the hospital to drive her to the children's home. Still, she was grateful to have his presence and knowledge as they entered through a gate into the small compound.

"Why the fence?" she asked. "To keep the children in?"

"Partially, but mainly to help keep thieves out. There are always people willing to steal when there is poverty and hunger."

"I can't imagine being so hungry that I would steal food from a child."

"Then you have never been starving," Dr. Lawrence said, his voice matter-of-fact. "Hunger can drive even good people to desperation and violence."

As they walked around the compound, Dr. Lawrence showed her the clean wooden buildings where the children lived. The sturdy cinder-block kitchen in which their meals were prepared. And of course, the schoolhouse where she could hear chanting as they approached it.

She peeked in the open window and saw children of all ages, dressed in crisp uniforms, books open in front of them, and a young woman who appeared to be about twenty-years-old standing in the front.

"That is Mimose," he said. "She came to this children's home twelve years

ago as a child and stayed to help. She's rather extraordinary. I'm not sure what we would have done without her since Erma had to leave."

At the sound of his voice, Mimose looked up, smiled, and waved. Bertha saw that the girl was quite lovely. Mimose gave some instructions to the children, and as their heads bent down to their work, she came to the open door to greet them.

"Mimose," Lawrence said "This is Bertha Troyer. She is a nurse from America who is willing to fill in for the headmistress."

"Hello," Bertha said.

"I am so glad you have come," Mimose said, gracefully.

"Mimose speaks three languages fluently," Dr. Lawrence said. "French, Creole, and English. This is a great thing for the school because even though the government insists that the children be taught only in French, Mimose can help the little ones who only know Creole."

"Why would the government do such a thing," Bertha said. "When Creole is the national language."

"Prejudice," Dr. Lawrence said. "Creole is based upon a combination of languages that developed between French settlers and Congo slaves with a little English thrown in. Therefore, French is considered the language of the elite, the educated. Even the president uses formal French when he addresses the nation, although most of the population does not understand it. Some of us are trying to get this changed as it applies to our school children, but so far we've not had much success."

"I'm grateful that you are here, Mimose," Bertha said. "I'm afraid I would be quite overwhelmed otherwise."

Mimose looked relieved. "I am happy to help."

Bertha suspected that the girl had been worried about the person who would replace the previous headmistress. She hoped Mimose sensed that they would work well together.

As Dr. Lawrence showed her around the children's home, she began to have the same feeling of panic she had experienced once as a child while wading in the creek behind their home. She had accidentally slipped into water over her head and nearly drowned until her father fished her out.

She was in charge of all these young lives whose language she could not understand, a culture with which she was not yet familiar, in a foreign country where the political situation was far from ideal. She knew there would be difficulties in coming to the aid of this country, but suddenly, the overwhelming importance of her task left her practically gasping for breath.

"It will be okay," Dr. Lawrence said, as though reading her thoughts. "These children have been used to so little. Many have been rescued from terrible situations. Even if you cannot communicate with them in words at first, love seldom needs much translation. More than education, almost even more than food, the children will need to be loved."

"But how do I communicate love to them if I can't talk to them?"

"Hold them," Dr. Lawrence said. "Try to make sure that each child, depending on their age, is touched by you each day. Hold the little ones on your lap, or carry one of the smaller children around on your hip. Braid a little girl's hair. Wash a child's face and kiss their forehead. Put an arm around the older children, or a hand on their shoulder when you talk to them. It does not matter whether you speak in French or Creole or English, speak to them with love written on your face, and it will translate just as well."

Bertha began to breathe a little easier. "I can do that."

"Mimose can take care of what little discipline or instruction is needed for now. She knows what sort of rules are in place, and she knows the type of discipline that is appropriate—assuming that it is even necessary. I would suggest that your job at first simply be to let the children know and be reassured that the person in charge, the strange blonde white woman who looks so different from them, has the love of Jesus for them in her heart."

As they stood in the middle of the small, baked-earth courtyard, Dr. Lawrence looked deep into her eyes as though trying to penetrate her soul.

"Can you do that?" he asked. "Can you love them? Can you cuddle those little black bodies with as much affection as you did the little white Amish children back home? If you cannot, I need to know now and I will arrange for someone else to come who might not have your medical training or knowledge, but who can genuinely care for them. I can always find a place for you

at the hospital, but if you have any misgivings about your ability to love these precious children, you must tell me now."

Without answering, Bertha walked over to the school window again. Mimose had resumed teaching. She could hear Mimose's lilting voice helping some of the little ones count.

It was easy to see why Dr. Lawrence would be concerned. Where she lived in Ohio, there was a great sameness in their northern European background. To see a person or child from a different race was rare.

She honored Dr. Lawrence's wishes by seriously searching her soul as she peered through a window of that primitive building at the neat rows of children. She saw the pigtails and barrettes, the earnest little faces, the trusting eyes, as they listened and responded to their teacher.

She turned to Dr. Lawrence and saw that he had been watching her, waiting.

"It will not be difficult for me to love a child," she said. "Any child. Any color. Thank you for your advice. Be assured that I will follow it. I'm very grateful for the chance to serve."

She saw him visibly relax.

"Then let me show you where you'll be staying," Dr. Lawrence said. "I need to get back to work, and you need to get settled. Let's go get your luggage."

Dr. Lawrence was stronger than she expected for such a slender man. He seemed to have no problem helping her with her luggage, although it was heavy. After all, she had packed with the idea of staying two full years.

The room that she would be using was small, but it did have a washbasin, a mirror, a desk, a chair, and a bed so narrow that it was more of a cot than a bed. She was not a small woman, and she knew that the cot would be uncomfortable, but she had no intention of mentioning it. She would make do. Remembering how sparse his and his wife's home was, there was no way she was going to complain about anything.

Dr. Lawrence noticed it, too. Silently, he stared at the small bed, and then his eyes swept her from the top of her head to her toes.

"That bed is not going to work," he said. "We'll have to find you something bigger."

It shamed her a little. She knew she tended to be larger than most women. At least she was taller.

"I will be fine," she said. "You shouldn't have to try to find something else. It isn't your fault that I'm such a big horse of a woman."

Dr. Lawrence shot her an angry look. "Don't talk about yourself like that!"

His words startled her because, in her mind, she had just been making a self-deprecating joke, but he seemed to be genuinely disturbed by her words.

"Excuse me?" she said.

"I'm sorry. It's just that I see too much," he said. "There are so many diseases and so much hunger here. To have a fine, strong body such as yours is a gift, especially on this island. You should cherish it and take good care of it. With your education, your health, and your training, you should be able to do much good here."

"I apologize," she said. "You are right."

It interested her that although a man not too far from her age, Dr. Anthony had only commented on her health and abilities. He had seen her body only as a tool for good. A tool for saving lives and for caring for the children who were now in her charge. She wasn't sure how to feel about that. Part of her wished he had said something a bit more complimentary than telling her that she was strong and healthy. But anything more than that would have been inappropriate. After all, he was a married man.

He left soon after, and she was relieved not only because she was anxious to get settled but because she felt so sorry for the line of people who were waiting patiently for him to get back.

There was no chest of drawers to tuck her things away in, but there were some shelves on the wall that she stacked the items she had brought with her. There was no closet to hang her clothes in, but there were nails that had been randomly nailed into the walls, upon which she hung her nurse's uniforms and her few pieces of off-duty clothing.

Once everything was unpacked, she squared her shoulders, put a smile on her face, and marched out to acquaint herself more fully with the small compound. She did not want to disrupt Mimose's teaching any more than she and Dr. Lawrence already had, so she stayed away from the school.

Tomorrow morning she would visit the classroom and ask Mimose to introduce her to the children. Then she would begin her ministry of getting to know and love each one.

CHAPTER 31

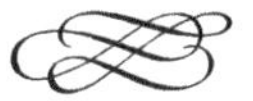

"How is our angel baby doing?" Joe washed his hands in the restaurant's stainless steel sink and dried his hands on his apron before taking it off, hanging it on a hook, and reaching for little Holly. She had fallen asleep in her car seat on the drive from the aunts' home to the restaurant. Now, still half-asleep, she tried to suck her thumb, but as sleepy as she was, she didn't have quite enough muscle dexterity to pull it off. With her eyes closed, she blindly worked at getting her thumb in her mouth.

"She was a trooper," Rachel said. "Bertha says she's an exceptionally good baby."

"Well, Bertha would know." Joe cradled their baby in his arms and crooned down at her, "Are you Daddy's good little girl?"

In answer, Holly screwed up her tiny face and passed gas.

"Well, I guess that answers that." Joe laughed. "How did Anna's doctor visit go?"

"Okay, I guess," Rachel said. "This one had a much different viewpoint about what Anna should be doing to get better."

"Oh?" Joe retrieved Holly's pacifier from its clip-on holder and successfully got it into her mouth.

Watching Joe with the baby in his arms, so tender with her, made Rachel's heart turn over. He had been one of the greatest pitchers in the world until repeated shoulder injuries took him out of the game. Instead of being bitter, he now flipped burgers and ran his own restaurant. No matter what Joe did for a living, he was still Joe—a family man who passionately loved his wife and son, and now also loved their daughter. There was just something about the image of this good man holding their baby that sent a powerful surge of love sweeping through her.

"Her old doctor emphasized the need for Anna to rest," Rachel said. "To not over-extend herself physically."

"I know," Joe said. "And?"

Joe's brother Darren walked in from busing tables in the dining room.

"I want to hear this, too," Darren said. "When I picked up the pies yesterday, Lydia told me about how concerned everyone was about Anna."

"Her old doctor recently retired, and a much younger doctor has taken over his practice," Rachel said. "He has a very different viewpoint about Anna's health."

"Did he change her medicine?" Joe asked.

"Not exactly," Rachel said. "He is keeping the medication the same for now, but he is recommending mild exercise. He does not feel that having her rest so much is a good idea."

"And how do you and Bertha feel about that?" Darren asked.

"Anna isn't getting any better," Rachel said. "She's getting worse."

"I've been so busy with the restaurant I haven't seen her for a few weeks," Joe said. "In what way is she getting worse?"

"She's tired all the time," Rachel said. "And she seems withdrawn and sad."

"I've noticed the sadness," Darren said. "I'm there nearly every day picking up pies. What did the doctor say?"

"Well, it's quite a prescription he wrote," Rachel said. "He knows a few things about the Amish, and he is recommending she go to Florida for the rest of the winter. He specifically mentioned Pinecraft."

"Isn't that the place where so many Plain people go for a vacation?" Joe said. "They've sort of established an Amish community there?"

"It is," Rachel said. "It's been an Amish destination for a long time."

"What made him think of sending her there?" Darren asked.

"While they were waiting for the doctor, Anna was playing with her seashells. Bertha said that when the doctor came through the door, he introduced himself, and then he started talking to Anna about them."

"He sounds like a very perceptive doctor," Joe said.

"That's just it," Rachel said. "I think he might be very good, indeed. He thinks Anna needs to be outside in the sunshine. He says taking slow walks will build up her stamina, and if she walks every day, the weight might begin to come off, which would be so good for her heart."

"Is it possible for her to go to Pinecraft?" Joe said.

"It's very possible," Rachel said. "We have a cousin, Rosa, who lives nearby. She's recently widowed, and she would love to have any of us come stay with her."

"With our new baby and Bobby in school, you aren't thinking of taking them, are you?" Joe said. "Couldn't we hire someone?"

"That's an awfully long trip. It's hard to imagine Bertha and Anna agreeing to go with anyone except me," Rachel said.

"Lydia isn't going, too, is she?" Darren sounded worried. "We can't keep the restaurant open without her pies. I think our customers would revolt if we ran out of Lydia's pies."

"He's got a point," Joe said.

"Aunt Lydia never enjoyed the beach," Rachel said. "She won't want to go."

"This restaurant can do without me for a few days," Darren said. "I wouldn't mind a change in scenery for a bit. I'd be happy to drive Bertha and Anna down."

"That would be wonderful," Rachel said. "Are you sure you wouldn't mind?"

"Not at all," Darren said.

"Wait," Joe said. "You will come back, won't you?"

Darren laughed and clapped Joe on the back. "Don't worry, brother, I have too much invested in this place to wander off. I'll take Anna and Bertha to Pinecraft, stay long enough to see them settled and then come straight back. What could go wrong?"

Joe and Rachel shared a glance. The thoughts of free-spirited Darren driving for two long days with Anna and iron-willed Bertha struck both of them as comedic. Rachel could see the corners of Joe's mouth twitch as they shared the same thought.

"Nothing at all," Joe said. "I'm not worried about a thing. It should be a breeze."

CHAPTER 32

"Of course you can come," Rosa said. "I'd be thrilled to have you. It's been lonely with Don gone. I would love it if you and Anna moved in with me permanently! Lydia, too. Sell the Sugar Haus Inn. Come live with me! I'm serious. I have plenty of room. You would love Florida. No more of those nasty Ohio winters."

Bertha was grateful for Rosa's enthusiasm for their visit, but sell their beloved Sugar Haus Inn? Move to Florida? Never again experience the beauty of an Ohio winter in Amish country?

"That's not going to happen," Bertha said, politely. "But thank you."

"Well then, don't forget to pack some shorts and your bathing suits," Rosa trilled. "It gets so hot down here. You'll be happy you have them."

Bertha, standing in their phone booth at the end of their driveway, rolled her eyes. That wasn't going to happen, either. Her in shorts? Rosa must have lost what sense she had back when they were girls and moved further away from her Amish roots than Bertha would ever have dreamed. Being married to Don must have thoroughly addled Rosa's mind over the years!

However, being given a free place to stay while Anna soaked up some sunshine and walked on the beach was very welcome.

"I have plenty of sunscreen," Rosa rambled on. "And a beach tent to keep the sun off of us when we take Anna to the ocean. And I have lots of beach towels. Oh, Bertha, I'm so glad you two are coming!"

Bertha heard the loneliness in her cousin's voice and chastised herself for having any negative thoughts about her. Rosa was a good and kind person. It was just that she'd always seemed a little bit silly.

Still, the shorts and bathing suits comment was a surprise. To Bertha's knowledge, the Beachy Amish didn't dress immodestly, but perhaps the ones in Florida were different. It would be good to know what she and Anna were getting into.

The only way to find out was to ask.

"Are you still Beachy Amish?" Bertha asked.

"No," Rosa said. "Not anymore. There's a wonderful Mennonite church up the road."

Well, that explained the shorts and bathing suits. The Mennonite church Rosa attended must be one of those liberal ones. When Bertha was a girl, shorts and bathing suits would never have been allowed in any self-respecting Anabaptist church community, whether it be Beachy Amish or Mennonite. Things were changing, though. Of course, none of that was her problem, although she did hope that Rosa wouldn't take it into her head to have any wild parties while they were there. With Rosa, one never knew.

After working out the details of when they would arrive, Bertha thanked her cousin and disconnected. As Bertha plodded from the phone shanty back into the inn, the sick feeling of apprehension she'd carried with her ever since Anna's visit with the doctor grew stronger. Florida was so far away, and Anna's health so fragile. The drive would be stressful, but the decision had been made and she would have to see it through. Bertha considered it one of her few strengths. She always saw things through, no matter how difficult.

CHAPTER 33

Haiti
1963

The morning after Dr. Lawrence dropped Bertha off at the children's home, she awoke early, stretched, yawned, then stared at the ceiling a few moments thinking about and planning the day. She could not remember experiencing such a bright feeling of sheer happiness ever before.

Her life had, indeed, begun, and she couldn't wait to start making changes. Oh, the things she was going to do to make the lives of her small staff and children better!

Although she knew nothing about running a children's home, nor had she ever taught a class, she was confident she would sort everything out in no time. Mimose was a jewel. Haiti was certainly different, but not quite the culture shock she had been dreading.

The structures that made up the children's home were shabby, of course, as was her own small room, but she hadn't expected to live in a sturdy farmhouse like her family had back in Ohio.

If there was one thing the Amish were good at, it was in their ability to build homes and barns and outbuildings that were strong.

The home her parents owned had been constructed in such a way that she would not be surprised if it still stood one hundred and fifty years from now. The room in which she and her sister slept was a marvel of near-perfect craftsmanship. Although quite plain, the woodwork was beautifully made. The bed they shared as girls was so strong it didn't even creak when they climbed in.

She knew building materials were at a premium here, lumber-producing trees were rare. It was probably a small miracle that these buildings were here at all. She wondered what missionary had sacrificed, coerced, and argued enough to get the funds and volunteers to build the place, but she guessed that lumber—assuming one could get some—did not last as long in the tropics as back at home in North America.

Staring up at the roof, laying on her narrow cot, she marveled at the twisted grass that comprised the roof over her head. She now realized that the rusted corrugated tin roof that the Lawrence's had—far from being a sign of poverty—was a bit of a luxury in Haiti.

As the dim early morning light began to slant into the room, she could see more clearly. To her surprise, she saw a glimpse of bright yellow up in the rafters directly below the grass roof. Why would that eye-catching color be way up there? Had the former headmistress left something behind? And if so, why had she secreted it in the grass roof?

Then the yellow began to move and unfolded into a fat boa constrictor that flashed across the grass ceiling. It caught a rat that had been using one of the rafters as a highway.

The rat struggled, the boa somehow lost its grip on the rafter, and both fell to the dirt floor in a deathmatch.

Bertha did not scare easily, but she sat up, her back pressed against the headboard, her legs and feet pulled up beneath her, terrified that the boa would lose interest in the rat, and come after her.

She knew how to deal with the various farm animals and wildlife back in Ohio, but she had no idea what to do with a boa constrictor. She only knew what it was because of a picture she'd seen in a handbook while trying to familiarize herself with the creatures of Haiti.

She bit the back of her hand, trying not to scream as she watched the boa thresh about on the floor. She did not want to awaken Mimose or some child who might come into the room, unaware of what was going on. They might inadvertently step on the thing. How dangerous were boas anyway? She didn't know, but she didn't want to accidentally find out.

The threshing stopped, and the boa began the slow process of swallowing the now-dead rat. Unwilling to disturb its breakfast, Bertha remained in bed, wondering how long this would take, wondering if the boa would be satisfied or if its appetite would be large enough to eye her as a potential meal as well. She would have fled the room except it had managed to start its digestive process directly between her and the only door.

As the boa concentrated on its breakfast, Bertha focused on the sounds of children awakening and of Mimose's voice responding to various childish requests. They would soon be wondering why she wasn't up already. She might even get an undeserved reputation of being lazy if she didn't get dressed and out there soon.

Had the room been larger, she might have attempted to by-pass the snake, but it was small, and the snake took up a rather large part of it. There wasn't room to walk around it. She would have to step over the thing. Never mind the need to move about the place to get dressed.

There was a quick knock on the door. Before Bertha could call out a warning, Mimose opened it, smiling.

"I have some breakfast for you..." Her attention dropped to the snake. "What are you doing here?"

The snake did not answer. Its mouth was full of rat.

There was a broom just outside the door that Mimose grabbed. She began to use it as a shovel as she tried to get the boa to move. It was reluctant.

"Get out of here!" She shoved at its heavy body with the well-worn broom. "I told you before, this is not your home!"

At Mimose's urging, the snake began to slowly slither across the floor and finally disappeared through a hole and was gone.

"You need to get up now," Mimose smiled at Bertha, cowering in the bed. "The children will begin their classes soon."

"You weren't afraid of that snake?" Bertha tried to keep her teeth from chattering

"I am a little afraid of that snake," Mimose said. "Although it is a gentle animal that helps keep the rat population down. But if you will forgive me for saying this, you need to learn that it is a mistake to show fear in Haiti. Ever."

"Why?"

"Because there is too much to be afraid of," Mimose said. "You must not appear to be weak. It will make you a target."

"A target of what?"

"Practically everything," Mimose said. "Now, let's get busy with the children. Knowledge is as important to giving them a good life as the food we give them."

A shy teenage girl brought a pan of warm water into Bertha's room just as Mimose was leaving. After washing up in it, and then a quick breakfast made up of a small portion of rice and beans that Mimose brought to her room, she followed the sounds of children singing from the open windows of the schoolhouse.

All sound ceased as she entered from the front side door. Mimose paused in her teaching, and a room filled with small black faces stared at her. Some open-mouthed.

Mimose said something in what Bertha assumed was Creole. The children said something in unison, and Bertha thought she had probably been introduced and greeted. Her ignorance appalled her. How on earth was she going to teach these little ones? Why had she not studied Creole before she came?

The answer was simple. There had been no one to teach it to her.

"Excuse the children's manners," Mimose said. "You are not the first white person they have ever seen, but you are probably the whitest person they have ever seen."

"Excuse me?" Bertha said.

"It is your blonde hair," Mimose said. "To our eyes, used to many different varieties of skin color, you are so extraordinarily white, you look strange."

Bertha had never given any thought to her whiteness. But now, dressed in her light tan cotton dress, she felt self-conscious and out of place.

"What would you like for me to do?"

"Take my teacher's seat and simply observe," Mimose said. "That's about all you can do for now. You will have to listen to Creole and French, but we will have an English lesson in a bit, perhaps you can help with that."

The teacher's seat was not much, a wobbly straight-backed chair behind a makeshift desk of concrete blocks and some boards. But watching Mimose teach was a revelation. As a whole, the Amish children she had known back home had been fairly obedient, but they were children after all. They had trouble sitting still through their extended church services and trouble leaving one another alone. But these children's eyes never left Mimose's face. There was little extra movement. They sat on the benches, the youngest and smallest feet did not touch the ground but dangled. The children did not have books or paper and pencils of any kind. Their lessons were learned by rote for the most part.

It pleased her when Dr. Lawrence showed up. He carried with him a large bag of rice, which she saw him drop off at the kitchen.

She left the classroom momentarily to go speak to him.

"How are things going?" he asked. "Do you think this is going to work out for you?"

"Everything is fine," she lied.

"What do you think of the children?"

"I've never seen children so well-disciplined," she said. "They seem content to just sit still and learn."

Dr. Lawrence looked at her with something like pity in his eyes. "What you see is not discipline. It is a lack of calories. Children who don't get enough food do not have the energy to wiggle or squirm. What you see is the listlessness that comes from hunger."

"But I thought the children had just had breakfast," Bertha said.

"They are on short rations for now," Dr. Anthony said. "The truck that usually brings their allotment of food is several days late."

"But I had breakfast this morning," Bertha said, confused.

Dr. Lawrence said nothing as Bertha realized that the small portion of food she had consumed without much thought this morning had been given to her at the expense of others' hunger. This could not go on. Children needed to be fed.

Almost as though it was in connection to her brain, her stomach gave a low growl that was audible. Embarrassed, Bertha quickly put her hand on her stomach.

"Excuse me," she said.

"No need to apologize," Dr. Lawrence said. "I am well acquainted with growling stomachs."

"What can I do to help?" Bertha said.

"Not much," Dr. Lawrence said. "Not until the supplies are freed up. There is some sort of issue with the government I need to go check on today. Papa Doc and his minions are more money-hungry at some times than at others. Often yet another bribe must be given before they will allow us to take the food that is waiting at the dock for the children. That's where I'm headed now. The rice I brought this morning is from our pantry at home. I hope it will be enough to tide you and the children over. Pray that everything will go as it should, and we can prepare full meals again by tomorrow."

Mimose released the children for a short recess, and as she was walking over to join Bertha and the doctor, she overheard his last comment.

"And we will pray that Papa Doc will not take offense at some small thing," Mimose said. "Be very careful, Dr. Lawrence."

When he had left, Bertha turned to Mimose. "How much danger is he in?"

"It is complicated," Mimose said. "Our president, Papa Doc, kills many people he does not like. There is a death squad called the Tonton Macoute, who do his bidding. It is best in Haiti today to live in such a way that one is never noticed by Papa Doc. It is best if he does not pay attention to your existence."

Bertha felt sick to her stomach, thinking of Dr. Lawrence having to put himself in danger to free up the food meant for the children.

"What can we do?" she asked.

"What we always do when this happens," Mimose said. "We pray without ceasing."

The rice Dr. Lawrence brought was cooked and parceled out to the children for their noon meal. Bertha chose to eat nothing.

There was nothing for supper for anyone. Some of the smaller children cried. The older children were more stoic and comforted the younger ones.

That night, as Bertha went to bed hungry, knowing there might not be anything for breakfast tomorrow, she gave thanks for her hunger but begged God to supply food for the children. For the first time in her life, the words from the Lord's Prayer about giving thanks for one's daily bread took on weight and substance.

And yet, for the first time in her life, she found herself fantasizing about how a few bites of bread would taste awfully good right now. Especially from one of the loaves Lydia made twice a week. Whether eaten with butter and jam or torn into chunks with cold milk poured over it for a quick supper, Lydia's bread was delicious. Especially if one came in from the outdoors to a kitchen filled with the scent of baking bread.

The next morning, Dr. Lawrence did not arrive with the supplies—he explained he was still wrangling over them—but he did bring enough cooked beans and rice from the hospital kitchen to put some warm food into the children.

Bertha refused to have any. She couldn't stand to think of eating something when the children needed food so badly.

For three days and three nights, Dr. Lawrence was barely able to scrape together enough to keep the children and staff alive while he pleaded with those who would not allow the American church-donated supplies to come through. He was putting himself at considerable risk, Mimose told Bertha.

Bertha continued to fast, and she did not stop praying.

"Our Lord didn't eat for forty days," she said to Dr. Lawrence when he encouraged her to at least have a few bites of the food the hospital had sent. "I think I can last a few more days."

"Yes, well, our Lord didn't have to keep up with thirty little children," Dr. Lawrence retorted. "He only had to withstand the temptations of the devil."

"True, but I've noticed something interesting during this time," Bertha said.

"What's that?"

"Remember how the devil tempted Jesus to turn stones into bread?"

"Yes."

"For these past three days, whenever I start fantasizing about food, all I can think about is bread. Thoughts of bread consume me. It's the oddest thing. Not my sister's cakes or pies or cookies. Just that crusty, delicious bread she bakes. Not chocolate or fruit. Just bread."

The next day, for lunch, which was day four of her self-imposed fast, the children ate well. The supplies got through. Dr. Lawrence did not disappear or get imprisoned for arguing with government officials. There was canned meat to mix with the rice. And a package waited for Bertha in her room. Inside was a loaf of crusty bread.

As the children enjoyed a full meal, she quietly closed and locked the door to her room. She took out the simple loaf of French bread, and stared at it, wondering what she should do.

It wasn't a particularly large loaf, but it was fresh, and it smelled divine. Dr. Lawrence's thoughtfulness staggered her.

She was so hungry, she could have easily consumed the entire loaf and another besides.

Permitting herself to consume the entire loaf—that was the problem.

Instead of tearing into it like the starving person she was, she broke off a small section at the end, knelt at her bed with the piece of bread held in both hands, and prayed her thanksgiving.

After her prayer ended, she very gratefully ate the morsel with more appreciation and enjoyment than she had ever felt about anything.

Knowing what a rare treat this bread would be to the others as well, she carried it to the kitchen and cut the remaining loaf into four pieces, enough to share with each of the staff. With all her heart, she prayed that their supplies would never again be held back for so long, and she intended to make sure she always had some food hoarded away for the children—whatever it took.

It was harder to see the children she loved go hungry than to starve herself, but she was determined that neither she nor the children would ever have to feel the bite of hunger again.

CHAPTER 34

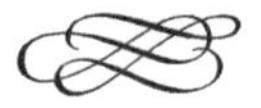

"Are we ready?" Darren asked as he entered the kitchen two days later.

"I guess so," Bertha said. It had been so long since she'd packed for a trip, it had taken quite an effort to get everything sorted out.

"My bag!" Anna said.

"What bag?" Lydia asked. "We've already packed everything."

"My shell bag." Anna plumped herself down on a kitchen chair and began to cry.

Darren looked confused.

"It's okay," Lydia reassured him. "Rachel bought her a bag yesterday to use for the shells she finds. It's mesh so the sand can fall through. It's upstairs in the bathroom last time I saw it. I'll go get it, Anna. Don't cry."

"Okay." Anna dried up immediately.

"Anna gets wound up sometimes when things aren't routine," Bertha explained. "She's very excited about the trip, aren't you, Anna?"

Anna nodded enthusiastically.

Lydia came back with the bright green mesh bag in her hand. "Here you go. Now you have everything you need!"

In Bertha's opinion, Darren, Joe's brother, was a mixed bag, and she wasn't thrilled with the fact that he was the one driving them to Florida. From what she understood, he had a somewhat shady past. Many failed business attempts. She suspected he had skirted around the edges of the law from time to time. And he didn't seem to have any loyalties to any sort of church, even though he and Joe's parents had been missionaries to Africa.

Despite past failures, Darren had somehow managed to come up with an excellent business idea and had executed it nicely. That restaurant, which they based on their mother's recipes honed in the laboratory of feeding a family in the African bush, had become a success.

She liked Darren well enough. He was a polite and cheerful young man. But she did not really know him. They had so little in common, she feared that spending two days on the road together while they made their way to Sarasota would be awkward as they clumsily tried to talk to one another on the way there.

She sighed as she contemplated the next two days of travel. This was not going to be easy. She loved and valued her family, but sometimes members of that family could create an enormous amount of inconvenience.

Now that the precious shell bag was found, Anna once again percolated with excitement. It was the most alive she had acted for quite some time. Perhaps this trip would be worth it, after all.

"We are going to Florida," Anna announced to Darren.

"I know!" He smiled. "I'm the one who is taking you."

Anna looked worried. "Not Rachel?"

"Rachel needs to stay home and take care of baby Holly remember?" Lydia said.

"I can help," Anna said. "Holly can come, too."

"It is best not to take babies that young on long car trips if you can help it," Lydia said gently.

"But..." Anna began to argue.

Bertha was not in the mood to deal with Anna's arguments. She had not slept well the night before, and there had been many bad dreams. She was feeling more than a little irritable.

"We cannot take Holly with us," Bertha said, with finality. "Darren is going to drive us instead of Rachel. That is the way it has to be. We will just have to make the best of it."

Lydia, Anna, and Darren all stared at her.

"What?" Bertha said.

"Darren doesn't have to take you," Lydia gently reminded her. "He is making this trip out of the goodness of his heart."

Lydia was right. Bertha deeply regretted the fact that she had probably just hurt Darren's feelings.

"Please forgive me," she said. "I appreciate what you're doing, Darren. I know you don't have to make this trip."

"No sacrifice for me." He shrugged. "I'm driving two lovely ladies to Florida. I will be getting out of the snow and ice for a few days. I will not be working in the kitchen at the restaurant. And my brother and sister-in-law are grateful to me for doing this. What's not to like?"

Darren was a charmer. Bertha smiled despite herself. She still did not want to go, and she was still not sure that this trip would do Anna any good, but it was her responsibility to see it through.

"I believe we are finally ready." She could not hold back a small sigh as she handed her suitcase to Darren.

As Darren carried their luggage to his car, Anna toddled out behind him, chatting a mile a minute about beaches and seashells.

Bertha and Lydia watched.

"I know this is a sacrifice for you," Lydia said. "But I believe it is going to do much good. Anna deserves this trip. I know deep in my heart that it will help her—if not physically, then emotionally. Cousin Rosa is beside herself with happiness that she's going to have house guests. Who knows, you might even have fun."

"I sincerely doubt it," Bertha said.

"I've packed food for the three of you." Lydia handed her a

medium-sized cooler. "There's plenty there, more than enough to share with Darren as well, at least for the first day. I packed some lemonade as well."

"Thank you," Bertha said.

"That way, you won't have to stop at any restaurants today. I have heard that the cost is great when one is stopping at places along the interstate roads."

Lydia and Bertha did not hug good-bye, that was not usually a part of their stoic culture, but Bertha's heart ached with love for her thoughtful younger sister.

"I will miss you, Lydia," Bertha said.

"As I will you," Lydia said. "Take good care of yourself and Anna. I do not know what I would do without either of you."

"Nor I you."

As their car pulled out of the driveway, Bertha looked back and saw Lydia smiling and waving good-bye from the porch. Such a gentle soul. She seemed so small and thin and fragile, standing there alone. Lydia was and always had been a much better person than Bertha knew herself to be. She would miss her.

As they drove out onto the highway, she closed her eyes and began to silently pray. She prayed that Lydia would be surrounded by God's special protection while they were gone, that the trip would go so well that Darren wouldn't regret having volunteered for it, and that spending time in Florida would create a vast difference in Anna's physical and emotional help. She prayed that Rachel and Holly would stay well, that God's perfect candidate to take over Rachel's police job would appear soon, and that Joe's Home Plate would continue to thrive. She also gave thanks for Rosa's willingness to let them stay with her and asked that their presence would help ease her cousin's loneliness.

Having been Amish for so long, it did not once occur to her to pray for anything for herself.

CHAPTER 35

Once Bertha finished her prayer, she felt more peaceful about going to Florida. The decision was made. The trip was inevitable. The Lord had been alerted about all her immediate concerns. She could relax.

That's the way it had always been with her. Lots of worry and soul-searching before a major decision, but once it was made, she put the fretting behind her and tried to enjoy the journey.

"Tried" was the operative word this time. Once Bertha opened her eyes, the lovely sense of peace immediately began to evaporate. It was Darren's fault. He did not drive to her liking.

Once they got out on the interstate and headed south, he sped up, and she was forced to remind him to slow down. Unfortunately, he did not want to listen.

"The speed limit is seventy miles per hour," he told her the third time she gently encouraged him to slow down before he got them all killed!

"That may be, but it is an ungodly amount of speed," she said, watching the trees whip by.

"I'm staying just under the speed limit," Darren said evenly.

She saw that his knuckles had grown white, he was gripping the steering wheel so tightly. He also had developed a habit of clenching his jaw. She'd never noticed that before.

"That may be," Bertha said. "But..."

"Please let me drive," Darren said. "I know what I'm doing. Honest."

Bertha wasn't so sure about that.

Anna was of no help. She didn't seem to care how fast they went. If there was one thing Anna enjoyed, it was a car trip. She loved watching the world go by as she gazed out the window. Now and then, Bertha could hear her give a pleased little sigh.

Bertha was caught between a rock and a hard place. She couldn't get Darren to slow down, and since he was the one driving the car, there was little she could do. Instead, she closed her eyes again and began to pray more fervently for their safety and for Darren to use good sense and keep his eyes on the road and not go so fast!

Route 77 went very straight for many miles after they left Sugarcreek. The hum of the engine, the sound of wheels flying over the pavement, plus her lack of rest the night before, lulled her into a deep sleep.

When she awoke, she was startled to discover that it was her own snores that had awakened her.

She sat up straight, glanced out the window, and was relieved to discover that they were still alive even though Darren hadn't slowed down one bit.

"Where are we?" she asked.

"West Virginia," he said. "You were asleep for a long time. Feeling better?"

Bertha wasn't sure. What she felt was uncomfortable.

"A bathroom break would be welcome," she said, with dignity. "Although it is not yet an emergency."

"Thank you for letting me know." He glanced at her, smiling

mischievously. "Whatever you do, don't wait until it is an emergency before you tell me."

A rest stop was coming up, and he pulled in. She and Anna went to use the facilities. It tended to take Anna a long time. Bertha hoped he didn't get impatient, but when they got back to the car, Darren had his head leaned against his headrest and appeared to be asleep.

She wasn't sure what to do, but the minute Anna opened the door to the backseat, Darren came instantly awake.

"Are you all right?" Bertha asked.

"I'm right as rain," he said, cheerfully, as he started the car engine. "That's a little trick I learned over the years. A short catnap every couple hundred miles or so, and I can drive almost indefinitely.

This made her nervous.

"Whenever you get tired," Bertha said, "We can stop at a motel. I have enough money to pay for two rooms. I don't want you to drive when you are tired. I have read that it is as dangerous as driving drunk."

"I'm not tired," Darren said, checking over his shoulder as he backed out of their parking spot.

"Would you like a sandwich?" Bertha asked. "Lydia packed a very nice lunch for us."

"I'm not hungry. When I do get hungry, I usually just go through a drive-through."

Bertha was appalled. Who knew if those Englisch teenagers who worked at fast-food places ever washed their hands? She thought the possibility iffy at best.

Bertha clucked her tongue. "Anna, please hand the cooler to me. We need to make sure our driver is fed."

"Peanut butter and grape jelly on Lydia's homemade bread?" she held up a thick sandwich wrapped in waxed paper.

"Wow," he said. "The good smells coming from that cooler has caught my attention. "What other kinds of sandwiches are in there?"

Bertha investigated. "Egg salad, ham, cheese, and meatloaf. Plus some fruit and fresh veggies and oatmeal-chocolate chip cookies."

"Meatloaf."

"Good choice," Bertha said. "Lydia's meatloaf is especially delicious."

Darren expertly unwrapped the sandwich without taking his eyes from the road. "It's been years since I've eaten a sandwich wrapped in waxed paper. Why doesn't Lydia use those little zip-lock sandwich bags?"

"She thinks waxed paper makes the sandwiches taste better," Bertha said. "I can't tell one way or another."

Darren's first bite brought an ecstatic roll of his eyes and a sigh of appreciation. Bertha wished Lydia was there to see him wolf it down.

"Lemonade?" she asked.

He nodded and finished chewing his last bite as she handed him a napkin, then a small bottle of lemonade.

"Is there anything that Lydia makes that isn't delicious?" he asked after he'd drained the bottle and wiped his fingers.

"Pizza."

"Pizza?"

"Yes," Bertha said. "She attempted pizza once, and that turned out very badly. We decided she would leave that dish to the experts, and we gave it to the chickens."

"Did the chickens like it?"

"Chickens eat bugs," Bertha said. "What do they know?"

He chuckled. "That's a good point."

"Do you want anything else?" she asked.

"I'm good for now. Aren't you and Anna going to have anything?"

"A little later," Bertha said. "We had a big breakfast."

She handed the cooler back to Anna, who sat it down on the seat beside her and then continued to happily watch the world whiz by from the back seat of Darren's car.

Satisfied that she had done all she could for now and that Darren wasn't going to slow down, no matter what she said, Bertha decided she might as well take another nap. She settled down, closed her eyes, lost consciousness for what felt like only a few minutes, and then startled herself awake again—only this time it was her mind that awakened her, serving up a new concern.

She was worried about Darren. He had been driving for a long time now, and she had read about how sometimes drivers fell asleep at the wheel and wrecked. Sitting up straight, she resolved to not let that happen!

Horses and buggies were so much safer! If an Amish person fell asleep, the horse either kept going and took them home, or it stopped entirely and stood still. At the very worst, wandered around a bit.

Horses did not crash into other horses while going seventy miles per hour!

Instead of napping, Bertha decided she needed to stay alert and make sure Darren did, too!

CHAPTER 36

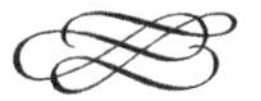

Haiti
1963

As Bertha got to know the children under her care, she learned that many who had come in off the street were not true orphans. Many had at least one living parent or grandparent. The reason they were there was that many of their relatives were subsisting on fewer financial resources than Bertha thought possible. Many of the children had been brought in by relatives who simply could not feed them.

Those first months, in addition to receiving a social and cultural education, she learned about health problems that went far beyond her training. Life was fragile in Haiti. There was so much that could take a person from being well one day to dying the next. There were diseases in Haiti that she'd never heard of in Ohio.

The more she learned, the more she fought to protect the children under her care from the ravages of all the germs and microbes determined to hurt them.

She rarely got a full night's sleep. Some viruses would sweep through the place, and before she knew it, several children would be feverish and calling for her. Or calling out for a big sister or brother or mother who was no longer in their lives. Rarely did they call out for a father, and that fact saddened her. So many men, unable to carry the physical and emotional load in this impoverished nation, abdicated their position in their children's lives and drifted away.

It was up to her and the small staff to cuddle them, wipe their noses, potty train them, and brush the tangles out of their hair. An elderly widow named Widelene came asking for work. All Bertha could offer was a place to sleep and meals which the woman gratefully accepted.

She had never expected braiding hair to be a problem for her. Every Amish girl and woman was used to braiding hair daily because it was the only way to keep long hair neatly coiled beneath their kapps. But Bertha soon learned that braiding a little Haitian girl's hair took a slightly different skill. It had taken a few days for Mimose to teach her how to do it properly.

The children's clothes became torn and needed to be mended. Bertha was no wizard with a needle and thread, but like every other Amish woman, she was raised to be at least competent enough to repair a rip, or sew up a torn hem.

As her mastery of Creole increased, she began to teach. Reading, writing, and arithmetic. There was so much more she wanted to show them, though. The children needed to know the history of their country and the victories as well as the mistakes their leaders had made and continued to make. There was a reason Papa Doc brought terror to the hearts of the Haitian people. She hoped to talk about this with the older children at some point. They needed to know these things so that when they became leaders, they wouldn't make the same mistakes.

She also longed to do something about the eroding hills, which had been deforested for charcoal and lumber. There was enough farm girl within her that she hoped to teach the poor farmers how to rotate crops. She longed to tamp the ground in around sturdy, transplanted fruit and nut trees and begin to grow forests that could provide lumber with which to rebuild this country. The soil was rich enough to sustain the population if it was treated with care, but the people were too desperate to give it time to rest and regrow.

In addition to all her other tasks, there were patients to tend to who kept coming. The hospital was several miles away by jeep or truck. Word had gotten out that there was a nurse at the children's home who had medicine and skill. Three days into her arrival, she awoke to find several Haitians at the gate with various illnesses and injuries patiently waiting to see her. She began to awaken earlier and earlier each day so she could tend to at least a few of them before the children awoke.

At least a third of the children in Haiti were infected with worms in their little bellies. Her children were not, but only because she and Mimose took strong measures to protect them.

She saw typhoid, tetanus, and tuberculosis. Malaria was also a problem. Bertha knew that people often inadvertently raised their own mosquitos, so she patrolled the area within and outside the perimeters of the children's compound, emptying various containers of stagnant water before more mosquitos could breed.

Charlotte came to help her as often as she could. On those days, she would take over some of Bertha's chores with the idea that Bertha could get some rest, but Bertha never rested. The bit of respite Charlotte gave her was much too precious for rest. She used that quiet time to sink into her Bible and prayer. It became food and drink to her because the work here was not just physically demanding, it drained her spirit if she didn't take care to refill.

Some days, it seemed as though she could not bear to have her heart broken one more time. A child too ill to save. An aging grandmother with tuberculosis and no living relative to care for her. A woman hugely pregnant, standing in line to see her and Bertha discovering there was no fetal heartbeat.

Precious people with nothing to work with, clinging to the hope that she would be able to help them. Many times she could. Much of the time she couldn't. Often, even Dr. Lawrence and the hospital staff could not help.

Sometimes the Haitians' resigned acceptance of terrible things—gangrene from a machete accident, the horrific-looking elephantiasis, dengue fever—broke her heart even more than the fact of the diseases themselves.

In addition to experiencing heart-ache daily, she often found herself dealing with intense anger. The toll taken by the Vodou priests on the Haitian people was enormous, both emotionally and financially. The priests often required money these people did not have to remove various so-called spells. The people were threatened with all sorts of evil things by the priests if any of them turned away from the dark religion to embrace the grace of Christ.

One day, only three weeks after she arrived, Dr. Lawrence dropped in to check on how things were going. She broke down when she saw him, and to her deep embarrassment, she started crying. Exhaustion, culture shock, a too-tender heart, her inability to communicate in the children's language as well as she needed to, was suddenly way too much.

Dr. Lawrence reacted to her tears like she was one of the children needing comforting.

"Come here," he said and took her in his arms.

As she sobbed out her feelings of inadequacy, of being overwhelmed, and of her great sadness over what she was seeing, he quietly patted her on the back and said soothing words.

"You are doing a wonderful job here," he said. "Please don't doubt that. But your first job is the children. Focus on protecting and caring for them. If you can just save and teach these precious little ones, you will have moved mountains and God will be glorified."

Although it had felt good to have him tell her that, she couldn't seem to stop crying.

"I'll ask Jane to come over in the early mornings and take some of the pressure off of you with the adults seeking medical attention. Would that help?"

She stopped crying and nodded. It would be nice to have Jane come every morning.

Dr. Lawrence stepped back and took a long look at her, making sure her tears had dried up. Then he kissed her on the forehead, told her she was an amazing woman, and the children were lucky to have her.

Later that night, she was a little surprised at herself for reliving that brief, physical encounter in detail. It had felt good to be held by someone stronger than herself. Perhaps a little too good even though Dr. Lawrence had meant nothing by it. He was only comforting a hysterical nurse. But she was wise enough to see the need to be careful. It would be entirely too easy to begin caring too much for Charlotte's husband, and that would never do.

Jane did come, and it did relieve much pressure. She heeded Dr. Lawrence's advice, but even just protecting the children took a toll. Rabies was yet another evil she had to fight. Jane told her there had been several cases of human rabies the hospital staff had dealt with. Beyond a particular stage, there was no cure.

Rabid dogs occasionally roamed the area. Sometimes leaving pups behind who were also infected. Of course, the children wanted to adopt every stray animal that came near the place. Bertha could not allow that if she was going to protect them. It was not a popular decision, but she knew she could not back down.

All of that in addition to protecting them from all the germs and microbes little bodies could pick up, and Haiti had some awful ones.

Two little girls, twins, maybe nine or ten years old, waited outside the gate as she walked across the compound after supper one evening. The girls wore identical tattered blue dresses and were barefoot. They were the same height, the same skin color, and the same hair.

That is where the resemblance ended. One was lovely, her face unmarred. Her sister, whose hands she grasped, was what Bertha would forever secretly think of as the girl with no face.

She had read about Yaws in her nursing classes, but it was not a disease of North America, and therefore the instructors had not focused on it in her studies for long. It was just part of a myriad of nasty tropical diseases.

Knowing she would be working in Haiti, she had studied these various diseases more than most of her classmates. However, as she looked at this girl, she knew she had not studied nearly enough.

Yaws was a bacteria that ate away at the flesh and bone. Papa Doc had supposedly worked with an American doctor to try to find a way to cure it. She did not know how much Papa Doc contributed to the research, but certain antibiotics had been found that could stop the advance of the disease.

Fortunately, she knew Dr. Lawrence had a supply of those particular antibiotics at the hospital.

The two girls were ragged, extremely hungry, and they had nowhere else to go. The non-disfigured girl explained to Bertha that her sister had been cast out by their parents, who could not bear to look at her. The non-disfigured sister could not bear to see her sister go away alone. She knew the other children threw rocks at her. The valiant little healthy sister had come along to protect her until they could get to the children's home where they had heard there was a nurse who would help.

A nurse was not supposed to flinch in the face of disfigurement or wounds, and Bertha had seen much suffering in the few weeks she had been here, but the sight and pathos of this poor child's face when she raised the thin veil she wore to protect herself from flies and prying eyes nearly made Bertha's knees buckle.

The Haitians had a strange medical folklore. They believed that a wound had to rot before it would get better. This, of course, was untrue. The wounds left to fester often turned into gangrene. Dr. Lawrence said he had been forced to perform several amputations because of that very philosophy.

There was so much ignorance on this island. Bertha knew it would take more time than she possessed to see that all the people learned the medicinal value of basic cleanliness, or even for them to have the supplies they needed to apply that knowledge. So many did not have the wherewithal to buy clean bandages and antibiotic ointments. Had they been able to do so, there would not have been so many cuts and wounds that became septic.

But to see a sweet child in this condition...

Bertha left word at the hospital asking Dr. Lawrence to stop in on his way home that evening. That she had a child he needed to see and to tell him she needed an injection for Yaws.

"Come with me," Bertha said.

She helped the little girls wash up, then fed them in her room, not wanting to subject the infected one to the stares of the other children. Both girls were exhausted, so after they had eaten and had a sponge bath, she tucked them into her bed and let them sleep. The poor things had walked so far and were so young.

Then she sat and watched over them, praying that Dr. Lawrence would come soon. He would know what to do. He always knew what to do.

He came a little later than she had hoped, but he did come, and he had brought the antibiotics with him.

"I am a doctor," he said to the girls, in soft Creole. "I want to help you. Can I look at your face, sweet girl?"

His tenderness and concern for the two girls was incredibly touching. What a saint this man was! How blessed she was to have someone like him to turn to when there were situations like this.

Dr. Lawrence's voice soothed the little girl. She didn't cry out when he gave her the injection. After he finished, he pulled her onto his lap and held her while he assured them that everything was going to be okay.

Bertha wondered how he could say that.

"I have a close friend in the states who is a plastic surgeon," he explained. "Sometimes, he makes third-world visits. I think his next visit should be here, don't you? And soon."

Bertha nodded, unable to speak, fighting back tears of gratitude.

Over the following days, as she cared for the two girls and Dr. Lawrence made arrangements for his friend to come, she wondered when it would be her time for illness to hit, but it did not. At least not for the first few months. It was as though the childhood she had received in the Holmes County area had given her such a good start nutritionally, her body could throw off any number of diseases. She was grateful but doubted her good luck would last.

CHAPTER 37

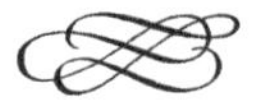

"You might want to slow down a little," Bertha suggested yet again, this time without even bothering to look at the speedometer. "I saw a sign back there that said the speed limit was sixty-five now. "I would hate for you to get a ticket."

"I *am* driving the speed limit, Bertha," Darren said. "I'll get a ticket if I go any slower."

They had made three bathroom stops so far. Two had been at McDonald's so Darren could get a large black coffee to go. They had eaten about half the food in the cooler. Darren had not shown any signs of accidentally falling asleep that she had seen. She was feeling much better about him.

"Where are we?" she asked.

"About half-way through North Carolina," he said.

"Are you still feeling all right?" She was concerned. "You've been driving an awfully long time."

"I've driven all over this country, Bertha," he said. "I haven't fallen asleep at the wheel yet."

"Would they really ticket you for going too slow?" She turned to check on Anna, who was lying on the back seat, sound asleep.

"Yes. Some people have gotten tickets for driving too slowly."

"That is a bad rule." She thought about it for a few moments. "But I trust you. I apologize for nagging so much."

Darren glanced at her. "You trust me?"

"Yes."

"That surprises me."

"Why?"

"Because I'm Darren—the black sheep of the family." He drummed his fingers on the steering wheel for a moment. "Joe was the brother people trusted. I was the prodigal who wasted my life in what the Bible called 'riotous living.'"

"I was the black sheep of our family as well."

"That's not the same thing," Darren said. "Leaving your church to become a nurse isn't exactly riotous living."

"Becoming a nurse did not go over so well with my family, that is true," she said. "But I have been disobedient in my own heart many times."

"Being disobedient in your heart doesn't count," Darren said. "You can be a little bossy sometimes, but overall I've never met anyone who lives with more integrity and righteousness than you."

Bertha gave a small snort of derision.

"What?" Darren asked. "Everyone respects and admires you."

"Then they are foolish," Bertha said.

"Come on, now. You've led an exemplary life."

"I have tried to, yes," Bertha said. "But sometimes a person does the very thing they think they will never do. That's scripture, Darren. The Apostle Paul wrote those very words about himself."

"I know," Darren said. "It's one of my favorite passages."

"You've read the Bible?" Bertha was surprised.

"I was a missionary's kid, remember?" Darren said. "Of course I've read the Bible. But you couldn't have done anything all that bad. It is not in your nature."

"Oh?" she said. "And you think you know my nature so very well?"

"I know what Rachel thinks of you, and that's enough for me."

"And what does my niece think of me?"

"She reveres you," Darren said. "And I revere Rachel."

"Rachel is worthy of your respect, yes," Bertha said. "But even our Rachel does not know me as well as she thinks."

"I imagine that's true with most people. There are always things that are best left between them and God."

Bertha glanced at him in surprise. Darren had mentioned God again. There was more to Joe's brother than she realized.

"Don't look so surprised, Bertha," he said. "I've done some things I'm not proud of, and I've made some stupid decisions, but I never stopped believing."

"I'm glad."

"Are we there yet?" Anna had awakened. She unbuckled her seatbelt and leaned over the seat.

"No," Bertha said. "We aren't even close. In fact, where are we?"

"Almost to South Carolina," Darren said. "Does anyone need to stop?"

"No." Anna shook her head, obediently put her seatbelt back on, and settled down to watch out the window again.

"What about you, Bertha?" Darren said. "Are you holding up okay?"

"I feel fine," Bertha said. "I almost always feel fine. Except for breaking my leg when I fell down the steps a couple of years ago, I've hardly had any issues with my health."

"Then you are fortunate," Darren said. "Hey, I see a McDonald's up ahead. You and Anna can use the bathroom, and I'll get another cup of coffee."

As Darren parked the car, Bertha realized that she had told Darren a lie. It wasn't deliberate, but sometimes her memory wasn't as good as it used to be. She had once become extremely ill, and it had been her own fault.

CHAPTER 38

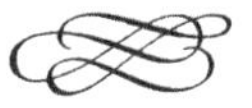

The tub was rust-stained as she stepped into the cloudy water. The water felt scalding hot, and she jerked her foot back as Charlotte steadied her.

"I don't want to do this," Bertha said.

"You are burning up," Charlotte said. "The water is barely lukewarm. It will help bring the fever down."

"No." She was chilling and just wanted to go back to bed. "Please, no."

"Trust me," Charlotte said. "Anthony says you have to do this."

Anthony?

Oh yes. Charlotte's husband. A doctor.

Bertha started shaking, and her teeth began to chatter.

"Anthony!" Charlotte shouted. "Come in here. I need help!"

That was the last thing Bertha remembered.

She was surprised when she awoke in the hospital with an IV emptying into her arm. Her nose itched, but when she tried to scratch it, she discovered that she barely had the strength to lift her arm. Every bone in her body ached. She glanced around and saw she was in a ward with other patients. Dr. Lawrence was talking to a woman several beds down when he glanced up and saw her watching him.

"Finally awake?" Dr. Lawrence finished with the other woman, came over to where Bertha lay, sat down on the side of her bed, and felt her forehead with the back of his hand. "How are you feeling?"

"Weak," she said. "What happened?"

"Malaria."

"Oh." She relaxed back against the thin pillow. "That makes sense."

"Did you forget to take one of your doses of Chloroquine?"

"I ran out."

"And you were too busy to come to me for more?" Dr. Lawrence's voice was stern. "Even though it is the rainy season and mosquitos are breeding like crazy?"

"Some of the children have been ill..."

"I know. An even better reason to keep yourself well."

"I've never been sick a day in my life."

"You never lived in Haiti before," Dr. Lawrence's voice was uncharacteristically bitter. "Apparently illness is what we do."

For the first time, Bertha noticed how weary he looked.

"What's wrong?" she asked.

"Nothing," Dr. Lawrence shook his head. "I'm just tired. I've been helping with the boys as much as I can. All three are home with diarrhea. Keeping them hydrated has been an issue. Neither Charlotte nor I have gotten much sleep."

"And I added to your burden," Bertha said, miserably.

He didn't bother to say that she hadn't. That wasn't the kind of man he was. Instead, he took her hand in both of his.

"Just remember to wear your mosquito repellent, continue to sleep beneath the netting and take your Chloroquine," he said. "We desperately need you to stay well."

After he left, she marveled over how warm his hands had felt as they clasped her cold ones. She wished he had held them for a few moments longer. Perhaps then she wouldn't feel so weak and disheartened.

Bertha vowed never to forget to take a dose of malaria medicine again.

The one thing she never, ever, wanted to do was become a burden to Dr. Lawrence and her good friend, Charlotte.

CHAPTER 39

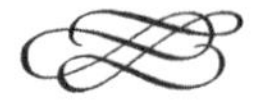

"It is very dark out," Bertha said after they got back on the road after their McDonald's break. "It must be hard to drive in the dark. I have enough money to pay for two hotel rooms if they are not too expensive."

"Funny thing about cars." Darren took a gulp of fresh hot coffee. "They have headlights, and I am wide-awake. I can drive all night."

Anna happily licked a McDonald's ice cream cone she had insisted on getting.

"You are sure you can do this?"

"I'm sure."

The car created a sort of private cocoon around them as they hurtled through the night. This was not something Bertha had ever experienced before, but she rather liked the sensation. Especially when Darren, without asking, turned the radio on and found a station that played lovely soft music. Although radios were forbidden in her sect, she secretly enjoyed hearing a little music now and then.

"So, as one black sheep to another," he said, "What is it that makes you think you are such a bad person?"

Bertha was silent.

"Oh, come on, Bertha," Darren said. "What commandments have you ever actually broken?"

Commandments? The question took her by surprise. She had memorized the Ten Commandments many years ago as she taught them to the Haitian children under her care. As the road spun beneath the wheels of the car, thrusting them through the night, she examined each one.

"Most of them," she confessed.

"You can't be serious." Darren sounded shocked. "I was joking."

"I am not joking."

"You took God's name in vain?"

"A couple of times when things did not go my way," she said. "I am very ashamed of that."

"You didn't honor your mother and father?"

"I couldn't help it if I was to become a nurse. I broke their heart with my choice."

"Covetousness?"

"Oh yes," she said. "I have often envied other women for having their very own children."

"Remembering the Sabbath?"

"I've not always gone to church every time I could."

"So, you're human," Darren said. "It's not like you're a murderer or anything."

Silence.

"Bertha?"

She still did not answer. Instead, she glanced into the back seat to see if Anna was listening and discovered that Anna had fallen asleep with a half-eaten ice cream cone melting in her hand.

"Can you pull over?" she asked Darren. "I'm afraid there is a bit of a mess getting ready to happen."

He pulled over, Bertha got out, threw away the soggy ice cream cone, wiped off Anna's sticky hands, reassured her little sister that she hadn't done anything wrong, and then they continued their journey with Anna drowsing in the back.

"So," Darren cleared his throat. "About that fifth commandment. You never actually killed anyone, did you?

"I thought I had no choice," Bertha said. "I'm afraid at that time in my life, I was not as good of a pacifist as I had been taught to be."

He stared at her. "Does anyone else know?"

"A few," Bertha said. "I doubt many of them are living anymore."

"Do you want to tell me about it?"

"I've not discussed it with anyone since I left Haiti. It is a complicated story that would take much time to explain."

Darren turned off the radio. "I don't have a lot of talents, but one thing I seem to be good at is keeping secrets. Maybe it's because I've had to keep my own for so long."

Bertha found herself actually contemplating telling Darren one of the two darkest secrets in her soul. Maybe it was because his own failures had been legion, and yet he never stopped trying. Perhaps it was because she did feel a bond with him over being the black sheep of the family. Maybe it was because she had come to a point in her life when she simply didn't want to be silent any longer.

To explain to Darren what it had been like, she allowed herself to sink back into that dark time when, because of Papa Doc's reign of terror, resources were sparse, and everyone was looking out for themselves...

CHAPTER 40

Haiti
1963

Bertha awoke from a deep sleep and bolted upright, listening. She had not dreamed that sound. Someone was trying to batter their way through the barred gate of the Haitian children's home compound.

It would not be the first time someone had tried to gain access, nor the last. The Haitian people were hungry.

She kept all the children's food securely locked in the supply room in the building they used as a kitchen and dining room. The key hung on a leather cord around her neck. If anyone wanted it, they would have to fight her for it. The few staples she'd managed to lock away was the only thing standing between full little bellies for her children and starvation.

The crops, such as they were, had not done well this year. Not that Haiti ever had a surplus of food, but this year had been worse than most. Were it not for the support of the Mennonite Central Committee and the sacks of beans, rice, and canned meat they brought over from the United States, her children would be in desperate need.

So far, her height and loud indignation had been enough to scare the would-be thieves away—but she wasn't sure how long that would work.

Grabbing her flashlight off the rickety nightstand, she scanned the floor of her room. Good. It was clear. Experience had taught her not to assume she could leap out of bed without the possibility of an unwanted surprise. A painful encounter with a brown scorpion had made her cautious.

Again—that sound of someone trying to break in. They must either be stupid, desperate or entirely fearless to make so much noise. The other two thieves she had faced had been more cautious.

She ran outside just in time to see the wood of the barricaded gate give way. Of course, it hadn't been all that strong, to begin with. Boards were hard to come by in Haiti, good, thick oak boards like her people used back home were nearly impossible to find.

The night sky was clear, and a full moon illuminated a large man stumbling through the broken gate and into the open area between them. Bertha played the flashlight over him and took a step back. His eyes were wild. His face was a grimacing mask. He looked stronger than most Haitian men.

Bertha's first instinct was to run, but she couldn't run. She was the only one standing between this intruder and the children.

"You need to leave." Bertha stood her ground, her voice strong and steady. "There is nothing here for you."

He plunged past her, headed straight for the building that functioned as the girls' dormitory. That was a surprise. She would have bet her nearly nonexistent pay that he wanted food.

"Please stop!" Bertha called. "There is no food in there."

The man ignored her and continued to stalk toward the building where seventeen precious and innocent girls slept.

Did he think that was where the food was kept? Or did he have something more sinister in mind?

His hair was long and tangled. He was ragged and barefoot, but he had a powerful stride, and Bertha, encumbered by the unforgiving skirt of her long, cotton nightgown stumbled as she tried to keep up with him.

"Please don't go in there," she begged. "The children are asleep."

His hand was on the doorknob. Thankfully, it was locked. Widelene, the elderly Haitian widow who helped Bertha and Mimose with the children, slept in the girl's dormitory. It was her job to keep the doors locked at night.

Bertha caught up with him just as he grabbed hold of the doorknob and rattled it.

"Please!" she shouted in Creole. "Please don't hurt my children!"

He began to heave his shoulders against the door. Bertha grappled at his arm to hold him back, but he shook her off.

Her righteous indignation, her tall, strong body, the desperate prayer running in her mind—nothing was holding him back.

The door began to splinter.

Bertha, like all Amish and Mennonites, believed sincerely in pacifism. It was her lifelong desire and intent never to hurt or cause pain to another person. It was practically bred into her DNA to turn the other cheek.

But her great fear for her beloved children created a blaze of anger that she could not see past. Her visual focus had narrowed down to one item—a Louisville Slugger, made from hardened maple, leaning against the side of the building. She had asked her sister to send it so she could teach the older children how to play baseball. The game quickly became a favorite. The baseball bat was in daily use. Both she and Mimose played it with the children frequently. She had never thought of using it as a weapon, but now she grabbed it and threw herself between him and the door.

"Leave my girls alone!" She brandished the bat.

He paused, seeming to truly notice her for the first time. Then with one quick move, he grasped the bat and tried to jerk it out of her hands, but Bertha held on. He was bigger and stronger, but she felt an almost supernatural strength as she fought him—a force drawn from her love of the children and her fear for them if he got past her.

Unable to wrestle the baseball bat out of her hands, he gave a mighty heave and shoved her away from him. She stumbled backward, fell to the ground, and the baseball bat skittered away across the bare earth.

She could hear the girls crying and whimpering from within the dormitory. He had already managed to do a great deal of damage to the door. It was nearly off its hinges. This time, nothing significant would be in his way.

Unless she acted.

It was at that moment, sprawled in the dirt, the last dregs of Bertha's firmly held pacifist beliefs drained away.

Baseball was a favorite sport among Amish boys and girls alike, and they played it often. During teenage games, there were always several farm girls who could knock a baseball out of the ball field just as well as a boy. Bertha had been the strongest of those girls. Helping her father on the farm had made her able to pluck a sixty-pound bale of fresh hay out of the field, lift it above her head, and toss it onto the wagon for her father to stack.

"Lord, forgive me," she said aloud as she rose to her feet.

Bertha scooped up the wooden bat, ran toward the man, and swung at his head with a strength fueled by anger and desperation.

She did not miss.

CHAPTER 41

The man crumpled to the ground and lay there unmoving. Mimose, who had been awakened by Bertha's shouts, came running.

"Oh!" Mimose said when she saw the man lying there in the dirt. "Who is this?"

"I don't know." Bertha dropped the bat and rubbed her hands on her nightgown as though trying to wipe them clean of her violent act.

Time stood still as the two women stood watching, still as statues, holding their breaths. Would he arise?

He still did not move. It appeared he had also stopped breathing.

Cautiously, she approached him.

"Be careful," Mimose said.

Bertha knelt and felt his neck for a pulse. There was none. She felt his wrist. Nothing. She moved his head, saw the damage the bat had done to it.

"I just wanted to stop him—to knock him out." Bertha felt a roiling in her stomach. "I never intended to kill the man."

Mimose took a step backward, as though trying to distance herself from the act.

As the magnitude of what she had just done hit with full force, Bertha ran to the fence, braced her hands against it, bent over and threw up violently and repeatedly until her legs could no longer hold her. She fell to her knees.

Through the roaring in her ears, Bertha could hear Widelene inside the bunkhouse calming down the girls.

"Everything is fine," Widelene kept saying. "Go back to sleep now. There is no danger."

Mimose brought a wet washcloth from somewhere and gently wiped Bertha's face.

"We need to call the police," Bertha said.

"That would be foolish," Mimose said. "Even though you are an American, they will take you to jail. Bad things happen to women in Haiti who are taken to jail. We must call Dr. Lawrence. He will know what to do."

Of course. Anthony always knew what to do.

"Call him." Bertha's aching heart was grateful there was someone as competent as Anthony to come to her rescue.

CHAPTER 42

"It was a terrible time in Haiti," Bertha told Darren. "People were hungry. The government—well, it was a dangerous time for everyone. Even at the children's home, we did not always have enough to eat. Without the food supplies that the Mennonite Central Committee sent, we would have been desperate, and those supplies were often withheld by dishonest custom officials. Bribes for necessities were an everyday reality."

"But you survived," Darren said.

"We did." Bertha realized she was unconsciously pleating and unpleating the skirt of her dress. This was something she tended to do only when she was extremely nervous. She forced herself to stop.

"How?" Darren asked.

"Lydia's husband had a good job and a generous heart. They frequently sent small packages to me, usually containing tins of commercially canned meat. Many of them got through to us. We hoarded them for the children. I also wrote letters to friends from nursing school and at home. They sent money with which I bought whatever I could find that was edible in the markets in Haiti. I became obsessed with collecting food that would keep well. Eventually, I had gathered what I believed was enough to sustain the children for two weeks without any outside help."

"Did you have any staff, or was it all you?" he asked.

"I had Mimose, a young woman who had grown up at the home and came back to teach. She and I shared much of the care of the youngest, and the older children helped as well. Widelene was an impoverished widow who offered to work in return for room and board. She slept in the girl's building with them. At the time, two of the girls were prone to sleepwalking, and she made certain they didn't accidentally go outside in the night. She was also skilled with a needle once we got her some eyeglasses. She helped keep the children's clothing repaired. Two women from the church came every day to cook and clean up afterward. They received a pittance, but they were grateful to get it. From time to time, Dr. Lawrence would pay a man to do repairs and whatever other work needed to be done."

"So, money was an issue. Food was an issue. The political situation was unstable," Darren said. "It was a desperate time. Things happened that might not have otherwise. I'm starting to get the picture."

"I had such grand ideas." She gave a mirthless laugh. "One month in, I decided to put my training as an Amish farm girl to good use. I asked Lydia to send seeds, and she did. We had enough space within the compound and enough willing hands to plant and tend a large garden. The seeds came and we had a marvelous time planting them. Our hopes were so high. I felt like I might be able to save Haiti all by myself with what I considered my superior knowledge about gardening. Amish women are noted for their gardens. We learn it from our mothers. I had no doubt my garden would be a success."

"I take it that things did not turn out as you'd hoped?"

"The seeds were good, our care was meticulous, but the garden did not grow a tenth of what the same work and seeds would have produced back in Ohio."

"What went wrong?"

"The earth was different, the sun was hotter, the children, fascinated with the plants that did manage to grow and hungry for fresh things, couldn't wait long enough to allow the vegetables to get fully grown. They were constantly picking and eating the unripe tomatoes, corn, and beans. Even the root vegetables were dug up and consumed before anything could reach full maturity."

"I'm sorry, Bertha," he said. "That must have been so demoralizing."

"It was. I'd had such hopes of recreating the abundance of my own childhood table. I dreamed of platters piled high with sweet corn, bowls of fresh-picked peas, creamed new potatoes, and radishes freshly washed and mounded in a bowl. It nearly broke my heart when I realized none of it had a chance of becoming a reality. At least not that first year. Eventually, I figured things out, but it took a while."

"I'm guessing more happened than just a bad harvest," Darren said.

"Oh yes," Bertha said, sadly. "Much, much more."

CHAPTER 43

"Do you feel like telling me the rest of the story?" Darren asked.

"I think I do." Bertha glanced over at him. "If you are still sure you want to hear it."

"I'm sure."

Bertha leaned her head back against the headrest and closed her eyes, remembering.

"I often had to deal with people who tried to steal food from the children," she said. "Can you imagine grown men that desperate?"

"I've seen worse—but not for food."

"Worse?"

"I've never been an addict, but I've known people who were. There is little they won't do to get a fix."

"There is much evil in the world."

"I agree," Darren said. "So, someone tried to steal from you?"

"That's what I thought," she said. "He was large for a Haitian man and...terrifying. He broke into our compound."

"Let me guess," Darren said. "You were the only thing standing between him and the children's food."

"I've never been certain what he wanted," Bertha said. "At first, I thought it was food. But when he started trying to break into the girl's dormitory..."

"Were you frightened?"

"*They* were frightened!" Bertha said. "I was *angry*! Oh, how angry! I could hear the little ones crying from fear. The rage I felt was ungodly. It made me go against my own beliefs."

"How?"

"I begged him to stop." She started pleating her skirt again. "Time and time again, I told him to stop. He wouldn't."

"So, you had to make him stop?"

"I thought I did."

"What did you do?"

The words she needed to say next felt like they were choking her.

"I killed the man. I did not mean to."

Darren stared at her for an instant, then turned back to watch the road.

"How?"

Bertha had not noticed until now, but a light rain had begun. The only sound within the car was the back and forth swish of the windshield wipers as the tires rushed through rain-slicked miles. She was grateful for the dark as she told him the whole story.

"Did any authorities come?" Darren asked gently. "Or did you have to deal with the man's body all by yourself?"

"Dr. Lawrence came immediately and took him to the hospital. It was there he was officially pronounced dead. The man's sister claimed the body. We waited, but there were no repercussions. You have to understand. People were disappearing in Haiti for the smallest infractions during that time. Ganash was just one more."

"Ganash?"

"The man's name. I found out later that he was known for being mentally unstable. Most of the time, he lived quietly up in the mountains in a makeshift tent. His sister brought him food and left it near the path where she knew he would find it. I never found out what he thought he was doing or why he had been so determined to break into the compound. His sister told Dr. Lawrence that he had lost his mind after losing a child, a little girl who succumbed to one of the many diseases that plagued children in Haiti. She said he'd been goaded by a Vodou priest to think American missionaries had stolen his child from him."

"So, you think he had come to find her?"

"Who knows?" Bertha shrugged. "Perhaps so. Or perhaps he had other terrible things on his mind that he intended to do. I will never know."

"You've never gotten over that experience, have you?" Darren said.

"Once the adrenaline subsided, nothing Dr. Lawrence could say made my soul feel any less soiled."

Darren changed lanes and merged with traffic into a different route. Bertha had no idea where they were. It almost felt like they were suspended in time.

"What did you do with the baseball bat?" he asked.

"I buried it as deep as I could manage to dig," she said. "It had taken a man's life. I could not bear to see it being used by children as a plaything ever again."

"I'm sure you didn't have many toys or athletic equipment for them," he said. "That must have felt like a sacrifice."

"Perhaps, but what else could I do?" Bertha said. "Afterward, I knelt beside my bed and begged God for forgiveness. I've been doing that practically every night since."

"Did the other missionaries in Haiti at that time know what you had done?"

"Charlotte Lawrence did. The doctor's wife who was my friend. I went to her the next day to tell her I did not think I was fit to continue at the children's home."

"How did she react?"

"Charlotte was so kind. She listened to all my words and sopped up my tears with a handkerchief. Then she fixed me a cup of tea with plenty of sugar and made me drink it. She gave me my heart back. Her loving sympathy made it possible for me to go back and begin to care for the children again."

Bertha lapsed into silence once her words were all out. It was then that he surprised her by reaching over and covering her hand, which had grown cold during the telling of her story, with his large warm one.

"You protected those little girls," he said. "There's no telling what that man had in mind. You saved the children even though it meant sacrificing your peace of mind. I'm proud of you."

He squeezed her hand once, then returned his to the steering wheel.

Bertha found herself feeling a little lighter. Perhaps this trip wouldn't end up being as hard or as awkward as she had imagined after all.

"Thank you," she said. "For listening."

"It was an honor," he said.

Anna stirred in the back seat. "Are we there yet?"

"Not yet," Darren said. "What do you think, Bertha? Do you want to stop somewhere for the night or keep going?'

"How are you feeling?" Bertha asked.

"I'm good for at least a few more hours."

"I think I would like to keep driving if you feel okay," Bertha said. "Are you hungry?"

"Do we have any more sandwiches?"

Bertha reached behind the driver's seat and checked the cooler. "We do. There is a bag of oatmeal cookies we haven't touched yet. Plus, some egg salad sandwiches and four bottles of lemonade still cold. Oh, and grapes."

"Egg salad sounds good," Darren said. "Let's keep going. As one black sheep to another, perhaps it might be a good time to tell you about some of the things I'm not particularly proud of. You know—to kinda even things out between us."

After handing him food and drink, Bertha prepared to listen. She was profoundly grateful that it was Darren who was taking them to Florida instead of Rachel, who could sometimes be quite critical.

It never failed to astonish her how God often sent just the right person at the right time. She was sure that after this trip, she and Joe's brother were going to be good friends.

CHAPTER 44

Alex could not sleep. He lay in bed, staring at the ceiling, wishing he was a better person. It was too bad that a nice little kid like Calvin had gotten stuck with a screw-up like him for a guardian.

He'd thought he was doing the smart thing moving his younger cousin to a rural area with an ultra-low crime rate. He figured Calvin would be better off if they lived in a place like this while he tried to pull himself together, but things weren't working out as he'd hoped. Mainly because so far, he couldn't seem to get his act together.

The sessions he'd been advised to have with the precinct psychologist hadn't helped much. She was a nice woman, but it was clear she had no idea the depth of anguish he was experiencing. Ultimately, the best she could do was recommend what amounted to time, distance, self-forgiveness, and medication.

The precinct captain, who was a bit of a jerk, gave him a short leave of absence, time to pull himself together, he said. He seemed annoyed that Alex hadn't shaken it off yet. The captain's annoyance hit Alex the wrong way. Instead of taking a leave of absence—he quit.

He took the medication the psychologist suggested. The self-forgiveness thing? Forget about it. That wasn't happening. Might never happen.

He still spent the biggest part of each day and night going through every detail, trying to figure out what he could have done differently, castigating himself for real and imagined mistakes. He was heart-sick and obsessed with what he had done, and his obsession wasn't easing up.

Funny how the number six kept jumping out at him everywhere he looked. Phone numbers. Grocery store circulars. Road signs. It was no mystery to him why the numeral six permanently burned itself into his psyche.

One deranged man. Six hostages. Six gunshots exploding in his ear.

One. After. Another.

He could still hear them coming over the phone, his lifeline to the gunman.

He also heard them echoing through the city air. His own body wincing at the sound of each one.

Six families devastated. All of them on Alex's watch.

Once upon a time, in an entirely different universe, he had enjoyed the reputation of being a good hostage negotiator. Once upon a time, he had felt confident in his abilities. Once upon a time, he would have made an excellent guardian for a ten-year-old boy.

It was too bad that Aunt Beatrice died less than a month after the hostage incident, forcing him to keep his word to her. He had taken on the care of a grief-stricken child when even the act of getting himself out of bed in the morning felt monumental.

Poor kid.

One of the hostages had been an elementary school-teacher with three small children at home. He watched her husband being interviewed the next day on the national news. The man looked stunned and helpless as he sat with their littlest girl, a two-year-old on his lap.

The child had been sucking her thumb and hugging a stuffed blue rabbit. The image was burned into his brain.

Another one was a neo-natal nurse who had a paraplegic husband at home for whom she was caring—a veteran who had sustained injuries in Afghanistan.

And a sixty-four-year-old security guard, a former cop only two months from retirement, had been killed. He had big plans for his retirement, his wife told the news anchor. They had been saving up for years to buy an RV and visit all the places he had always wanted to go.

A sixteen-year-old girl had also been one of the six. She was so smart she was already a college freshman. Pre-med. She had wanted to be a doctor from the time she was five. Her mother was so distraught Alex feared she might try to harm herself.

There were two others with dreams also cut short and people who loved them.

How could he have misread the situation so completely?

The counselor told him it wasn't his fault. She reminded him that the killer was much more unpredictable than anyone thought. She said he could not expect himself to be a mind reader.

The problem was, that's precisely what he was supposed to be. A mind reader. That was his job—to read a killer's mind and anticipate what he might do next. He didn't have a crystal ball, but he had studied hundreds of cases of hostage situations. Had helped defuse dozens. He'd known the man was unstable and unpredictable. He'd known anything he might say was a calculated risk.

He should have sent in the swat team immediately. Caught the man off guard. Some of the hostages might have survived. But his calculations were off. The guy was even more deranged than he had thought. He could still hear the man's laughter as the gunshots were fired.

CHAPTER 45

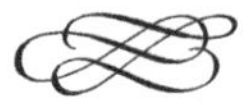

Seventeen hours after leaving Sugarcreek, with only five bathroom breaks, eight cups of coffee, and Lydia's cooler empty, Darren, Bertha, and Anna pulled into Rosa's driveway.

It was 4 a.m.

"We're here." Darren put the car in park, took his hands off the wheel, and wearily leaned his head back against the headrest.

It had somehow not occurred to Bertha that in driving straight through, they would wind up at Rosa's at such an inconvenient hour.

Anna, who had spent the hours sleeping, staring out the window, and doling out sandwiches, felt great. She popped up from the backseat.

"Can I find seashells now?"

"Not now, Anna," Bertha said. "Let's just rest and wait for Cousin Rosa to wake up."

"I don't want to," Anna whined. "I want to go to the beach!"

Darren turned to look at Bertha in the semi-darkness of very early morning. "I don't suppose your cousin would be awake yet?"

"I don't see any lights on," Bertha said. "Rosa always liked to sleep late when we were kids, and I told her we were going to stop and get a hotel about half-way. I don't think she's expecting us for a while. I didn't even think about that when we were driving."

"I want to find seashells." Anna's voice began to rise. She had been so complacent all the way here that Bertha was surprised at the passion in her sister's voice. "I want to go to the beach! I want to go now."

It was the most animated and passionate Bertha had heard Anna sound for months, maybe years. Too bad it was happening when she and Darren were completely drained.

"We can't go now," Bertha said. "Try to be patient, Anna."

Darren started the engine again and backed the car out of the driveway.

"What are you doing?" Bertha asked.

"Taking Anna to the beach," he said. "The beach will be packed later in the day. Anna has waited a long time. By the time we get there, the sun will be almost up and she'll probably have the beach to herself. Morning is a better time to go shell hunting anyway. It isn't far."

"But you have to be exhausted."

"I'll nap while you take her shell hunting."

Bertha found herself liking Joe's brother even more. What a compassionate and thoughtful young man he was!

It wasn't far. Darren found a place to park, she pulled Anna's seashell collecting bag from beneath the seat where it had fallen. Both Anna and Bertha took their shoes off and left them in the car, and in the quiet of the early morning, they went to collect seashells while Darren crawled into the back seat and napped.

The sun had not yet risen, but the sunrise was imminent and the sky was starting to lighten as they walked toward the sound of waves.

"We might have to wait a little bit before we can see the shells well enough to find any," Bertha told Anna.

"I don't care." Anna gave a sigh of contentment.

At the place where the water touched the sand, just before it got wet, Anna plopped herself down and began to cry softly.

"What's wrong?" Bertha sat down and put her arm around her. "Why are you crying?"

"I'm here!" Anna said.

The pathos in her voice nearly crushed Bertha because she finally understood. Anna had gotten to enjoy the beach only once, back when she was a little girl, and their parents made their first and only visit to Pinecraft. Everyone had thought that her fascination with seashells was adorable, but no one had ever realized that her need to count and collect them had held so much nostalgia for her.

Apparently, the memory of being here was more important to her than any of them had ever known. It wasn't just about seashells. It was the sound of water, the scent of the ocean, the view of seagulls flying overhead. It was the feel of sand beneath her feet. Had Bertha known, she would have turned heaven and earth to make sure that Anna got to travel to the beach every year of her life.

She thought back on how reluctant she had been about coming here, how annoyed she had been, and she felt ashamed. When was she ever going to get things right? Was God never going to be finished teaching her?

Silently, she gave thanks that He had created a situation where even against her will, she was doing the right thing for her little sister. She would have happily endured an even longer trip had she known how important this was to her.

"Look!" Anna said, pointing.

Bertha looked.

The sun was beginning to show a few beams of gold and pink as it peeked over the horizon of the ocean.

"Oh, so pretty!" Anna said. "I remember!"

Anna had always talked slowly. It sometimes took a long time for her to say her words. It was easy to grow impatient. It was also easy to dismiss her words because they usually had to deal with wonder over such mundane things as a new litter of kittens, or a pretty flower, or a cricket chirping on the porch.

Bertha wondered if Anna had ever tried to tell them how badly she wanted to come back here, and no one had taken the time to hear.

She wordlessly reached for Anna's hand and held it as Anna marveled over yet another seemingly mundane thing—the brilliant, spectacular, breathtaking gift that God made every morning. A gift that so few people ever bothered to notice.

"So pretty." Anna sighed.

And that was how Bertha and Anna spent their first morning in Florida. Two elderly, barefoot Amish women, sitting in the sand, holding hands while they watched the sun come up.

CHAPTER 46

It was eight o'clock on a Saturday morning. Alex was still asleep, but Calvin had been up since six.

The cartoon tapes had become boring and he was hungry. Calvin wanted to eat a bowl of cereal, but they were out of milk. He hated cereal without milk.

Saturday mornings shouldn't be like this. When Grandma was alive, Saturday mornings were nice. She would make them pancakes and sausage, and they would take their plates into the living room and watch cartoons together.

Cartoons weren't boring when Grandma was alive. Calvin didn't know why that was, except having Grandma watch them with him made them seem a lot more fun, probably because they laughed at them together.

He pulled some Cheerios out of the box and ate a handful, but without milk and sugar, they were dry and tasteless.

There was milk at the grocery store in town. He passed by it every day on his way to and from school. He knew he could easily walk there and back, probably even before Alex woke up, but...he didn't have any money.

Alex had money, but it was in his wallet, which was just sitting there on the TV. Did Calvin dare help himself to a few dollars? He only intended to get a half-gallon. He wasn't sure he could carry a whole gallon that far.

He looked at the box of cereal. He looked at the wallet. His stomach growled. Alex wouldn't even notice or care if he took some money to buy breakfast, probably. This was not the first time there had been no milk for Calvin's cereal.

One thing Calvin did not want was to get into any more trouble. He really wasn't a thief, even though he did manage to consume a pie that was not his. Would helping himself to a few dollars out of Alex's wallet really be stealing?

There were just so many things he didn't understand. So many pitfalls. He wasn't even sure if Alex would get angry if he woke him up. He wished he knew what all the rules were.

His stomach growled.

He looked at the wallet. He looked at Alex's bedroom door. He looked at the box of cereal. In the background, cartoon characters made silly noises.

Calvin finally decided that he would rather irritate Alex by waking him than risk getting any more of a reputation as a thief. He softly knocked on Alex's door. There was a muffled "come in."

He opened the door carefully and tiptoed over to the bed.

"We are out of milk," he said in a soft voice, as though to keep from waking Alex completely.

"I'll get some in a little bit," Alex said.

"I'm hungry now." Calvin's voice grew impatient. "We have cereal but no milk. I want to go to the store and get some."

"Okay." Alex turned over in bed.

"I don't have any money."

"My wallet is in the living room," Alex said. "Get what you need."

"Thank you."

There was a five-dollar bill in Alex's wallet, and Calvin took it. He was fairly sure it was more than enough, but not so much that Alex would think he was taking more than he should. He wasn't sure how much a half-gallon of milk cost, but he thought it wouldn't be any more than that.

It was blustery outside, and so he tried to dress warmly, but he still couldn't find his gloves, and there were no extras in the house. In fact, there wasn't much in the house at all.

Grandma's house had felt soft and comfortable. He had liked it even though there was an awful lot of purple and lavender and pink. There were lots of doilies, too. He overheard one of Grandma's friends say his grandma's house looked like the inside of a fancy candy box. Grandma took it as a compliment. He wasn't sure it was meant as a compliment, but he didn't mind living inside a house that felt like a candy box. He liked candy, especially the kind that came in frilly paper cups.

When he got to the store, he got the milk, but when he got in line to pay, there were some awfully tempting things crowding around him. The cashier gave him enough in change after paying for the milk that he knew he could purchase several candy bars if he wanted. Alex probably wouldn't even care, but he had asked for enough money for milk, and that was all he intended to get. He wanted Alex to know that he was a man of his word.

It was the walking uphill back home that was rough. The plastic sack with milk in it was heavy. It started spitting snow only a few minutes after he left the IGA.

As he passed by the Sugar Haus Inn, he tried not to even look at the place where he'd eaten that pie. If anyone in there was watching him, he didn't want them to think for a minute he was contemplating breaking in and eating another one!

The less he had to do with those women, the better. It had been embarrassing having them catch him in the act. He never wanted to have that sick feeling in his stomach again.

He was just about even with the house when he heard a loud

rapping sound on the window. He glanced over and saw one of the old Amish women at the window waving and motioning for him to come to the door.

He didn't know what to do. It would be hard to run with a half-gallon of milk in his arms.

As he hesitated, she rapped on the window again and motioned again. He noticed she was smiling. If she was smiling, there was a slight chance she wasn't still mad at him. There was also the fact that Grandma had taught him to be extra polite to old people.

Reluctantly, he trudged through the snow to the doorstep. The old woman opened it. He staggered backward a step because of the wonderful smells rushing out at him through that open door.

"I have need of a small boy to help me with something," she said. "Do you think you could be that boy?"

"I don't know," he said doubtfully. "I could try."

His nose was practically twitching from the smell of bacon wafting out.

"My niece tells me that your name is Calvin," she said. "Is that correct?"

"Yes."

Could that be pancakes he smelled, too?

"Well, my name is Lydia," she said. "And I have a rather large favor to ask."

He wondered if there was real maple syrup to put on those pancakes. His grandma had always insisted on real maple syrup.

"This is my problem." Lydia wiped her hands on her apron. "I fixed a large breakfast this morning for guests who were staying with us, but they had to leave early and didn't have time to eat. It's just me here by myself this morning. I was just thinking how nice it would be to have a boy with a big appetite who might like to help me eat it. Do you suppose you know anyone like that? I hate to see all this food go to waste."

Calvin could not believe his luck. How amazing was it that he was walking past their house just as she needed someone with a big appetite. It was mind-boggling.

"I do know someone like that!" he said. "Me!"

She stood back away from the door and asked him to come on it. He handed her the carton of milk while he politely took off his coat and shoes and hat.

"I will put this in our refrigerator until later," she said. "Then you can take it home with you. In the meantime, go on in and choose a seat at the table."

He took one look at that table, and his jaw dropped. He was hungry, all right. But he wasn't *that* hungry. There were biscuits and gravy, pancakes, a platter of bacon, a pitcher of syrup, sliced fruit, and a large bowl of scrambled eggs.

Culinary heaven.

"It looks awfully good," he said. "But I don't think I can eat all this by myself."

"I don't think so either," Lydia said. "Do you know anyone else who might be willing to help me out?"

"Alex might," he said. "But he's not up yet."

"Alex is your guardian?" Lydia asked."

"Yes, ma'am," Calvin said. "And my cousin."

"Do you suppose you could run up there and invite him?" Lydia asked.

"I sure can!"

"Then hurry," Lydia said. "Tell him that he would be doing me a great favor."

CHAPTER 47

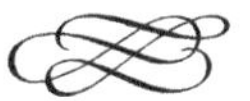

Alex got out of bed after Calvin left, and stood at the window, watching Calvin's small figure walk down the road to the IGA. It wouldn't hurt the boy to walk to the grocery store, but he regretted the fact that it was because of him that the child had to.

What time was it, anyway? He glanced at his watch.

8:30.

Good grief. Back when Alex was normal, it was rare for him to sleep past five a.m. The sleeping pills the doctor gave him did help, but the effect didn't go away soon. Perhaps it was time to stop using them altogether, no matter what the outcome. He couldn't allow himself to stay in a fog forever. He just couldn't. Not with a child depending on him.

As soon as Calvin got back, Alex resolved to be showered and dressed and at least able to pretend some semblance of normality.

He undressed and dropped the jogging pants and t-shirt he had worn to bed on top of the pile in the corner. How long had he been wearing the same clothes? A week maybe? That had to stop. He found one remaining pair of fresh jeans in a bureau, and a clean shirt. Underwear, socks. Then he started the shower.

While he waited for the water to heat up, he glanced around the bathroom. It had been clean when he rented the place. Now it was grungy. This also was not acceptable.

As he stepped into the shower and lathered up, he wondered why he had allowed himself to go so many days without bathing. What was that all about? Punishing himself? Perhaps. He certainly didn't feel like he was worth the effort of getting cleaned up.

He had been frugal and banked enough of his salary back when he was working that he and Calvin had enough to live on here for a while, even without a job. Eventually, he would have to go back to work, but never again as a hostage negotiator. Never that. He had no intention of ever allowing himself to hold the fate of so many people in his hands.

As he was buttoning up his shirt after his shower, he glanced out the window again, and to his surprise, he saw Calvin running up the road toward their house. This scared him. Was Calvin running from something? He rushed to the door just as Calvin threw it open and stood on the front step, panting.

Alarmed, he pulled Calvin inside and closed and locked the door behind him.

"What's wrong?"

"You gotta come, Alex." Calvin bent over from the waist, still panting, trying to get his breath. "Lydia needs our help. You gotta come. It's an emergency!"

By the time Calvin had gasped all that out, Alex had his boots and coat on and was holstering his gun.

Calvin looked up at him. "No, it's not like that. Lydia cooked too much food. Her guests didn't stay for breakfast. She needs help eating it."

Alex slowly began to put the gun away and took his coat off.

"No, no, no," Calvin said. "You have to come with me. I promised her I would bring you to help." He tugged on Alex's hand, impatiently.

"Come on. There's biscuits and pancakes and sausage, and...she says she wants to meet her new neighbor. And that's you. And Alex?

"Yes."

"I'm hungry!"

And that is how Alex was reluctantly pulled into the Sugar Haus Inn a few minutes later where he found warmth, laughter, companionship, and renewed hope in the form of a hot cooked breakfast and a kind, elderly neighbor awaiting him.

CHAPTER 48

"Does this happen to you very often?" Alex asked, after consuming the last tasty morsel on his plate. "I mean, your guests not staying for breakfast?"

It had been one of the most satisfying meals of his life. In addition to the excellent food, there was something about the warmth of the wood cookstove and the kindness of their elderly Amish neighbor that filled his heart even as he and Calvin filled their stomachs.

"It is rare," Lydia said. "The Sugar Haus Inn has a bit of a reputation for its breakfasts. Would you like more coffee?"

"Yes, I would, but it's my turn." Alex rose from his chair. "I'll get it."

Lydia did not protest as he filled her coffee cup and then his own from the brown spackle-ware pot on the woodstove.

"How are you doing there, buddy?" Amused at the satiated look on Calvin's face, Alex returned the coffee pot. "Do you think you finally got filled up?"

"I can make more pancakes," Lydia teased the stuffed boy. "I would not want you to go hungry."

"I tried," Calvin said earnestly, one hand on his belly. "But I don't think I can eat another bite. I'm sorry, Lydia."

"That is fine," Lydia said. "You and your cousin have done a wonderful good job of helping me with this breakfast my guests did not want. Now, my chickens also want their breakfast. Perhaps you would not mind feeding them?"

"Your chickens?" Calvin sat up straight. "I'd be happy to!"

"Then I will get you their bucket of feed," she said. "You don't mind, do you, Alex?"

"Not at all."

Lydia returned from a pantry with a small tin bucket of chicken feed. "The chicken yard is behind the pie house. You do know where the pie house is, don't you?"

Calvin blushed and looked at the floor. "Yes, ma'am."

"I thought you might." Lydia chuckled at her little joke. "Do not go inside the chicken yard. There is a new rooster out there, and he is very protective. Just toss the feed in through the chicken wire a handful at a time."

After Calvin shrugged into his coat and grasped the bucket, Alex watched him strut out to the chicken pen with purpose written all over his small body.

Lydia was already running water to start washing dishes.

"Let me do that," he said. "I'm no cook, but I'm a whiz at washing dishes. Why don't you sit down and rest?"

"I do not need to rest yet," she said. "But, I will welcome your help. While you wash the dishes, I'll pack up the leftovers for you to take home."

"You don't have to do that," he protested.

"Of course I do," she said. "You have a growing boy living with you. I do not, and I do not believe in waste."

He could faintly hear Calvin talking in a high pitched sing-song voice to the chickens while he fed them. The boy was definitely enjoying the chore Lydia had given him.

"Thank you for this morning," Alex said. "I appreciate it more than you can know."

"What did you do for a living before moving to Sugarcreek?" She slid their drinking glasses into the soapy water.

"Me?" he said. "I was a hostage negotiator."

"Oh? And what does a hostage negotiator do?"

"We try to defuse dangerous situations." He carefully rinsed the soapy drinking glasses with hot water, then sat them upside down on the wire drainer.

"That sounds interesting." Lydia brought the stacked dirty plates to him. "How do you go about doing that?"

"Well," Alex washed a plate until it was squeaky clean, then rinsed it and placed it in a slot on the drainer. "First, we try to establish contact with the person. Once we can begin to talk with them, we gauge their state of mind and try to make them feel like they are being heard and understood."

"How?" Lydia began using aluminum foil to create neat packages of leftover food.

"By listening," he said. "And by treating them with respect. When I was training for the job, one of the instructors said that it is amazing how powerful, unconditional respect can be. Especially to those who rarely receive it."

"I can see the wisdom of that," Lydia said. "Were you good at your job?"

Alex's hands paused in the soapy water. "I thought I was."

"But?"

"I found out that I wasn't."

Lydia glanced at him. "Oh. I'm sorry to hear that."

She did not pry or ask for details, which he much appreciated.

"Why did you choose to come to Sugarcreek?" she asked. "With no connections to this place, it seems like an odd choice."

"I used to live here once."

"Really?" She glanced at him in surprise. "When?"

"I came here when I was seven. I left when I was nine."

"Who were your parents?"

"My real parents didn't live here. My family kind of fell apart—what there was of it. Long story short, I ended up with an Amish couple near here who were willing to foster children. They had qualified to be in the system, and they were extraordinarily kind to me. Some of my best childhood memories are from those two years. I loved living here. I hoped, perhaps, Calvin would too."

She thought this over. "Do you remember your foster parents' names? I might know them."

"I was a child. I called them *maam* and *daett* like their natural children. I don't think I ever knew what their real names were."

"Why did you leave when you were nine?" Lydia grabbed a clean dishcloth and began to dry.

"A relative, my Aunt Beatrice, found out what had happened and came to get me. She was my grandmother's younger sister and a good person. I stayed with her until I entered the police academy. When she asked me if I would take guardianship of Calvin after she was gone, I could not refuse."

"Of course, you couldn't."

Alex noticed that Lydia had become quite preoccupied during their conversation. She was probably worn out. It was time for them to go, but there was one chore left.

"I'll fill the wood box before I leave," he said. "Is your firewood out back?"

"Yes, it is," Lydia said. "And I would very much appreciate you doing that."

"No problem."

After Alex filled the wood box in the kitchen, a job he had as a child when he lived with his Amish foster parents, Calvin came in and proudly handed Lydia the empty chicken feed bucket.

"You were right. That rooster didn't like me, and he flew at me a couple of times, but I wasn't scared. I fed the chickens just like you said."

"That rooster scares even me a little," Lydia said. "You were brave to stand your ground. Thank you."

"I'll help you any time you want!" Calvin said.

Lydia smiled and touched his rosy cheek lightly with her fingers. "You are a good boy."

"Time to go, buddy." Alex opened the door. "Thank you so much, Lydia. For everything."

She laid a gentle hand on his arm. "Before you go, can I ask you something?"

"Of course."

"Do hostage negotiators have to be police officers first?"

"I was," he said. "Ten years in Chicago."

"How very interesting." Lydia smiled. "Do you believe in prayer, Alex?"

"Why do you ask?" he said.

"I plan to be praying very hard for you."

"Thank you, ma'am," he said. "Calvin and I could use some prayers."

"I often have chores that would be perfect for a boy your age," Lydia told Calvin. "You must stop by often."

"I will! I think your chickens like me," Calvin said. "Except for the rooster."

"Not liking people is a rooster's job," she said.

As he and Calvin walked home, Alex felt more hopeful than he had for a long time. It was nice to know that there were still some very good people in the world. He had just met one of them.

CHAPTER 49

"I made an appointment with my doctor for Anna," Rosa said, over breakfast.

It felt odd to be eating a bowl of fiber cereal while sitting on the couch, but that was Rosa's routine, and Bertha was trying not to disrupt her cousin's life any more than she and Anna had to.

The fact that a morning news show blared from the big-screen television, also felt quite odd. Rosa seemed to need TV on all day, or she got nervous. She called it "background noise" and said it was a comfort to her. It was a terrible annoyance to Bertha, but she was trying hard to be a good guest.

They had only been here two days, and Bertha did not yet feel comfortable enough to take over Rosa's kitchen to cook something more substantial. Besides, what with walking the beach and the reduction in calories, Anna was already acting like she felt better.

Darren had left after one night on the couch. Even though he didn't stay long, he so thoroughly charmed Rosa that she had offered to adopt him. Anna seemed happier than Bertha had seen her in years. Everything was going well, although it did surprise Bertha that Rosa had made a doctor's appointment without checking with her first.

"Oh?" Bertha said. "Why?"

"Because if anything happens while she's here, it would be good for her to have a doctor. I've already talked to Gwen, and she understands the situation. She said she would be happy to see her."

"Gwen?" Bertha asked.

"Dr. Gwen Thomas. She's my doctor, but she also goes to my church. A general practitioner. If Anna has any heart issues while she's here—God forbid—Gwen will be able to get her in to see a specialist. Otherwise, you might be out of luck."

It made sense. Rosa might wear shorts, have dyed red hair, and wear lipstick and earrings, but she wasn't a stupid woman. Nor was she without compassion. She had been wonderful with Anna.

"What day is the appointment?" Bertha asked.

"Gwen's office called a little bit ago and said they'd had a cancelation and can get her in today." Rosa checked her watch, which she wore on her wrist instead of having it tucked away in her pocket as a good Amish woman would do. The timepiece was a pretty thing—cobalt blue with fake diamonds around the face of it. Bertha's cousin was most definitely no longer Plain. Not in any way, shape, or form.

"It's in two hours. Plenty of time to get ready," Rosa said.

One of the things that Bertha had noticed about Rosa was that she was seldom still. It had been so long since Bertha had seen her cousin she wasn't sure if this was Rosa's way of not thinking about having lost her husband, or if it was just her nature to be continuously involved in some activity. Except for breakfast, they had rarely eaten at home since she and Anna had arrived. It seemed like they were continually coming and going to various restaurants. Making this appointment just felt like more of the same, but Bertha did think it was a good idea.

Bertha supervised Anna's dressing until she was ready to go out in public, then she braided her own hair and wound it tightly around her head before anchoring it with bobby pins.

Anna, who was seldom shy, did not have a problem with meeting new people, not even a new doctor.

After they arrived, when the nurse ushered them into the small examining room, she had Anna climb onto the examining table, which left one chair for a visitor and a stool for the doctor. Rosa motioned for Bertha to take the chair.

"No," Bertha said. "I would rather stand."

"Are you sure you don't want the chair?" Rosa said.

"I am sure." It was a matter of pride for her. Rosa wasn't that much younger than Bertha, and yet she seemed to want to pretend that there was at least a decade between them.

Bertha was stewing on that when Dr. Gwen came in. The late fifties or early sixties. Small in stature, graying hair, kind, but weary-looking eyes. She was wearing a salmon-colored dress under a white lab coat. She also wore earrings, but they were small. Barely noticeable. Bertha wished that Rosa would be inspired to do the same.

"Hi, Rosa," she said. "These must be your relatives from Ohio?"

"My cousins, Anna, and Bertha."

"It's good to meet you finally," Dr. Gwen said, glancing at Anna's chart. "Rosa often speaks of her family."

"Thank you for taking the time to see us." Bertha meant it. It wasn't every doctor who would see a patient who had no insurance whatsoever.

"Now," Dr. Gwen said, smiling at Anna. "Who do we have here?"

"I'm Anna!" Anna said beaming.

"It's good to meet you, Anna," Dr. Gwen said. "I think we are going to be friends."

As Dr. Gwen examined Anna, Rosa mentioned to Bertha that Gwen's father had once been a medical missionary in Haiti. Then, for reasons Bertha couldn't fathom—it certainly had nothing to do with Anna's health—Rosa found it necessary to tell Gwen that Bertha had also once been a medical missionary in Haiti.

The doctor was concentrating on listening to Anna's heart. For a few moments, she did not seem to be listening to what Rosa was saying.

"When were you there?" The doctor removed the stethoscope from her ears. She had heard Rosa after all.

"Early sixties to the mid-eighties," Bertha said.

Dr. Gwen had been reaching for a thermometer. She stopped, turned, and gazed at her.

"Could you possibly be the same Bertha, who worked with my father and mother?"

"I don't know," Bertha said. "Who were they?"

"Anthony and Charlotte Lawrence."

Bertha felt her stomach clench.

"Yes," Bertha said, evenly. "We worked together for a few months before I went back to the states. I returned later."

"This is remarkable," Gwen said. "I've heard stories about you from my mother. Mom used to talk about the amazing nurse from Ohio, who helped Dad get through the aftermath of hurricane Flora. She almost made me want to go into nursing, myself because she made you sound so heroic. Dad insisted I become a doctor, though.

Bertha was dumbfounded. Why would Charlotte speak so well of her to her daughter? Had Charlotte not known what had sent her scurrying back to the states after the hurricane?

"Anna," Dr. Gwen said. "It looks to me like Florida agrees with you. Are you enjoying your walks on the beach?"

"I like it here!" Anna said. "I pick up seashells."

"We do have quite a lot of seashells," Dr. Gwen said. "If you keep doing what you are doing, I think your doctor back home is going to be very pleased the next time you see him."

"Thank you." Bertha hoped they could leave now without any more conversations about Dr. Gwen's parents.

"If my father knew you were here," Dr. Gwen said, "he would insist that you come over to the house for dinner. Since he quit practicing medicine, he's become quite a cook. Tonight we are having smoked salmon. It's one of his specialties."

Bertha began to protest, but Dr. Gwen wouldn't hear of it. "It would do Dad so much good to visit with someone who was such a good friend to our family. He's a valiant man and pretends to be fine since Mom's death, but I know he struggles with loneliness, even when I'm there."

"Oh, Bertha! You have to go," Rosa said. "Think how wonderful it will be to relive old times."

For the life of her, Bertha could not come up with a good reason to refuse. At least nothing that wouldn't make her look foolish. Apparently, she was not going to get out of this easily. Perhaps, after all these years, it would be best to face him again finally.

"I will look forward to it."

It was the first lie she had told in a very long time.

CHAPTER 50

Rachel was washing off tables at Joe's Home Plate, with baby Holly sleeping peacefully in her wrap. She'd seen another young mother at church using one, and it seemed like the perfect way to help Joe out at the restaurant while Holly was still so young. It freed up her hands so she could do a few easy tasks with Holly's tiny warm body tucked safely beneath her heart.

The dinner crowd was long gone, the rest of the staff had left, and Joe and Rachel were preparing to lock up the restaurant and go home.

She wondered how Darren's trip to Sarasota was faring. It took a lot of patience to deal with her aunts. Even a trip to a local doctor's office was cause for a great deal of flurry and packing. Then there was Bertha's nervousness if Rachel dared drive much faster than the speed of a fast buggy horse.

Poor Darren. It was kind of him to volunteer to take them, but she was pretty sure he had regretted it by now.

I'm finished," Joe said. "You about ready?"

Rachel glanced around for Bobby. She hadn't heard his boisterous voice for a few minutes. "Where is our son?"

"He was here just a moment ago," Joe said.

They stared at one another in alarm. After almost losing him to kidnappers the year before, they were extra sensitive when Bobby wasn't in sight.

Their hunt took them into every corner of the restaurant and finally up the stairs to Darren's one-room apartment over the restaurant where they found their son curled up in his bed sound asleep. The apartment key was still clutched in his hand.

Rachel guessed that he had gotten sleepy, had not wanted to bother her or Joe, knew where they kept Darren's key hidden and had taken care of putting himself to bed—even if it wasn't his own bed. He'd taken naps up there a few other times. Bobby was such an independent little guy.

Silently, she chastised herself for having let him get out of her view so easily. She heard a slight cough behind them and turned to see who it was.

"Well, well, well," Darren said, standing at the door with a small suitcase in his hand. "Look at that. My family decided to move into my apartment while I was gone."

"You're home!" Joe said. "And in one piece. How did the trip go, brother?"

Darren dropped his suitcase on the floor, collapsed on a chair and dramatically dropped his head into his hands.

"That bad?" Rachel asked.

"It wasn't easy," Darren said. "I can say that much. I definitely earned my pay."

"You aren't getting any pay," Joe said.

"Oh yes," Darren said, peeking up at them through his fingers. "I forgot. I volunteered. Don't let me do that again."

"How hard was it?" Rachel sat down on the edge of the bed and gently patted Bobby's leg. "Time to wake up, son."

Bobby was so sound asleep he didn't move.

"How bad?" Darren considered. "Well, Bertha doesn't feel comfortable driving more than fifty-five miles per hour. I bet you knew that and didn't tell me. She sat in front and watched my speedometer like a hawk."

"She actually allowed you to go fifty-five?" Rachel marveled. "I usually have to keep it under forty when I'm driving her. You have to remember that she's used to a buggy speed. Forty is fast to her."

"Yeah, I know. I tried to be sympathetic, but after a while, I felt like the Israelites wandering around in the desert. I told her that if we were going to make it to Sarasota before next January, I'd have to speed up."

"So how did she take it?" Rachel asked.

"I set the cruise control on the legal speed limit and convinced her she would have to deal with it."

"Seriously? And how did that work out?"

"What could she do? She dealt with it."

"Impressive! I'll have to try that. How was Anna?"

"Quieter than usual. Just kept her nose to the window, watching the scenery. Now and then, she would pull out her little purse of shells and count them or look at that book about seashells she's always carrying around."

"What about food?" Rachel asked, although she was reasonably sure of the answer.

"I think Lydia loaded more food into that cooler than Bertha and Anna packed clothing in their luggage," Darren said. "It was like she was afraid they might go into a restaurant and eat."

"It's just the Amish way to pack plenty of food for a trip. They are a frugal people. I'm sure Lydia had been planning for days what she would send."

"Oh, I'm not complaining about the food," Darren said. "I'm wondering if we should start carrying Lydia's meatloaf sandwiches for the restaurant."

"How long did it take you to get there?" Joe asked.

"About seventeen hours. We didn't stop much." Darren said. "Bertha didn't want to overnight any more than I did, and Anna just napped in the back seat."

"Do you think Rosa's will be a good place for them?" Rachel asked.

"I think so," Darren said. "I didn't stick around long. I just slept on the couch for a few hours and then headed back home.

"You drove straight back, as well?" Rachel said.

"I was afraid Joe might do something stupid if I didn't get home soon."

"Like what?" Joe asked.

"I don't know. Hand out pieces of raw bass and try to call it a sushi bar?"

Rachel patted the little boy's leg again. "Come on, Bobby. Time to get up and go home."

Bobby stirred sleepily, then he opened his eyes, saw Darren, and was instantly awake.

"Uncle Darren!" he shouted. "You're home!"

Darren was obviously weary, but he still had enough energy to catch Bobby as he catapulted off the bed into his arms.

Bobby got a hug, then Darren tousled his hair and set him down. "Seems like the older I get, the more it matters having a family to come home to. How have the receipts been the past couple of days?"

"We survived without you, brother, but just barely," Joe said. "Business has been good, but we had a busload of tourists empty out here yesterday, and we weren't expecting them. We managed to make everyone happy, but it wasn't easy."

"Who do they think we are?" Darren said indignantly. "McDonald's? What was the bus driver thinking?"

"Apparently, we have managed to become a tourist attraction, thanks to my baseball history and Lydia's pies," Joe said. "They cleaned us out, and we had to close early, but we made a nice profit. We may need to rethink some things in case that starts happening more often. The biggest problem was the seating. Some of the locals who were here saw the problem and had us package their orders to go just to give us room. But we do need more space."

"We only need more space during tourist season," Darren said. "And that tends to be the warmer months. I wonder if we could manage to put picnic tables in the back."

"It would require landscaping," Joe said. "And we'd have to find a different place for people to park."

"Or we might consider expanding into the empty store next door. If we could afford to buy it, we could open up that wall and add another thousand square feet or so to our restaurant," Darren said.

"I'm not sure our kitchen could handle that many people," Joe said. "We would have to expand it also."

"As fascinating as this conversation is," Rachel said. "We need to get the children home, Joe."

"You are absolutely right," he said. "And we need to let Darren get some rest."

As Joe took Bobby downstairs to the car, Rachel gave Darren a sideways hug with Holly still sleep in the wrap. He placed a kiss on top of the baby's fuzzy little head and smiled down at her.

"I'm so happy for you and Joe. You have the sweetest children."

Rachel could hear the heartfelt sincerity of his voice. Darren might've been Joe's ne'er-do-well brother for a while, but he had definitely redeemed himself. Had he not been willing to sell his fancy car and invest all the money into their restaurant startup, she wasn't sure where she and Joe would be right now.

"I love you, my brother." Rachel said. "Thank you for what you did for my aunts. I'm grateful that it was you who took them. I knew they would be safe with you."

Darren's eyes softened at her words.

"It wasn't as bad as I made it sound," he said. "I was just trying to make you and Joe laugh. I enjoyed the trip. Once Bertha began to relax, we had a good talk about her early days in in Haiti. I'd never heard much about that part of her life. It was fascinating."

"I'm surprised she talked with you about it."

"Me, too," Darren said. "Listening to her made the miles go faster. Bertha was quite a woman in her day."

"She still is," Rachel said.

CHAPTER 51

Bertha lay back in Rosa's deep bathtub, wondering what her life would have been like had she never read Charlotte's letter about dirt cookies.

Would she have remained Amish and married one of the nice young Amish men who had shown interest in her, and would she have been content with such a life? All her other friends had seemed to be. By the time she got back to Sugarcreek after her second sojourn in Haiti, many of her friends had large families. Many were the grandparents of young children. Many had created family businesses that successfully employed many.

She, on the other hand, had nothing to show for the twenty years she had spent on the mission field except her memories and the knowledge that she had made a difference. There had been some victories. The little girl she had once thought of as the girl with no face had lived at the children's home after her surgeries until long after she was grown. Missionaries from the states purchased a sewing machine for her, with which she started a small business—enough to sustain herself. Bertha remembered her as scarred, but so joyful it only took a moment to look past the ravaged face and see the beautiful spirit within. Her twin sister eventually went into business with her. By the time Bertha left Haiti the second time, both women had good husbands and families.

It was one of the successes Bertha often thought about when she was feeling down and needed to remind herself that she had done some good—that she had lived a life that mattered.

Several of the children she helped raise and educate got higher educations and became school teachers. Three of the girls managed to get nursing degrees. One little boy who was so skinny and sick when he arrived that he almost didn't survive, turned out to be quite brilliant. He now worked as a doctor in the slums of Port au Prince—a brave man and highly revered. Bertha remembered walking the floor with him in her arms night after night, willing him to live, praying that he would make it.

Bertha received many letters over the years from the children for whom she had cared, and she treasured each one. Still, she often regretted not having had the resources to accomplish more.

While Bertha bathed before her dinner, Rosa took Anna to the beach again. Bertha appreciated the fact that Rosa was giving her the privacy and time she needed to prepare for an evening she was dreading.

She was also grateful for Rosa's large bathtub. Warm water was comforting, and she needed comfort right now. Seldom had she ever experienced so many emotions at once as tonight. Gratitude to Rosa for finding a doctor for Anna. Irritation with Rosa for inadvertently bringing her together with a man she had hoped never to see again.

The Mennonite/Amish community in Florida was not all that large. It had probably been inevitable that she would run into him or someone who knew him, but it was unfortunate it had to be his daughter, and that his daughter would feel compelled to invite her to dinner.

Bertha had a headache, which was rare to her. No doubt, it was from all the stress of the day. As she lay in the warm water, she felt it begin to ease up. She wished the water could rid her of her heartache as quickly.

Eventually, Bertha finished her bath and began to dress. Her heavy black socks and black tennis shoes that she usually wore seemed absurd in the Floridian heat. Rosa had loaned her a pair of tan-colored flip-flops to wear. She slipped those on now.

She didn't think she would need a purse unless it would be to hold a handkerchief. A handkerchief might be necessary, though. Although she hoped not, there was a chance she might be in tears before the evening was over. She did not like tissues—they tended to disintegrate.

Her dress did have a side pocket. She pulled a clean hanky out of the dresser, folded it, and put it in the pocket. Then she went into Anna's room. Anna had a great affection for things that smelled good. She loved any kind of perfume with the scent of flowers. For Anna's sake, Bertha was grateful that scented bath oils and soaps and perfumes were not forbidden in their particular Old Order Amish sect.

Apart from being clean, Bertha rarely cared if she smelled good. But tonight—oh, it was an old woman's sheer foolishness!—she went into Anna's room and put a tiny dab of orange blossom perfume behind her ears and on her wrists. It was the perfume that Rachel had gotten Anna for Christmas this year. Just a tiny bit.

Then she changed her mind. What was she doing? This was ridiculous! She was an old woman! It irritated her that she was acting like a nervous teenager about to go on a first date. She went into the bathroom and scrubbed the perfume off with soap and water, then she prayed that God would keep her from making a complete fool of herself tonight.

CHAPTER 52

Alex was on the computer again. Calvin was grateful Alex had finally gotten around to getting Wi-Fi put in. Still, it seemed like whenever Alex wasn't sleeping or watching some stupid TV program or trying to cook something inedible, he was almost always on the computer.

It was annoying because they only owned one, and Calvin liked to play games on it. It soothed his nerves after a hard day at school—and being the new kid at school, he needed his nerves soothed rather badly most school days.

"You about done?" Calvin asked, dumping his school bag on the couch.

"Sure. Just looking for a job," Alex glanced up from the computer.

"Do you have to do that now?" Calvin allowed some of his irritation to show. "I want to play a game."

"It's all yours." Alex clicked out of the site he was on and stood up. "You can have it. I'll go start supper."

Calvin's stomach twisted into a knot when he heard this. Was Alex going to try to cook again? This did not bode well.

"What are we having?" Calvin climbed into the chair.

"Fried chicken, mashed potatoes, and green beans."

Calvin glanced up at Alex in surprise. "Really?"

"I bought some microwave dinners today for our supper." Alex shrugged. "I figured I couldn't mess that up too bad."

"Well, okay. I guess." Calvin tried to force some enthusiasm into his voice, but it came out flat.

Alex gave a little sigh and then squatted down where he could look Calvin straight in the eyes.

"Look, buddy," Alex said. "I know living with me hasn't been a lot of fun."

"It's been okay." Calvin shrugged.

"I...went through something right before you came to live with me. I haven't been dealing with it well. I'm sorry. I'm trying to do better."

Calvin didn't know what to say. Alex seemed to be actually looking at him instead of walking around in a fog. He squirmed a little, uncomfortable. He wasn't sure he liked Alex paying attention to him. But if Alex was going to apologize, he guessed he probably should as well.

"I'm sorry, too," Calvin said.

"For what?" Alex acted surprised. "You've done nothing wrong."

"You had to take me in after Grandma died," Calvin said. "I know you didn't want to."

Calvin was surprised to see Alex's facial expression crumble at his words.

"Is that what you really think?" Alex said.

"Yeah," Calvin said. "I guess so."

Alex scrubbed his face with both hands and stood up. "That's it. No TV dinners tonight and no more of you playing videogames while I sleep."

"Did I say something wrong?" Calvin asked, worried. "I didn't mean to. Honest. Please don't get rid of me. I'll be good."

"What are you talking about—get rid of you?"

Calvin kept silent. He was afraid to answer. He didn't want to make Alex mad.

"Is that what you've been thinking?" Alex's voice rose. "That I would get rid of you if you weren't good enough? Oh, you poor kid!"

Calvin was astonished when Alex plucked him up off the chair like he weighed nothing and gave him the biggest hug. Calvin was small for his age, but he hadn't been picked up and hugged like that since he was in kindergarten. Grandma hadn't been real strong. For a moment, he resisted, then he realized how badly he'd needed a hug and allowed Alex to hold him for a few moments before he squirmed to signal he wanted to get down.

When he was back on his feet, he glanced up and saw that Alex's eyes were all red and watery.

"For your information," Alex said. "I'll fight anyone who tries to take you away from me. Got it?"

Calvin hadn't expected Alex to say something like that. He felt a choking sensation in the back of his throat and knew he was about to cry, too. He didn't want to act like some sort of crybaby in front of Alex, so he swallowed the tears, wiped his nose on his shirt sleeve, and said, "Got it."

"Good. Now—let's forget frozen TV dinners tonight. There's a place in town called Joe's Home Plate. Want to try it out?"

Calvin nodded.

"Then go get your coat on."

"Okay."

Alex looked him over before they went out the door. "Where are your hat and gloves?"

"I lost them."

"I don't remember purchasing that coat."

"Some church gave a bunch of new coats to the teachers at my school to give to needy kids."

"They thought you were needy?" Alex looked like he had been struck. "They thought I couldn't afford to buy you a decent coat?"

"I don't know what they thought."

Alex looked down at the sodden tennis shoes. "Where are your boots?"

"I outgrew them before Christmas."

"And you didn't say anything?"

Calvin shrugged. "I didn't want to make you mad."

"I just lost my appetite," Alex opened the door. "Before we eat, we're going shopping. This is not acceptable. A kid needs decent clothes. Especially when he's the new kid in school. Where has my mind been?"

CHAPTER 53

Rachel didn't mind helping out at Joe's Home Plate. Having been raised Amish, one of the first things she had learned was how to work. In fact, not working felt odd to her unless she was just enjoying being with her children.

Ever since Joe and his brother, Darren, had opened the restaurant, she had jumped in whenever she could. She'd done everything from clearing tables to taking out the trash, to cleaning the grill, to flipping burgers.

Now that she had little Holly, though, she was limited in the jobs she could do while carrying the baby. Once again, she had her tiny daughter nestled in the stretchy wrap, and Rachel loved having her there. This left Rachel's hands free to do the more manageable jobs, one of which was to work behind the cash register.

It was seven o'clock on a Friday night, and Joe's Home Plate was filled with patrons, mostly locals. The receipts would be good tonight. There were already several hundred dollars in cash Darren would need to take to the night deposit at the U.S. Bank down the street after they locked up.

Standing behind the counter, she could also keep an eye on Bobby, who was coloring with Calvin, the little boy who had stolen one of Lydia's pies. From what she could see, the child had also managed to steal Lydia's heart. Most children would have had no interest in a woman of her aunt's age, but Calvin followed her around like a puppy, eager to help.

She'd heard Calvin slip up a few times and call Lydia "grandma." It didn't take a psychiatrist to figure out that Lydia had become a grandma substitute to a heart-hungry little boy. From what Rachel had seen, Lydia didn't mind one bit.

Rachel suspected that having Calvin drop in after school every afternoon was a great comfort to her aunt, and vice-versa. Last night when Rachel had stopped by, Calvin was doing his homework at the Inn's kitchen table while Lydia oversaw it. There was, of course, a small plate of cookies on the table. Lydia had been too engrossed in the child to spend much time with her.

The only issue she saw about this arrangement was that she had no idea how long Alex and Calvin would be sticking around. She had the feeling that Calvin's guardian was somewhat rootless and aimless at the moment.

He did seem to be a perfectly decent man, though, albeit a tad overwhelmed by being thrust into the role of guardian. Calvin was looking better tonight than the last time she saw him, though. He was wearing new jeans that were long enough for him, and he had on brand new, boot-type shoes instead of those old tennis shoes with the raggedy shoestrings he'd been wearing.

He looked much happier, too, and so did his guardian. In fact, they seemed to be genuinely enjoying having dinner together.

The baby began to squirm, and Rachel was about to go warm up one of Holly's bottles when a man came through the door whom she did not recognize.

He didn't strike her as a tourist or a local, and she immediately felt the hair on the back of her neck stand up. He seemed jittery. A baseball hat was pulled low over his eyes. He came to stand in front of the cash register, but he didn't look her in the eyes when she greeted him.

Instead, in a low voice, he said words that made her blood run cold.

"I have a gun. Put all your cash in a paper bag. Hand it over. Pretend I'm picking up a to-go order. Now!"

She placed a hand protectively over the baby while she quickly took stock. He was wearing a plain wool jacket with deep pockets. Both of his hands were thrust deep into those pockets. There could be a gun in there, or a knife, or nothing. He might be bluffing. Or not. She had a strong feeling that he was not bluffing.

Had she not been encumbered with an infant, she would have immediately gone over the counter at him. She would have the element of surprise and enough know-how to subdue him.

But with little Holly nestled against her, she was virtually helpless. Joe and Darren were both working in the kitchen with no line of sight to where she was standing. Two high school girls were waiting on customers. All the locals were chatting and enjoying their meals. They were decent, everyday people who probably wouldn't notice something was wrong. Nor would any of them have the skills to help her without getting themselves hurt.

She was not armed. Nor did she have a weapon beneath the counter. Joe and Darren had decided against it because, in a crowded restaurant, the chances of an accidental gunshot would be a greater danger than a thief. Besides, this was Sugarcreek. It was a good place filled with decent people. The chances of being robbed were small—until it happened.

There was also no silent alarm button to push. No way to alert anyone to what was happening. Joe had meant to take care of that small detail, but they had been so busy, he hadn't quite gotten around to it.

Furious, but frightened for her family, her patrons, and herself, she pulled a white to-go bag from beneath the counter, opened the register, and placed a stack of ones inside the bag.

"Larger bills, first," the man shifted his weight from one leg to another and glanced around. "Hurry."

It was infuriating to know that some stranger was stealing the money from all their hard work, but there was absolutely nothing she could do about it.

She reached for another stack of twenties when she felt eyes from across the room. Glancing up, she saw that Alex was staring at her. He was frowning, and one of his eyebrows was cocked.

The look of understanding in Alex's eyes gave her a jolt. He'd seen what was happening and understood the ramifications. She quickly lowered her eyes before the thief could see the hope there.

Alex quietly rose from the table. One moment he had been supervising Bobby and Calvin's play. The next moment he was leaning against the counter, next to the stranger.

"Excuse me," Alex said. "I need to pay. My cousin isn't feeling well, and I need to get him home."

Rachel glanced at Calvin, who appeared to be fine.

"I was here first," the stranger said. "Go back to your table and wait your turn."

Rachel knew it would be hard for anyone to miss what was happening. She had a paper bag in her hand stuffed with bills, and the cash drawer was open and empty.

"I don't think I'm going to do that," Alex said. "Does he have a gun, Rachel?"

"I'm pretty sure," Rachel said.

"That's what I thought."

Before the stranger could react, he was face down on the floor with Alex holding both of his wrists behind his back. The man was wiry, young, and strong, and he fought hard to throw Alex off.

"A little help here?" Alex said, calmly.

She rushed out from behind the counter, knelt, and helped subdue him.

"Bring me the diaper bag," she said to Bobby, who was watching wide-eyed.

He ran into the kitchen and brought it back to her. Rachel reached in and pulled out a pair of handcuffs.

"Wait. You carry handcuffs in Holly's diaper bag?" Darren wiped his hands on a dishtowel as he followed Bobby out of the kitchen.

She didn't bother answering him. Instead, she snapped the cuffs on the thief's wrists, and then she and Alex pulled him to his feet.

Rachel patted the guy down and stopped. "I've found something."

Gingerly, she reached into the man's right coat pocket and lifted out a loaded Ruger 9mm semiautomatic pistol.

"He wasn't bluffing," she said, as she laid the lethal weapon on the counter.

The struggling wanna-be thief let loose with a string of words Rachel sincerely hoped would not make it into Bobby's vocabulary.

"Watch your mouth," Alex said. "There are children here!"

The man lapsed into a simmering silence.

One of the patrons had already called the police. The station was less than two blocks away. Ed, lights flashing, siren wailing, screeched to a stop in front of the restaurant. It had taken him approximately two minutes to arrive.

He burst through the door. "Everyone okay?"

Various customers nodded their heads.

"What about you?" Ed glanced at Rachel.

"I'm fine."

"Is that his weapon?" Ed nodded at the handgun, laying on the counter.

"It is."

"Who are you?" Ed asked Alex.

"He's a customer," Rachel said. "And a neighbor."

As Ed took over, Rachel went to a nearby booth and sat down

before her legs could give out. The more she thought about what had just transpired, the weaker her knees felt. The man was armed! Her children had been within a few feet of a man holding a loaded weapon with intent to harm!

"You're trembling, sweetheart." Joe wrapped his arms around her and the baby. "Are you and Holly okay?"

"I've faced a lot of criminals," Rachel said. "But I never thought I would have to do so holding my child. I was so angry, Joe, and so helpless. Then Alex stepped in."

"I think he and Calvin will be getting some meals on the house for a while," Joe said.

"Most definitely."

Then she saw Bobby standing near watching her, fear and concern written all over his little face.

"Come here, son," she said.

He went to her, and she pulled him into an embrace. He was shaking.

"Everything is fine, Bobby," she said. "There is no reason for you to worry. Your little sister didn't even wake up."

How she wished their son had not seen what had just happened! Bobby had already dealt with more trauma than adults had to endure. His mother's death, the paparazzi following him and his father everywhere afterward, and the kidnapping last year. Now, this. He had seen too much.

"I'm okay." Bobby pulled away, a stern look of determination on his face. "I'm going to grow up big and strong, and then I'm going to learn how to be a policeman, and then I'm going to protect you and daddy and Holly, and Aunt Lydia, and Aunt Bertha, and Aunt Anna, and my friends and everybody else. I'm going to keep everybody safe."

Rachel saw his lips tremble as he said this, and her heart broke for her brave little boy because she knew he wasn't okay. No child Bobby's age should feel so much responsibility. But she understood his emotion. Most of her life, she had felt a need to protect everyone she cared about, as well.

She loved her job and was good at it, but if she had harbored any doubts about giving it up, they had evaporated as of this instant. She had some repair work to do. Bobby might, indeed, become a cop. But right now, protecting everyone he loved was not Bobby's job to do. It was hers.

She was going to start right now by taking him home, putting him to bed, hearing his prayers, and reading him a bedtime story. In the coming days and weeks, she was going to do everything possible to make things feel normal, and help him feel safe.

It was time to get very, very serious about finding someone to replace her.

CHAPTER 54

"Hey, Rachel," Ed glanced up from his lunch, a sandwich obviously brought from home. Tuna from the smell. "You aren't on duty for a few more hours. What's up?"

Rachel knew he was not by nature a frugal man, but he was saving up for another fishing trip to Canada.

"What have you found out about our prisoner?"

He took one last bite and used a paper napkin to wipe his fingers while he chewed and swallowed. "He's in the county jail. Shot the last person he tried to rob. You were lucky a customer was able to help."

She sat down in a seat across from him. "How is the search for my replacement coming?"

"Not well." Ed pulled a stack of papers out of a drawer and tossed them onto his desk. "These are the resumes I've received so far."

"What's wrong with them?"

"What's wrong with them? They aren't you!" Ed said with frustration. "Are you sure you can't just get a babysitter."

"I'm sure," Rachel said.

She grabbed the stack of applicants and began to shuffle through them. "Anyone look good?"

"No," Ed said. "Sugarcreek's a special place. You know that. Not just any Tom, Dick, and Harry can waltz in and start dealing with these folks. The wrong move with one of the patriarchs of a large Amish family, and they would shut us out for good. You know how hard it's been to build trust with them."

"I have an idea I'd like to explore," she said.

"What?" Ed peered over his glasses at her.

"I have a hunch."

"Uh, oh." Ed tossed the sandwich wrapper into the trashcan beside his desk. "The last guy you had a hunch about was Joe, and you ended up married to him. What was it you told me about Joe the first time you met him? Something about him looking suspicious?"

"I'd like to forget that conversation, Ed."

"Nope, I plan to tease you about it for a few more years," Ed said. "So, what's your hunch?"

"I just had a nice visit with Lydia."

"Oh?" Ed said. "Lydia's hiding a cop we need to hire?"

"No, but she may have fed him breakfast. It turns out that Alex—the guy who helped me out at the restaurant--worked as a cop in Chicago before he became a hostage negotiator."

Ed leaned forward, both elbows on his desk. "Tell me more."

"That's pretty much it," Rachel said. "The only other thing she knows is that something happened in Chicago that messed him up. He's not working as a cop or a hostage negotiator anymore."

"I wonder why?"

"So do I."

"Worth looking into, I guess," Ed said. "I'll make some calls. Shouldn't be too hard to find out."

CHAPTER 55

Bertha always tried to be punctual, if not early. She was completely ready and nervously waiting on the front porch when Dr. Gwen came to pick her up.

She was far from an expert in cars, but even she could tell the vehicle that pulled into the driveway, although an older model, was expensive and well-cared-for.

She began to walk toward the car when a gray-haired man unfolded himself from the driver's side. This was definitely not Dr. Gwen.

"It's good to see you again," Dr. Anthony Lawrence said. "It's been a long time."

Bertha couldn't move. It took a moment to absorb the fact that Anthony was standing right there in front of her—the man she had spent a lifetime trying to forget.

He was still tall and lanky, but there was a bit more stoop to his back. It was probably from carrying so many people and their illnesses around on his shoulders all these years. How well she knew how much care he had devoted to others.

"Thank you for agreeing to come tonight," Dr. Lawrence said, breaking the silence.

Bertha shook off the momentary paralysis that seeing him again had created.

"I was so sorry to read that Charlotte had passed," Bertha said. "She was a good friend to me."

"There are times when all one can do is view death as the ultimate healing," Anthony said. "That was how it was with Charlotte in the end."

The worry lines etched upon Anthony's face were deeper now, more pronounced, but he still looked very much like the man she had once known.

"You will see Charlotte again," Bertha said.

"And that is the knowledge that helps me get up and face the day each morning," Anthony said. "I'm grateful you are here, Bertha. It will be a joy to get to talk with you about those days when the three of us were young and trying so desperately to save the world."

"Yes," Bertha said. "I'm looking forward to it."

She meant it. Seeing Anthony again was bringing back the feelings of the great friendship they once had shared.

He walked around to the passenger side of the car and opened the door. She climbed in and fumbled for her seatbelt, and then they were off.

"You've been well?" Anthony asked.

"Very well," Bertha said.

"I'm not surprised," Anthony said. "You were truly blessed with good health most of your time with us in Haiti, except for that bout you had with malaria."

Bertha remembered being filled with energy, while poor Charlotte wilted in the hot sun and often apologetically took to her bed with migraines.

As though reading her mind, Anthony said. "One of my biggest regrets is that I was not more considerate of her. She suffered much as

I dragged her from one place to the next. Somehow she always made a home for us wherever we were. The day she died, she told me that she was looking forward to finally being able to rest and be pain-free."

His voice broke on the last sentence as he wheeled the car into the driveway of a pretty, two-story house.

"Is this where Charlotte grew up?" Bertha asked. "The house her grandparents built?"

"It is," Anthony parked the car and opened Bertha's door.

"The house is what people around here refer to as 'Old Florida,'" he said, as she got out. "It was built before air conditioning was invented, so it was designed to be as cool as possible without it."

Bertha thought the design was charming. A rambling two-story with a deep porch. Some sort of blossoming vine trailed bright pink blossoms over the white clapboards of the house. Comfortable-looking wicker furniture with bright-colored cushions hospitably invited guests to relax.

No wonder Charlotte had loved it so and often longingly described it to Bertha.

"This is where Charlotte brought the boys to ride out Hurricane Flora?"

"It is," Anthony said. "One thing I've never regretted was getting them out of Haiti before the hurricane hit."

"Charlotte didn't want to go."

"No," he said. "She didn't, but I needed her to leave. Besides wanting to make sure my family was safe, I knew that if the storm was as bad as I feared, I would be hampered in my work by trying to look after her and the boys. I didn't want to have to choose."

"It was a terrible time," Bertha said.

"And that is quite an understatement." Anthony led her up the walkway. "On so many different levels."

She was grateful he was in front of her, so he couldn't see the quick flush she felt bloom upon her face. Apparently the evening was going to be as difficult as she had feared.

CHAPTER 56

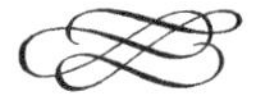

Gwen greeted her warmly as Anthony led the way into his cool, quiet home.

"It is going to be so good to visit with someone who worked closely with Mother and Father during their years in Haiti," Gwen said. "I was born after they left. I can't wait to hear the stories."

"I remember how much Charlotte longed for a daughter," Bertha said. "I'm sure she was thrilled when you were born."

"I would love to hear your memories about her while we have dinner," Gwen said. "Dad already had most of the preparations made when I got home. I finished up because he insisted on being the one to go get you."

"Shall I tell you about the first day I met her?" Bertha asked as they sat down to dinner. "It was not a great time for your mom to have three nurses from the states show up to be fed and spend the night, but she was so gracious."

"If I remember right," Anthony said. "Much of our furniture had not arrived yet, and the three of you had to sit on the floor. You looked like three lost waifs sitting there."

"And you sat on the kitchen table and swung your legs while the boys came home and put away their school things."

"The three of you were a godsend," Anthony said. "Even Darlene, although I had my doubts about her that first night."

"As did I!" Bertha said.

The meal they had was simple and delicious. Fresh melon and cheese. An interesting-looking salad with greens that Bertha did not often see. Grilled pork chops and rice pilaf. The conversation was an easy sharing back and forth. She liked Gwen very much, which was no surprise. She had loved Charlotte, and Gwen was so much like her mother.

The sun slowly began to dim as she and Anthony shared memories of the work in Haiti, with his daughter hungry to hear every word.

"Under the circumstances, what the three of you managed to accomplish was truly extraordinary," Gwen said. "You do realize that, don't you?"

"Extraordinary?" Anthony said. "How?"

"The primitive work and living conditions. The political unrest. The difficulty of getting medical supplies. Living through Hurricane Flora. The lives you saved. It was heroic."

Bertha and Anthony glanced at one another. Neither had thought of their time there as particularly heroic. For the most part, it had always seemed like something best forgotten.

"It's cooling down outside," Gwen said. "Why don't the two of you go out on the porch and visit while I wash up?"

"Oh, no," Bertha said. "I'll help you with the dishes."

"You will not," Gwen said. "Dad doesn't often get a chance to talk with old friends. At least not anymore. There are so few of them left."

"It's true, Bertha," Anthony said. "I don't know if you've noticed, but we've managed to outlive so many of our peers."

Bertha was not at all sure that she wanted to share private memories with Anthony. Those last few hours together were so painful that they still haunted her, but to turn down Gwen's kind invitation would be rude. She and Anthony went out onto the long porch that faced the water.

At home in Ohio, it would be winter and freezing cold. Here the air was balmy and soft. The house was built near the ocean with a long lawn leading down to the beach. The night sky was filled with stars, and the ocean, quiet tonight, reflected the starlight. It was a magical place. She could understand how hard it must have been for Charlotte to leave it, and yet she had and made a home in Haiti for her husband's sake.

"Charlotte was never strong," Anthony said, as though reading Bertha's thoughts. "She should have lived her life here in Sarasota. It was incredibly selfish of me to take her into the harsh realities of third-world mission work."

"Then, why did you?"

He didn't take offense at her question. Instead, he answered with such honesty that she knew he had asked himself the same question many times.

"I was young and selfish," he said simply. "I needed a wife, and Charlotte was a pretty girl and very much in love with me. I was so egotistical at the time I thought I deserved her."

"But you were not in love with her?" Bertha had always wondered.

"How could I be," Anthony said. "I was so in love with the image I had of myself as a great doctor and missionary, there wasn't much love left for anyone else. Even for my long-suffering wife."

Had Charlotte been long-suffering? Bertha had never thought about it at the time. She'd been too busy being envious of Charlotte for having such a saint of a husband.

"I do remember those headaches she used to have," Bertha said.

"You mean the agony she endured without complaint because of my impatience with her?" Anthony's voice was bitter.

Bertha thought about that. Had he been impatient? She hadn't seen it at the time. She had been too enmeshed in her hero-worship to see any flaws in him. Besides, deep down, she had not given Charlotte's headaches much thought. Her own health had always been so robust,

Now, from the distance of many years, Bertha remembered Charlotte, pale and shaky, attempting to take care of her family before she had fully recovered from yet another vicious migraine. She had even come to help Bertha with the Haitian children whenever she could.

Bertha stole a glance at Anthony. Age had not changed the underlying bone structure of that face. He had achieved the impossible—still attractive in his eighth decade.

"Do your boys still favor you?" she asked.

"Pretty much. It is Gwen who took after their mother."

"She does remind me so much of Charlotte."

"I've always thought so," Anthony said. "Gwen's divorce took a toll on her health. It was not what she wanted, and she grieved terribly for a while. After she moved in to help me with Charlotte's last illness, she didn't seem inclined to move out afterward. Selfishly, I'm very grateful she is here."

They lapsed into silence, listening to the soft lap of waves against the shore. Somehow, as they looked out over the ocean, the silence seemed appropriate.

Then Anthony broke the spell by bringing up the one thing Bertha did not want to discuss.

"Ever since Gwen told me you were coming tonight, I've been having flashbacks to that desperate time we endured during Hurricane Flora," he said. "Do you remember?"

"I remember it well," she said carefully. "I wasn't at all sure we would survive."

"I've often wondered how we did," he said.

She knew, and he knew that he wasn't referring solely to the hurricane. Sitting beside him, watching the ocean, so many memories came rushing back.

Hurricane Flora hit the coast of Haiti only six months after she first arrived. Not only did she and Anthony nearly lose their lives, but in the aftermath, they came close to losing their souls.

CHAPTER 57

"I won't go," Charlotte said. "That's all there is to it."

Bertha had never seen her friend so resolute. In fact, she had never heard her have even a mild argument with Anthony. Charlotte usually simply agreed with everything he said as though Anthony's words were inspired by God.

But not this time.

Bertha hesitated in the open doorway of the Lawrence's small house. She didn't know whether to go or stay. She had a small bag of apples with her. A gift. Charlotte had expressed a longing for fresh apples earlier in the month, and Bertha had just received some of the precious fruit from home.

The Lawrences were too involved in their argument to notice her.

"Yes, you will go," Anthony thundered. "You will take the boys back to Florida. If the hurricane is as great a monster as they are saying it is, I want you safely out of here."

"No."

"Charlotte..." His jaw clenched.

Bertha saw him visibly fight to stay calm. The information about the hurricane must indeed be dire.

"I was raised in Florida, remember?" Charlotte faced off against him. "I

am much more familiar with hurricanes than you. They do not always travel on the trajectory the meteorologists predict. Flora might pass right by Haiti and head for Sarasota for all anyone knows. You could be putting the boys and me in its direct path."

"And if the predictions are wrong, and if that does happen, you will sit out the storm inside your parents' solid house," Anthony said. "If there are medical emergencies, there will be dozens, maybe hundreds, of doctors and nurses on hand. In the states, there are people with resources to help. There are shelters to which you can run if necessary. If it makes landfall here in Haiti, there is no place to go. No place where you can effectively shelter. There will be only a handful of doctors and nurses to deal with the injuries afterward."

In Bertha's eyes, his arguments were unanswerable, but Charlotte didn't back down.

"I don't want to go, Anthony," Charlotte said. "I don't believe it is good for us, nor is it wise for our family. Please don't make me."

"I cannot do my job if I have to worry about you and our children," Anthony said. "Do not make me have to choose between taking care of you and helping the Haitian people. Take our sons to your parents' home and keep them safe."

Charlotte hesitated, as though having not yet spent all her arguments.

"I've arranged seats for you on the last commercial flight out." Anthony sounded weary. "It leaves in three hours. Go pack, dear."

Charlotte had tears in her eyes as she left the room. She barely glanced at Bertha.

"Can I help you with something?" Anthony asked Bertha.

"For Charlotte." She handed him the bag. "Winesap apples. She'll be pleased. They are from our orchard back home. Lydia packed a small barrel of them. They actually made it through customs to me. They will make a nice snack for the boys while they are on the plane."

"I'm certain she will appreciate them." He glanced at the bedroom where Charlotte had disappeared.

"Is it that bad?" She asked. "I've been listening to our little radio, and I've heard hardly anything."

"Of course you've heard nothing," Anthony said. "The Haitian Red Cross has prohibited radio broadcasts about the hurricane."

"Why on earth would they do that?"

"For fear of panic among the citizens," Anthony said, with disgust. "Of course there's going to be panic, but the people deserve a chance to get ready the best they can. The decision should not be taken from them."

"But it might not come?" she asked.

"Barring a miracle, it's going to come, and soon," he said. "We've been working on the hospital for the past two days, trying to get it ready. I was planning to head over in a few minutes to check on you and the children. I've hired a couple of men to start nailing what lumber and plywood we can find over the windows and doors at the compound. If you want to jump in the jeep, I'll run you back."

"May I talk to Charlotte first?"

He glanced at his watch. "No more than five minutes. She needs every second to get packed."

She had never seen him so worried. "Okay."

The door was open, so she hurried into their bedroom. Charlotte was folding clothing and placing it into a suitcase haphazardly. Tears were coursing down her cheeks.

"Are you okay?" Bertha asked.

"Of course I'm not okay," Charlotte said. "He's sending me away."

"For you and your children's safety."

"You don't understand," Charlotte said. "When the hurricane hits, assuming he survives and doesn't get killed running out into the storm trying to rescue someone, there will be no stopping him. He is not like other men. He'll work night and day trying to patch people up and save lives. He won't even notice whether or not he's eaten. The only reason he doesn't collapse now some weeks when there is much illness is because I know how to watch after him. I monitor him. I watch for the signs of exhaustion, of dehydration, and I make him rest and eat. He will listen to me, but if he sends me away,

who is going to watch after him? I'm afraid I'll have no home or husband left when I bring the boys back."

"Maybe the hurricane won't come," Bertha pointed out. "Like you were just saying. Perhaps it will miss Haiti."

"Oh, it's not going to miss," Charlotte said. "I've heard the reports and seen the maps."

"Where?"

"One of the men at the hospital has a short wave radio. He's been keeping us informed. Those who live near the beach have been seeing six-foot swells. That's always a solid indicator."

She stopped in her packing and glanced up at Bertha. "You have your own children to protect. Go back and get ready. This is going to be a dangerous time for Haiti."

"How do I get ready?"

"Anthony will make certain the outside is tightly buttoned up, but many of your buildings aren't all that substantial. Except for the kitchen. They built it with concrete blocks, bless them. The food is already there. As soon as you get back, start moving the children's bedrolls and some toys into the kitchen. This is where you will want to run as soon as the rain starts up. There will be torrents of rain and strong winds. Expect the winds to howl. The sound will frighten the children and you. When it is over, if you survive, you begin to rebuild."

Charlotte opened her arms, and Bertha stepped into them. The two friends hugged one another tight. As they did so, Charlotte whispered in Bertha's ear, "Take care of him, Bertha. If you can, keep my husband safe for me."

As they parted, Bertha saw that Charlotte had grown pale, and had begun to rub her temples with her fingers—an indication that another migraine was coming.

She stepped outside the bedroom and saw Dr. Lawrence pacing the floor.

"Your wife is getting ill," Bertha said. "You need to see to her. I'll walk back to the compound."

"All right." He abruptly strode toward the bedroom, but not before she saw a look of annoyance cross his face.

CHAPTER 58

Upon arriving back at the children's home, she began working non-stop. Fortunately, they had recently gotten in a shipment of food, which was already stored and locked away in the building that housed the kitchen and dining room. They were not on low ground, where the rush of water might drown them, but they would undoubtedly be susceptible to the punishment high winds could inflict.

Mimose led the younger children in their classes, while three of the oldest children helped fill every available container with water from the well that Mennonite volunteers had built.

Once the physical needs for food and water were taken care of, Bertha and Widelene began carrying bedding and clothing into the kitchen/dining house along with all the various medicines Bertha usually kept locked away in her room.

With what scrap lumber they had—which wasn't much—she and the two Haitian men whom Dr. Lawrence had hired, nailed what protection they could against the wind.

It felt like so little compared against the strength of the monster storm predicted, but as she worked, she prayed that the storm would stay far away from their poor island. Barring that, she prayed that the preparations they were making would be enough.

On Thursday, October 3, 1963, after all the frantic activity, after all the hopes and prayers that it would veer off its path and turn back out to sea, Hurricane Flora hit Haiti with a vengeance.

At first, it was just a few drops of rain pattering on the tin roofs. It was such a normal pitter-patter, Bertha found it difficult to believe the sound was ominous. Perhaps they were just going to have an ordinary rainstorm.

Then a breeze picked up. On the horizon, white cirrus clouds from the outer band of the storm appeared. The skies became overcast.

Bertha heeded Charlotte's advice to get the children to shelter as soon as she heard the first drops. Older children carried younger ones, and toddlers dragged worn blankets behind them. All made their way into the one truly solid building in the compound.

As the last child made it into the kitchen along with Mimose, Widelene, and one of the cooks who chose to shelter with them, Bertha stopped to look out over the hills. Clouds, thick and close, were bringing intense bands of rain toward them. It was a fascinating and unnerving sight, and it was hard to pull her attention away. By the time she closed the door, gale-force winds were pushing against her, forcing her to use more strength than she expected.

After the door was closed and locked, she pressed her back to it and was greeted with a roomful of wide and worried eyes watching her.

"We will be all right," she reassured them with as much faith as she possessed. "Everything will be fine. God is watching over us, and we have worked hard to prepare."

Exhausted, she slid down the wall onto the floor. A toddler crawled onto Bertha's lap, needing a cuddle. She drew the little girl to her, wanting the contact as much as the child.

"What can we do now?" one of the older girls asked.

"What do we do?" Bertha said. "We pray, and we wait."

The wind escalated.

Something hit the door with a thump. Everyone jumped, including Bertha.

"What was that?" Mimose asked. "It sounded heavy. Should we go see?"

The wind began to howl as it raced around the corners of the building.

"No, we can't afford to go look." Bertha raised her voice so she could be heard over the wind. Another small child crept into her lap, and she held the two children close. These innocent, trusting, babies were everything to her. She had to keep them safe. "If I open that door to look outside now, I'm not sure I can shut it again."

Massive torrents of rain beat down upon the corrugated tin roof, the rain thrummed so hard, it made communication impossible, their voices were drowned out. The hard concrete floor, the concrete walls, and the tin roof created a sort of large box of sound, frightening the children, and making Bertha feel as though they were caught inside a giant drum.

One of the children in her lap began to cry. Bertha held her closer and began to rock back and forth. Back and forth. It was all she could do not to burst into tears, herself.

Although it seemed impossible, the wind grew even louder, turning into a wilder, more menacing sound. Instead of howling, it screamed. To Bertha's ears, it was like a living thing, a prowling predator determined to tear through the wood, concrete, and tin that protected them. Her greatest fear was that the roof would be torn off, utterly exposing them to the elements. If that happened, she did not know what to do. There was no place to run, no place to hide.

She found herself envious of Charlotte and her built-in knowledge of living near an ocean. Bertha did not have that sort of wisdom about hurricanes. Back home in Ohio, they only had to deal with the occasional tornado, during which one went into the root cellar, waited for it to pass, hoped, and prayed that the house and barn would be standing when it was over.

This was a different experience entirely. For one thing, the children's home did not have a cellar, and even if they did, one might conceivably drown in it with rain this heavy.

After many interminable hours, the rain and howling wind died down.

"Do you suppose it is over?" Bertha wondered aloud. "I thought hurricanes lasted longer."

"It is the eye of the storm," Widelene said. "I have seen it before. It will come again."

"Is it safe to open the door?" Bertha asked.

"For a short time."

The two children on her lap had fallen asleep. She carefully eased them down on the floor beside her, then went to open the door.

The change was astonishing. The sky was blue, the sun was shining, the wind was calm, there was no rain, but no matter where she looked, there was destruction. Debris was strewn everywhere. Some of the buildings around her were standing but badly damaged. Three of their precious trees were uprooted.

"Can we see?" Several of the older children crowded around the opening, blinking from having spent so much time in the darkened building. They wanted to go outside.

Bertha did not trust the eerie calm, but she allowed everyone to come outside, stretch their legs for a few minutes, and marvel at the changes. The toilet was close by, and she had the children line up to use it before the hurricane closed in again. The children, sensing the strangeness of the moment, did not attempt to run or play. After using the toilet, they crowded around the four adult women and gazed out over the devastation. Bertha found herself wishing she had been born a boy. Had she been an Amish boy, she would have carpentry skills. She would know how to rebuild and repair damaged buildings.

She glanced at her watch. The eye of the storm had lasted just under seventy minutes so far.

A droplet of water hit her, and then another.

"It is coming again," Widelene said.

"Get back inside, children," Bertha said. "Hurry!"

They barely had time to scramble back in before the hurricane attacked again. Bertha leaned the back of her head against the wall, closed her eyes, and tried to ignore the catastrophic noises outside while she prayed for continued deliverance.

CHAPTER 59

By the time the wind quit howling, and the rain finally stopped, Bertha's nerves were strung as tight as a drum. The children got hungry. She and her staff managed to feed them despite what sounded like a war outside. The food was a welcome distraction. From time to time, she thought she heard screams, but hoped that was her ears playing tricks on her.

For hours and hours, it felt like a group of angry giants were trying to tear their way into the building. All she could do was encircle as many frightened children as she could with her arms. Mimose and Widelene and some of the older children did the same. No one sat alone. All needed the comfort of one another. Bertha drew strength and courage from the tiny bodies pressing against her, whom she loved so much.

Empty buckets were used as latrines. They were difficult for the younger children to manage, but it was all they had. She stored them in a corner and barricaded them with a wooden table turned on its side so that no one would accidentally stumble into them in the dark. The smell grew rank, but there was nothing she could do.

She dozed while sitting upright, jerking awake every time a particularly loud sound permeated her consciousness. It was almost as though time stopped. It felt like they had been trapped inside this building forever.

Eventually, the wind and rain died down. Not abruptly, like when the eye of the storm passed over them. Gradually, as the outer edges of the hurricane drifted over and off the island.

The silence, when it came, felt strange. Bertha's ears had become so attuned to the carnage that they seemed unwilling to accept the quiet. She tried to crack the door open a few inches, but it had somehow become barricaded with something—she had no idea what.

Now, she had a new issue. How to get out of the building when she wasn't strong enough to move whatever was lying against it. With the windows nailed shut and the door barricaded, she wasn't sure how they were going to get out. After the combined efforts of her, Widelene, Mimose, and the cook couldn't make the door budge. She didn't know what to do.

"Help us!" Bertha shouted, banging on the door. "We're trapped. Help!"

Her attempt to get attention frightened some of the children, who began to cry.

Eventually, she heard men's voices, a scraping sound outside, and then the door swung open. It took a moment for her eyes to adjust to the light, but when she did, the most welcome sight awaited her. Anthony and the two Haitian men who had helped nail boards over the windows stood there.

"You are okay." Anthony's voice shook with relief as he took her hand and helped her outside. "I was so afraid we had lost you, but you are okay."

She glanced around. The broken body of a cow lay to her right. "Is that what was blocking the door?"

"Yes,"

"Is there anything left of the compound at all?"

"There is much to repair, but I believe some of the buildings can be salvaged."

"What about the hospital?" she asked.

"By God's grace, it is badly damaged but still in operation."

"I'm so glad!"

It was then that she realized she still clung to his hand, and she dropped it.

"You have food, water, and shelter," Dr. Lawrence said, ignoring that

small bit of awkwardness between them. "You and the children are better off than most. For now, I will leave one of the men to help you begin the process of salvaging and rebuilding. I'll be back as soon as I can. Others are trapped and hurt. I must go try to save as many as I can."

She watched him confer briefly with one of the men who had helped them prepare for the hurricane. The man nodded, then began prying off the boards covering the windows of the building in which they had sheltered. Behind her, light entered the building that had felt like a cave.

After talking with the children and making sure they were unharmed, Dr. Lawrence left. As she watched him hurry away, Bertha decided that if she should ever find a man even half as compassionate and talented as Dr. Lawrence, she would marry him on the spot.

As he left, she turned in a slow circle and took stock. Then she began to roll up her sleeves. The challenge before her was great.

Over the next two days, as news filtered in, she discovered that while they were huddled in the kitchen, the hurricane had dumped nearly five feet of rain as it slowly passed over the beleaguered island. Twelve-foot storm surges had bit into the fragile land.

The great deluge of water triggered landslides so catastrophic that some towns and villages were completely buried in mud and debris. Others were swept away in flash floods, which were also caused by the heavy rainfall.

In many villages, not only were most of the buildings gone, the few that remained upright had lost their roofs.

Crops, including banana and coffee, were destroyed by flooding. Flash floods washed out roads and bridges, leaving them unpassable for months.

The hurricane killed approximately five thousand Haitians. Some drowned, some were covered by avalanches of mud, some were killed by flying debris or by homes collapsing, and some who could not find shelter died from burns caused by being scoured by strong winds gusting up to two-hundred-miles-per-hour.

No one, no matter how hard they tried, could have prepared for the utter devastation that Hurricane Flora brought upon the already struggling country of Haiti.

CHAPTER 60

The massive loss of life was only one factor in the devastation that surrounded them in the aftermath of Hurricane Flora. Thousands survived but were left wounded and helpless by the storm.

"I need your help," Dr. Lawrence said.

The sound of children's voices singing filled the air as Mimose held classes in a schoolhouse where half of the roof was torn off.

"I don't know how much help I can be." Bertha blew a strand of hair out of her eyes. She and Widelene had been sorting through debris to see what was salvageable.

"I'm getting a team together to go into some of the more remote areas. I'd like you to come with us."

"Why me?"

"Because you are one of the most competent people I know." Dr. Lawrence said. "And you have the constitution of a horse when you remember to take your malaria medicine."

Despite her respect for Dr. Lawrence, she wondered if he had lost his mind. Didn't he realize how much work she had here? Widelene and Mimose couldn't handle this alone.

"The children need me," she said.

His face, ravaged with worry and overwork, softened. "Of course, they do, but Darlene has offered to come take your place temporarily.

"Darlene?"

Despite Bertha's original assessment of Darlene, the woman had stayed. Once she got over the culture shock, Darlene had shown herself to be a competent nurse with a flair for administration duties. She also loved the children and visited frequently.

"Darlene is trying hard, but she isn't as emotionally strong as you. I have found her to be quickly overwhelmed by the never-ending stream of hurricane victims. It isn't easy for any of us, but she's broken down crying repeatedly. I can't depend on her."

Bertha thought it over. She had noticed that Darlene had a strong maternal side. Whenever she visited the children's home, she reveled in interacting with the children.

"What does Darlene say about this?" Bertha asked.

"She's more than willing to come," Dr. Lawrence said, "In fact, she's eager, and I desperately need nurses with me who have the stomach to help without falling apart."

"You honestly think this is best?" she asked.

"I do. Pack only those things you truly need and can carry," he said. "Before this is over, you will have a chance to apply every last ounce of nursing knowledge that you've ever learned. I'll be back with Darlene within the hour. Be ready."

When he came to drop off Darlene, he picked Bertha up in the dependable old jeep he drove.

"Thank you for changing places with me," Darlene told Bertha, gratefully. "I couldn't have taken much more at the hospital."

The children seemed pleased to see Darlene as Bertha left with an impatient and focused Dr. Lawrence.

"How is Charlotte?" Bertha asked. "Was she ever okay about leaving the island?"

"No." Dr. Lawrence raised his voice over the whine of the hardworking vehicle as he shifted into a higher gear. "But she understood the necessity. I

am willing to sacrifice much for this country, but not the lives of my sons and their mother. They were not the ones who chose this work. I did."

"Where are they staying?" Bertha held on tightly as he maneuvered around several potholes.

"Charlotte's family owns a home near Sarasota, Florida. There is room for her and the boys. When things are clear here, they can come back."

"How long do you think that will take?"

"A month, maybe." He shrugged and glanced around at the devastation. "Here we are. This is where we are setting up our field clinic for now."

Canvas tents had been erected in some places, just tarps, and poles in others.

As Bertha, Dr. Lawrence, and a team of Haitian helpers fought their way through the damaged island, Bertha's heart broke repeatedly. There were times when she wondered if the search, rescue, and need for immediate medical relief would ever end.

It would have been hard for anyone not to have admired Dr. Lawrence during this time. Never had she seen a man more passionate about caring for others. Two days passed before he even allowed himself a quick nap, and then only because surgical instruments began to slip from his hands.

"Let me finish," Bertha whispered, as he swayed slightly.

It was not usual for a nurse to finish stitching a patient up, but these were not normal times. As Dr. Lawrence stumbled to his sleeping tent, she dealt with the victims the best she could until he had napped and returned, and then she took her turn to collapse into her sleeping tent. She had hoped to lose consciousness immediately. She was beyond tired. Nearly numb with fatigue, but her mind wouldn't quit. It kept playing the past two days over and over, while she mentally calculated how much she, Dr. Lawrence, and the others could do.

Long lines of wounded made their way to their makeshift clinic over ravaged mountain paths. Untrained and ill-equipped search and rescue teams did what they could. The number of desperate people who came to them seemed endless.

Her stamina was extraordinary, but it did have its limits. Every now and then, she would almost literally crawl into her tent, collapse onto her pallet, spread the mosquito netting around her, and simply lose consciousness for a few blessed minutes. Her waist-long hair came undone and badly tangled. She did not want to take the time to comb out the knots. Instead, she took a pair of surgical scissors and asked one of the Haitian women to hack it off until it was shoulder-length. Then she pulled it back with a handkerchief and forgot about it while she struggled on.

Her dresses became dank and torn, but she covered them with hospital gowns and kept working. She watched Dr. Lawrence wipe his forehead with his shirt sleeve so many times, it grew dark with grime. He kept his hands clean and was careful to wear sterile gloves, but she was reasonably sure he hadn't washed his face or his hair since they'd set up. People were dying. They had the skills to save some of them. There was no time for niceties like showers.

Her respect for him grew with each hour that they worked together. Because her energy and endurance were better than most, she soon became the one he depended on and preferred to have at his side.

As she grew able to anticipate what he needed, sometimes before he even asked for it, she began to feel like they were working together as one person. Never had she felt so close to anyone. Never had she admired anyone more. It was an honor to be by his side in this desperate struggle. As they fought together to save lives, her habit of calling him Dr. Lawrence fell away. He simply became Anthony.

She was too smart not to see the danger in this, but she assured herself that she was strong enough and moral enough to be content with the honor of merely getting to work with such a man.

As many women had discovered about themselves from the beginning of time--when it came to the man she loved, Bertha was a fool.

CHAPTER 61

It took several weeks, but there came a time when the frantic pace of all the humanitarian efforts began to drop off.

It was a Saturday night, very late, when Anthony prepared to go to a nearby village to attend a long-laboring Haitian woman. It was her first baby, and her husband came to the clinic, begging someone to help her.

"I'll go instead," Bertha offered. "It's been a long day. You need to rest."

"As do you," Anthony said. "But I want to go. I think it will be healing to help bring new life into the world after all the death we have experienced."

She quickly gathered some supplies and prepared to accompany him. They took the long-suffering jeep, hoping it would hold together long enough to get them there and back. The rest of the staff stayed behind.

"Let them sleep," Anthony said. "They've earned it."

Five hours later, in a poor farmer's hut, with an anxious father looking on, Anthony gently eased a slippery baby into the world. After clamping and cutting the cord, he placed the squalling, healthy baby boy into the towel Bertha held out. As she wrapped the baby in the clean cloth, they shared a look that was so intimate with joy over the miracle they had experienced that she felt shaken by it. Had they gotten so close that a mere look was enough to make it feel as though they shared the same soul?

They finished their task, and as night lightened into day, they drove into the early dawn. Suddenly, as they crested a hill, they saw the most magnificent sunrise spread out in all its glory upon the ocean below.

It was so sudden and so beautiful, she gasped and grabbed Anthony's arm.

"Oh!" she said. "Please stop! I want to get out."

"Of course." He pulled off the road, threw the jeep into park, and switched off the ignition.

They climbed out and stood at the top of the hill, reveling in the majesty of the view.

Bertha knew that as soon as they descended back to their life below, they would be hemmed in by people, most of whom would need attention for one reason or another. Up here, there were no houses, no people, only fresh air and that brilliant view. Their lives had been so staggeringly harsh since the hurricane, she craved just a little more time here before they went back.

"A new day," she said. "A fresh beginning. Do we have a few minutes to spare so we can just enjoy this show God has spread out for us?"

"Of course," Anthony said. "I think we've earned a few minutes?"

"It's amazing, isn't it," she said. "How vicious the ocean and weather can be one day, and how perfect and beautiful it can be the next?"

He didn't answer.

She turned to look at him and realized he wasn't drinking in the beauty of the sunrise at all. He was drinking in the sight of her. Bertha had never seen such a raw look of longing on a man's face. It was so intense, she immediately knew that this incredible man wanted her. Not as a nurse, not as a helper, but as a man wants a woman. It both frightened and thrilled her.

In that moment of revelation, she finally acknowledged to herself that she desperately wanted him too. It had not been deliberate. Never had it been deliberate. Her feelings for him had transpired slowly, unconsciously, but the fact was there. She was absolutely sick in love with another woman's husband.

Frantically, she tried to distance herself emotionally.

Anthony was a good man. A spiritual man. A disciplined man. A family man. A man who deeply loved his wife and children.

And yet...

He took a step toward her. There was such depth of love in his eyes that it made her feel weak. She should have backed away and insisted he take her back to camp. Instead, seeing Anthony looking at her with such hunger made her stomach churn with anticipation.

She needed to get away from him. She was better than this. Better than what she was feeling right now.

And yet...

He was exactly what she wanted. More than she had ever known could exist in a man.

And yet...

Intimately being with him was impossible. As long as he was married to Charlotte, it was wrong to even think of him in those terms.

And yet...

She stood perfectly still. Trying to will herself not to touch him. Thinking of the devastation it would cause if she were to give in to her love for him.

And yet...

She was so lonely! Even with the children filling every moment of every day, she had reached an age where she longed for a true mate. Someone with whom she could share every aspect of her life. Someone like Anthony.

"Bertha?" His voice was halfway between a question and a caress. He reached out and gently touched her face with his fingers.

At the touch of his hand, those skilled hands that alleviated so much pain and healed so many people, she could not help herself. She took his hand in both her own and kissed his palm.

She heard his sudden intake of breath. Then he pulled her to him, wrapped his arms around her and held her close—so close.

"Every time you came to my house, it felt as though a streak of sunshine had somehow entered my home, and my life," Anthony said. "I find myself thinking about you constantly. I've tried to keep my love for you hidden. I've fought it. Lord knows I've fought it. But today..." His voice broke. "I'm just so tired of fighting."

Bertha's mind echoed with his words. It felt as though she had been starved for them. Visions flew across her mind, memories of his many kindnesses, the intelligence in his eyes, the way they flashed if he thought a child was being neglected or mistreated.

She had always taken pride in her strength and integrity. She had always had contempt for those weak women who gave into men's advances without the advantage of marriage, and she had judged them severely. But at this moment, she had nothing but sympathy for the women to whom she had once felt superior. She never had, until this moment, experienced the type of passion that could cause a woman to throw her morals, beliefs, and good intentions to the wind.

For one moment, she felt a hot rebellion against God rise in her heart. It was fiery and deep, surprising in its intensity. What right did someone else have to be with this man, to be loved by him, to bear his children?

Everything she had seen and endured during these past horrific weeks, all the heartbreak they had experienced together, had created a deep knowledge of how fragile life could be, how quickly it could be over. That knowledge was like dry kindling thrown upon living embers, so strong was her need to live and express her love for him.

This moment in time, this precious bit of privacy was so rare. If she did not grasp this opportunity, she suspected Anthony would make sure such a moment never came again.

It was almost as though Satan, himself, had created this opportunity for them, catching Anthony in a moment of weakness. Oh, the devil was most definitely alive and well this morning, roaming about seeking whom he should devour, but at this moment, she simply did not care.

She almost didn't hear the sound of a vehicle coming toward them, but Anthony did. He lifted his head.

"That's George's truck!"

George was one of the volunteers from the Mennonite Central Committee who had come to help during the hurricane rescue. He was also head of the MCC relief agency. If he so much as caught a whiff of what was in Bertha and Anthony's hearts, he could have Anthony's funding cut immediately. The

Mennonites did not play around when it came to adultery or even the possibility of it.

Anthony stepped away from her.

"Get in the jeep." All traces of love for her drained from Anthony's voice. "We have to go!"

The road was narrow. Less than a minute later, Anthony inched the jeep around George's truck as they tried to pass one another.

"I have brought good news to you," George said, as their vehicles came to a stop and idled beside each other. "Charlotte just got word to us that they are flying back tomorrow. One of her father's friends made arrangements for military transport to bring your family over. I came to camp to tell you as soon as I heard, but the rest of the staff said you two had left late last night, headed in this direction, and hadn't returned."

"One of the local women was having a difficult birth," Anthony said. "Her husband came to get me. Bertha was awake and offered to come help."

Bertha immediately saw that Anthony was making a mistake in adding that last bit. Assisting him was her job. To explain her presence sounded suspicious.

George looked at Anthony, and then he looked at her. She knew she was disheveled from the long night. She could feel that her cheeks were flushed. There had been no time to go from being passionately in love with a man to professional nurse mode.

"Does your house still stand?" George asked Anthony.

Perhaps it was her imagination, but she felt like the older man was asking a question far deeper than inquiring about the state of Anthony's physical home.

"I have no idea," Anthony said. "I've been too involved in trying to save as many lives as possible. I have not taken the time to check."

"That's understandable," George said. "But I think it's time you go home—if you still have a home—and begin getting it ready for Charlotte and the children."

"Of course," Anthony said. "You're right."

"Good," George put his truck in gear. "I would hate for that good woman to have nothing to come home to."

As they drove off, Bertha hoped it was only her guilty conscience reading more into those words than George intended, but she couldn't get over the feeling that he was quietly giving her and Anthony a warning.

CHAPTER 62

As the day drew on and the temperatures rose, the heat of Haiti felt like a living beast hovering over her, breathing down on her neck with its hot breath. She went about helping break down and pack up the field hospital and camp, deeply aware that Anthony had barely glanced at her since George had interrupted them. She was sick at heart with the guilt of what she had almost done, how quickly and utterly she had responded to him—and yet despite her shame, Bertha was still a woman in love.

Methodically both she and Anthony helped finish up, acutely aware that George's eyes were upon them. When they got ready to leave, she deliberately chose to catch a ride back with George. She hoped it would deflect any suspicions he had formed.

"I'll go check on the house for you before I go back to the children's home," she told Anthony in George's hearing. "You have so much else to do. If there is anything I can do to make it more habitable for Charlotte and the boys, I will."

Anthony's and Charlotte's house was still standing but damaged. A small portion of the roof was torn off, and two of the windows were shattered. The rain had gotten in, and the boys' beds were sodden, but all in all, they had been lucky.

"I have some tools in the truck," George said. "You clean up inside, and I'll see what I can do about the roof and windows."

Although hot, the day remained clear. Bertha spent the day washing bed linens and hanging them out to dry. With the laundry water, she scrubbed the mud off the worn, tile floors and set to rights what else she could. It was a humid day, and it took the sheets and blankets longer to dry than she'd expected. They still weren't dry by the time George finished.

"That ought to hold things for a while," George said. "Are you ready for me to take you back to the children's home?"

"I had hoped to have clean beds all made up for the children when they got home," Bertha said. "They'll all be so tired from their trip. I'll wait until the linens are dry, and then I'll find another way back to the children's home. It isn't so far that I can't walk."

"You're sure?" he asked.

"I'm sure," she said. "I've had word that Darlene and the rest of the children's home staff are managing well, and Charlotte gets migraines. If she gets one during the trip, I don't think she'll be able to manage, plus she'll be exhausted." "

George seemed tired and sad. He was a good man who had seen too much in his lifetime of disaster relief and working with third world countries.

"I'm going back to help with the temporary clinic Dr. Lawrence is setting up tomorrow," George said, as he left. "I'll let him know that you have things well under control."

The heat was still beating down on the roof that George had repaired, and there wasn't much breeze. By the time she finished everything, her clothes were sticking to her skin like paste. Once George was gone, while she waited for the boys' sheets and coverlets to dry, she went to the bathroom, undressed, and began to wash the sweat off herself. Charlotte had some bath soap setting out that smelled like lilac, and the scent of good soap paired with the lukewarm water comforted her.

When she finished, she could hardly bear to put the soiled clothing she'd been wearing back on. Charlotte had left so hurriedly, many of her dresses were still in the bedroom closet, but she was a smaller woman. Even though

Bertha knew Charlotte wouldn't mind if she borrowed a clean dress, there was no way anything Charlotte owned would fit her.

Anthony, however, did have a brown robe hanging on a hook in the bathroom that was large enough to fit her. She looked at it longingly. It would be so good to feel clean cloth against her skin once again. Neither Anthony nor Charlotte would mind if she slipped into it for a bit before donning her dirty clothes again, and so she did.

She felt the boys' bed linens again. Still damp.

It had been quite a while since she had eaten, but even more than hunger, she was tired. She knew that once she got back to the children's home, there would be no sleep. The children would want her immediate attention, and it would be wise to be rested enough to rise to their needs.

Longingly, she glanced at Anthony and Charlotte's bed. It wouldn't hurt if she lay down for a few minutes, she decided. Just until the boys' laundry was dry.

Anthony had mentioned that he intended to stay at the hospital for tonight. He had access to a room and bunk bed there. She thought this gave her the freedom to rest for a few minutes undisturbed. Alone in Charlotte and Anthony's home, she crawled into bed. It felt so good. It was large enough for her to stretch out. She lay there, physically comfortable for the first time in weeks, taking stock of her life and all that had happened in the past few hours—starting with the near-miss with Anthony.

Bertha's heart still sang with the knowledge that he loved her. If she were a different sort of woman, she would use his passion to wrest him away from his wife and children. But as she thought about those three precious little boys--who practically worshipped their father—and the toll it would take on Charlotte--she knew she could never do that.

If she gave in to her great love for Anthony, it would devastate four innocent lives. No matter how deeply she loved him, it was not within her to bring about that much suffering. Nor was it within Anthony.

There was also his work. He had grown so important to this place. The people depended on him. The ramifications of what would have happened had George not interrupted them was unnerving.

They were better people than this. Much better.

And yet...

She tossed and turned, wrestling with her love for him as she faced the inevitable. It was not within her to break the hearts of his three sons and their mother. She would prefer her own heart be shattered than to cause that much pain to people she loved.

Alone in the darkness, she resolved that she would not destroy a family—not even to be with the only man she had ever loved.

Exhausted by lack of sleep and hard work, she made one final decision before closing her eyes for a much-needed nap. She was going to have to leave the island. Leave the children and people she had grown to love at the children's home. Leave Anthony and Charlotte and their boys. If she stayed, the temptation to give in to her love for him would be too great.

She knew her departure might break Anthony's heart—it would most certainly break hers--but he would ultimately feel relief over her decision to remove herself from his life and Charlotte's. Memories would fade. He would sink back into his work and forget her.

Tomorrow, she would look for a way to get off the island. In a few minutes, she would go back to the children's home and pack. It was the greatest gift of love she could give him—to protect him from losing his family and his reputation. For him, she would leave the work for which she had sacrificed so much.

Having made her decision, feeling noble and pure of spirit, she closed her eyes, planning to rest just for a few minutes.

CHAPTER 63

The last thing Bertha expected to do was to fall so deeply asleep that she didn't awaken until hours later. Long after night had fallen. Long after she should have retrieved the bed linens.

Unfortunately, Anthony chose not to sleep at the hospital that night.

"Why are you wearing my robe?" he said sternly. "And what are you doing in my bed?"

Bertha felt disoriented as she looked around the darkened room. Anthony shined a flashlight in her eyes.

"I-I..."

The realization of how this must look to him came flooding in and along with it, humiliation. How terrible this must look! He must think she was waiting here to seduce him, instead of having made the self-sacrificial decision to leave as soon as possible.

"I'm sorry," she said. "I didn't think you were coming tonight. My clothes were so dirty. I was so tired, Anthony..."

He cut her off by tossing the keys to the jeep to her. "If I had known you were here, I would never have come home. You are too great a temptation. Get out of here, Bertha. Right now. Before I do something that I will regret for the rest of my life."

His undeserved anger struck fire in her own heart. He was acting as though she were the one to blame, and she wasn't. It was he who had allowed her to see the love he had for her.

She had done nothing except work next to him these past few weeks, trying to anticipate every surgical tool or medicine he might need. She had gone beyond what any nurse should have to endure, taking on tasks that she should not have had to do, trying to make things easier for him.

"I don't need your jeep!" She threw the keys at his head, he ducked, and the keys clattered against the wall. "I'll walk back to the children's home."

He looked concerned. "The Vodou drums have started. The people are anxious. Some of the priests are telling them they have angered the spirits. You shouldn't be out alone tonight."

"That's not your problem, is it!" she stormed at him, jerking the belt of his robe tighter. "I am not your concern. I will never be your concern."

He retrieved the keys and held them out to her. "Act like you have some sense, Bertha. Take the jeep."

"You egotistical idiot!" She grabbed her dirty and stained dress off a chair in the corner. "I was not waiting here for you! I fell asleep and didn't wake up because I was so tired from trying to help you and your family."

She went into the bathroom, closed the door, and yelled at him as she dropped the robe and jerked her soiled dress on over her head. "I've done your laundry, scrubbed your floors, and got the house ready for Charlotte and the boys. My sin is that I took the time to wash up and put on your robe—the only thing in the house I could fit into!"

"Bertha."

"The boys' bed linens are on the line. Make up their beds before you go to sleep. I don't want Charlotte to have to do it!"

"Let me drive you back," he said worriedly. "I can't sleep with you wandering around after dark. There is real danger out there, Bertha. You know that."

She crashed out of the bathroom and threw the robe in his face. "Here. Forgive me for borrowing it. By the way, I'm leaving Haiti. And the children.

And you. For your family's sake. I wouldn't want to be a distraction. Not to the great Dr. Anthony Lawrence!"

"Bertha..."

"I think that's an excellent idea," A quiet voice said.

Both Bertha and Anthony turned to look.

It was George. Standing in the doorway, watching and listening.

Bertha covered her mouth with the back of her hand. Anthony turned pale.

"George!" Anthony said, "I never..."

"I don't care what you did or didn't do," George said. "What matters is what happens from here on out. I've heard and seen enough to know that you two need to get away from each other. I'll be making arrangements for you to leave, Bertha. Hopefully, tomorrow morning if I can arrange it. I'll take you back to the children's home now."

"Thank you," Bertha said, trying to regain a modicum of dignity.

"Anthony," George said. "I suggest you spend the night in prayer. Pray for your marriage, your children, and your soul. Pray for the great good being done here in Haiti that Satan has tried to destroy through you.

"I do love her," Anthony said, heatedly. "But in my defense, I have never touched her in any forbidden way."

"And I don't care!" George snapped. "What you feel or don't feel is unimportant. I'm sending Bertha home, and I strongly suggest that neither of you has contact with one another again. Bertha, go get in the truck."

Walking out of the Lawrence's house, believing she would never see Anthony again, she felt such a mixture of grief, loss, humiliation, and anger that she felt sorry for any Vodou priest who might attempt to stop her.

CHAPTER 64

"What happened when you went back," Anthony asked.

"Excuse me?" Bertha had been wool-gathering. Remembering. It seemed strange to come back to earth and realize she was sitting on a porch in Florida with him.

"After you left Haiti before we left and you came back to the island, what did you do?" he asked.

"I rented a little house in Millersburg." She gathered her wits and concentrated. "I worked at the hospital there for a couple of years."

"Your family was okay with that?"

"Of course not, I had still not chosen to be Amish, but they were pleased I was closer to home."

"Why did you go back to Haiti after Charlotte and I left?"

"I like to finish what I start," she said. "I'd promised God that if He helped me become a nurse, I would do what I could for the Haitian people, and so I did."

"How long did you stay?"

"Twenty years."

"Good grief!" Anthony stared at her. "I didn't realize you stayed that long. That's a remarkable amount of life to devote to a mission work."

"It didn't seem remarkable at the time," Bertha said. "Once I became acclimated, it was the happiest time of my life."

"And this?" He touched the sleeve of her dress. "You became Amish again. When?"

"My mother and father were needing care, and so was Anna. There was the inn to run so that they would have a livelihood. I couldn't leave all the responsibility to Lydia. My father was still upset with me for leaving the Amish. Since I would be living at home, taking care of my family, it seemed less awkward to simply be baptized into the church. Besides, I had always admired and loved my culture. I only left in the first place because I felt it was the only way for me to be obedient to God's call."

"Are you sure that in taking your vows," Anthony's voice was quiet and thoughtful, "you weren't doing penance?"

"Penance?"

"For falling in love with a married man."

The question jarred her, but considering all that had happened, it seemed silly to deny what they both knew was true.

"Yes," she said. "I suppose, in a way, I was doing penance."

"Did you ever wish you had made a different choice and stayed on the island with me once we knew how we felt about each another?"

"There were times," Bertha said. "But in the end, I knew I could never be so selfish as allow myself to take a man away from his family."

"I often wished you had made a different choice," he said. "But I was not that selfish either, and I was grateful you left."

"I have discovered that life, if one lives long enough," she said, "tends to burn the selfishness out of you."

"For a good person, that is true," Anthony said. "But some people carry selfishness straight into their graves. I've seen it."

"As have I."

Once again. Silence.

What did one say, when there was so much to say? How did one even start? A lifetime lay between them, and yet the memories of what had happened between them were still fresh enough to cause pain.

"If you had not left the island," Anthony said, "You know that I would have had to."

"I know," Bertha said.

"I did love you," he said.

"And I loved you, but the memory of that last night together still stings. What I was not given a chance to tell you when you showed up so suddenly, was that I had already resolved to leave the island." Bertha said. "With or without George intervening. Your anger was not necessary. I already realized that if I destroyed your family, there would come a time when you would grow to hate me. I could not bear the thought of that."

"It's hard to imagine ever hating you," he said.

"Perhaps," she said. "But ultimately, I could not see any way to build a good life on the embers of so many innocent people's pain. Your sons revered you. They wanted to be like you. Where would the infidelity of their father fit into that? They loved their mother. How could they not hate you for hurting her? They would most definitely have ended up hating me."

Words she had never spoken aloud to anyone, she was now free to say to the one person who could truly understand.

"Had we stayed together," she mused, "I think we would have ended up two sad old people, estranged from our families, who in the end didn't even like each other very much. Nor would we have liked ourselves very much. Instead, you have this beautiful home. You have your wonderful daughter. You have sons and daughters-in-law and grandchildren who no doubt admire and love you."

"I've seen too much of the wreckage people make of their lives to disagree with you," Anthony said. "You saved us both by walking away. But what do you have? Did you ever marry? Do you have any children?"

"No," Bertha said. "I couldn't."

"Couldn't have children?"

"Couldn't marry." Bertha smiled. "There were men who were interested down through the years, but how could I ever love someone else when I measured them against you?"

His shoulders slumped. "I wanted you to have a good life, even if we couldn't be together. You deserved a chance to raise your own children."

Bertha lifted her chin in defiance to his pity. "I have had a happy life. A rich life."

"I'm glad." Anthony placed his hand over hers. "The sun is starting to set. Let's go for a walk before it gets dark."

He rose and helped her to her feet, but he did not let go of her hand, nor did she let go of his. They held on to one another as they walked down to the beach together.

It was so different from her regular life—this feeling of holding hands with a man for whom she had once harbored such deep feelings. But somehow, it felt exactly right.

When they arrived at the edge of the ocean, they stopped and gazed out at the ocean as the sun began to slip below the horizon, streaking the sky with vivid colors.

"It is so beautiful here," she said.

"Would you do me a favor?" he asked.

"What is that?"

"Would you take off your kapp and let your hair down? That is how I always think of you. That day after helping with that birth, for instance. You were so young and earnest. You had worked so hard to help. Been so kind to that laboring woman. So tender with the new baby. It was hot. You'd pulled off the headscarf that you wore. Your hair was so bright and lovely, and it floated on the wind flowing up from the ocean. It looked like spun gold, and you were utterly unaware of how beautiful you were."

She felt foolish, but the balmy air, the scent of the ocean, the sunset, Anthony standing so close...should she?

"I'm an old woman, Anthony," she said. "My hair is far from golden."

"I know exactly how old you are," Anthony said. "But I watched you fight to protect the children in your care. I've seen you comfort the dying. I've watched you bring new life into the world. I watched you walk away from me when I knew you loved me. I know your soul. You will never, ever, be anything but beautiful to me."

Mesmerized by the passion of his words, she took her kapp off, dropped it on the sand, unpinned her braid, ran her fingers through it, and shook out her hair. The gentle ocean breeze captured it.

"I remember everything." Anthony took her face in both hands. "I tried hard to hide it, but as we worked together, I became so obsessed with you, I could hardly eat. There was a window of time when you could have had me with a snap of your fingers. And yet, once you knew that, you chose to leave. You kept me from destroying myself. Thank you for what you did."

He wrapped his arms around her. She leaned her face against his shoulder, breathed in his scent, absorbed the delicious feeling of being held by this man whom she had loved most of her life. Finally, with a sigh, he released her, picked up her kapp, took her hand in his, and they began to walk along the edge of the water together. Each deep in thought at the wonder of this night.

For the rest of her life, she knew that she would forever remember this walk with Anthony, feeling—just for a short while—as though she were young again, and this time he was free to be hers.

CHAPTER 65

The U.S. military had managed to patch the airport tarmac enough that there was a commercial flight available for George to secure a seat for her the next day. Bertha packed her bags, said a tearful good-bye to the children and the staff. The trip to the airport with George was spent in awkward silence. What could she say? He knew what he knew. All she could hope for was that in deference to Anthony and Charlotte's marriage, he would keep that knowledge to himself. The Amish and Mennonite were a large but close-knit community—which often made them a gossipy bunch.

When she took her seat on the first plane to leave the island, she was no longer the idealistic young woman who had arrived. She felt like a battle-scarred soldier who had lost the war.

There was no doubt about it. She had failed. All the training, all the sacrifice, all the years of hard work to fulfill her dream—and she had failed. After only six months of service, she was going home in disgrace. Even if George never told a soul about what he'd seen and heard, she knew in her heart that she was disgraced.

As her plane lifted from the tarmac, she cried harder than she had ever cried before. Her heartbreak was so profound that the French woman sitting beside her excused herself and found a less emotional seatmate in the back of the airplane.

Bertha, feeling like her life was over, did not care.

CHAPTER 66

Calvin was a man with a plan that evening as he readied himself for his new job tomorrow morning. Aunt Lydia had confided that she was in great need of help. A young couple was coming from Alaska to spend the weekend at the Sugarhouse Inn, and there were floors to be swept and firewood to be brought in, plus all sorts of other interesting things for him to help her with that he had never done before.

He had been too young to help when he lived with grandma, or at least it seemed that way because grandma had pretty much done everything. But Lydia said that at ten, he was old enough, and since these were paying guests, she intended to pay him for his services.

He glanced at the silent television as he went through the living room to the bathroom. Usually, he would spend half of Saturday morning watching cartoons and spooning cereal into his mouth. But he was so excited about spending an entire day with Lydia that he didn't care if he didn't get to watch TV all day.

He carefully laid out his clean clothes for the next day on a chair in the bathroom just to be well prepared for the morning. Calvin's clothes were a pair of jeans, a Spider-Man T-shirt, some Spider-Man underwear, and the new socks and boots that Alex had purchased for him.

"Hey," Alex said, as Calvin came out of the bathroom.

"Hey," Calvin said, as he headed for bed.

"Want to watch a movie?" Alex said. "I'll pop some popcorn."

"I don't like burnt popcorn."

"It's not burnt yet!" Alex said.

Calvin shrugged. "It will be."

Alex laughed. "You're probably right. Want to watch a movie, anyway?"

Calvin was tempted. He liked this new Alex, who was awake so much more often these past few days, but Aunt Lydia wanted him to come really early tomorrow morning.

"I'd better get to bed," he told Alex. "I've got a big day tomorrow."

"Oh?" Alex said. "What's going on? It's not a school day."

Calvin sighed. Goodness. He was on an important mission. He needed to get to bed so he would have lots of energy tomorrow. There was no time for idle chitchat. Then a chill hit. What if Alex didn't want him helping Aunt Lydia? What if Alex told him he couldn't go?

With terror in his heart, he told his guardian about his plans to spend most of tomorrow at the Sugar Haus Inn. If Alex didn't allow him to work for Aunt Lydia, she was going to be awfully disappointed. She needed him!

But Alex was pleased.

"I'm proud of you, buddy," Alex said. "I can't think of a better use of your time than to help that sweet lady."

Calvin felt a surge of love for his cousin. Alex had been through a tough time, and so had he. But things were looking up.

Although he was only a kid, Calvin knew there could have been a lot worse places he could have ended up.

"Thank you for taking care of me," he said.

"I'm not sure who took care of whom there for a while," Alex said. "But I think we're going to be okay now."

"Me too."

Fifteen minutes later, Calvin, with his teeth brushed, face washed, and pajamas on, climbed into bed, and was saying his prayers in which Aunt Lydia and Alex were prominent. He also included a request that he wouldn't be scared of the mean rooster tomorrow when he gathered the eggs.

CHAPTER 67

It was later than Rachel would have liked, but Friday nights were always crowded, and Joe was short on staff. After a full day of being on duty as a cop, Rachel was needed to work the cash register again. As long as all Holly needed was to be fed, diapered, and held, Rachel could handle nights like this. But time was running out. Very soon, Holly would start crawling, then walking. A crowded restaurant was not a safe environment for a crawling baby or a toddler, especially if their mother and father were distracted by work.

By eight o'clock, the crowd had thinned out enough that she felt comfortable leaving little Holly in the arms of one of the waitresses who was thrilled to cuddle a baby instead of her regular duties for a while. Of course, Joe and Darren were there as well to watch over the baby.

It took less than five minutes for her to drive to Alex and Calvin's home. If the lights were off, she wouldn't bother them, but if the lights were on, she hoped to talk with Alex, and this time it wouldn't be about Calvin.

The lights were on. Rachel parked in the driveway, walked to the porch and knocked.

She saw Alex come to the window, glance out at her squad car, and then the door opened.

"Has my little cousin been stealing pies again, Officer?" Alex was smiling.

"He told you?"

"Yes," Alex said. "Calvin has quite a conscience. Neat kid."

"Yes, he is," Rachel said. "I'm glad he and my son are friends."

"But that isn't why you came." Alex crossed his arms and leaned against the door frame.

"No. I came to thank you for your help the other night at the restaurant. Can we talk for a few minutes?"

"Of course." He moved out of the way. "Come on in."

As Rachel entered their home, she was impressed. Not with the furnishings—those were worn and shabby and had probably come with the house—but with the order and cleanliness she saw. Clean dishes were stacked neatly in a drainer in the kitchen that she could see as she walked over to the couch. The old linoleum flooring looked like it had recently been mopped.

Alex took a seat in an armchair across from her. Then he realized the TV was on and turned it off. She detected the smell of slightly scorched popcorn.

He did not offer coffee or soda, which was appropriate because this was not a social visit, and he seemed to realize that. Instead, he waited quietly. This impressed her. Most people were too quick to chatter about trivial things when around a cop. Alex didn't try to start a conversation, nor did he seem at all nervous.

"Do you have any idea why I'm here?" Rachel asked.

"Is that a serious question?"

"Yes."

Alex calmly studied her before he spoke. "You are an attractive woman, but you are wearing no makeup. You did not take the time to brush your hair this morning before you pulled it back into a ponytail.

You are only wearing one earring. The other one is either lost, or you got distracted and forgot to put it in."

Rachel's hand jerked to her ear. He was right. Darn it! She had not lost the other earring. She knew exactly where it was—still on her dresser where it had been when Holly woke up and started to cry. She removed the lone earring and slipped it in her breast pocket as Alex continued.

"The night of the attempted robbery, you were carrying your newborn daughter. You also have a small son, a full-time job, and a husband who is running a successful restaurant. Your aunt, Lydia, has probably told you by now that I used to be a cop. You've had two full days to look into my background." He hesitated. "By any chance, are you here to offer me a part-time job?"

"No."

He looked surprised. "Oh?"

"We need someone full time," Rachel said. corrected. "Are you interested?"

Alex closed his eyes and leaned his head against the back of his armchair. "When you looked into my background, did you read about my big screw up?"

"The hostage situation?" she said. "Yes, I did. You were in a tough spot, you made the best call you knew. It didn't go well. I get that. You were also awarded the Medal of Heroism for a former hostage situation where you excelled and saved lives. We need a seasoned cop here in Sugarcreek to take my place, at least until my children are older. Cops with training and background like yours don't grow on trees. The job here doesn't pay as much as larger cities, but you are already here, and there are perks."

"And what would those perks be?" He smiled as though already anticipating her answer.

"Dealing with some of the most decent people you'll ever meet," she said. "Working with Ed, our police chief, who is a great guy and an excellent cop. Raising Calvin in a town where most of the people still go to church on Sundays and who try to live what they believe the rest of the week. It is far from perfect, but it's a good place to live and work."

"Those are some excellent perks," he said.

"You need to talk to Ed, of course," she said. "But your qualifications are better than any candidate we've seen so far. If you come down to the station tomorrow morning, he'll be there. At least come and talk to him before you make a decision."

"I'll talk with Calvin about it."

"Sounds good," she said. "And now I need to go pick up my kids at the restaurant and get them ready for bed."

"Calvin is already dead asleep," Alex said. "He went to bed early because he's helping your aunt tomorrow morning, and he wants to get there early."

"That's very thoughtful of him," Rachel said. "Most boys his age are not anxious to get up early on a Saturday morning to help an old lady."

"Calvin can be thoughtful," Alex said, "but I suspect he is also hoping to have a seat at Lydia's breakfast table."

Rachel grinned. "I guarantee that Lydia won't mind that a bit."

CHAPTER 68

"I can't tell you how much I have enjoyed our evening together," Anthony said, as he walked Bertha to Rosa's door.

"It's been wonderful," Bertha said. "Please tell Gwen how much I appreciated her hospitality. If she had still been awake when we came back from our walk, I would have told her so myself."

Bertha wasn't sure what time it was, but the lights were off inside the house, which meant that Rosa and Anna were sleeping. Under the circumstances, she was grateful not to have to deal with Anna's curiosity. If her little sister were awake, she would be openly peering out the window at them.

"How long are you staying here with your cousin?" Anthony asked.

"Rosa is insisting that I stay as long as possible. I think I'll stay until the weather warms up enough back home for Anna to continue her walks outdoors."

"May I see you again?" Anthony asked. "Tonight went by much too quickly."

"It did go by awfully fast," Bertha agreed.

"We have two lifetimes to tell each other. I want to tell you all about our sons and boast about how smart the grandchildren are.

There are places here in Florida that I would like to take you that I know you would enjoy."

"I would like that very much." Bertha hoped she didn't sound too eager, but really, at their age, what did it matter?

"Would you mind if I came back tomorrow?" he asked. "I'd like to bring you and Anna back to the house. She might enjoy having a more private beach to walk on instead of the public ones. They get so crowded this time of year."

"I think Anna would love that."

"Then, it's a date," Anthony said. "I'll come for you a little before noon. We'll pick up some take-out and have a picnic out on the porch."

"Anna loves picnics."

"I am so grateful you are here," Anthony said.

"As am I."

"Oh." Anthony slapped his trouser pocket. "I forgot to give you something. I put it in my pocket when Gwen told me you were coming tonight."

He reached into his pocket and brought out a small envelope with the words "For Bertha" inscribed on the front.

"What is this?" Bertha asked.

"Charlotte wrote it a few weeks before her death," Anthony said. "She told me that she'd had a succession of dreams about you and had something she needed to tell you. I was supposed to make sure you got it someday, but she made me promise not to read it."

"Charlotte wrote to me?" Bertha said, in wonder. "Why would she do that?"

"I don't know," Anthony said. "She asked me to find out your address and get it to you. I kept intending to, but considering the way we parted, I never quite got up the courage to get in touch. When Gwen told me you were going to be here tonight, I knew it was time."

Puzzled by Charlotte's actions, Bertha took the envelope. "Should I read it now?"

"No, not while I'm here." Anthony shook his head. "I'm not sure I want to know what's inside."

"Good-night, then," Bertha said. "I'll look forward to seeing you tomorrow."

She did not relish opening the envelope or reading this letter from a dying woman. But it was necessary to do so. It was her duty, and Bertha never shirked her duty. Using a knife from the kitchen, she slit it open.

Dear Bertha,

My doctor says I have only a few weeks left at most. His face was grim when he told me that. It was a shock at first, and then the most wonderful feeling of relief flooded over me. It won't be long now before I can finally be at rest and see our sweet savior.

It is a blessing having these last few precious days to say good-bye to my four children, our nine grandchildren, and three great-grandchildren. I hope I've left nothing but good memories for them behind me. I am grateful that I was able to tell each one how very much I love them. Some of them wept, of course. But I believe with all my heart that we will see one another again.

I have searched my mind and heart to see if there is any unfinished business to tend to before I go, and I keep coming back to all the words left unspoken between us.

You have often been in my mind and heart over the years. I've often wondered if you ever realized how very grateful I have been to you.

Yes, in case you've ever wondered, I know what happened. I knew the danger my marriage was in from the moment you walked into our home. I knew even before either you or Anthony had any idea of the situation into which we had been thrust.

Wives tend to pick up on such things.

You were so astonishingly beautiful the day you strode into our lives. I remember it so well. You were flushed from the heat, and the humidity made your lovely bright hair curl and escape the bun you had twisted it into. I had hoped physical beauty was all there was to you, but your goodness shone through as well. You were smart and kind and utterly dedicated to serving the Haitian people.

Anthony was captivated.

I knew him so well. I saw it immediately, but I also knew that he was a truly good man and would fight any attraction he might have toward you.

There was no way I could ever compete with you, so I prayed for God to give both you and Anthony the heart and strength to withstand the temptations that I knew might lay before you.

It would have been easy to resent you, except you had no idea. You were so gloriously in love with your work and the children and with God that you were oblivious to my husband's struggle. For a while, I thought we were safe.

Then he forced me to leave with the children to escape the hurricane, I was terrified to go. I was afraid with you staying behind that when I came back, I would no longer have a marriage.

I was right to be concerned. I came back to discover that you had left abruptly without giving anyone a good reason, and I came back to a husband who was not much more than a grieving shell. He tried to blame it on the tragedies he had seen, but I knew he was grieving the loss of you.

I confronted him with what I suspected, and he admitted his strong feelings for you. He also told me that you had chosen to leave rather than betray your friendship with me and destroy his relationship with his children.

Never have I been so grateful to another person.

With all my heart, I thank you for caring about me and my children enough to deny yourself the love of my husband.

Anthony is not like most other men. There is no guile or selfishness in him. He promised me he would have no more contact with you, and he kept his promises.

From that moment on, we began to try to rebuild.

It was not easy. For a while his grief over your absence was hard to watch. He did not talk about it, but I saw it in his eyes and face. He even showed it in his tenderness with the children and with me. It was that of a man who has been through a significant loss or illness, trying to learn to walk again on unsteady footing.

We have had a good life. Our children grew into strong believers and have done much good. None of them have ever had an inkling of what their father and I went through. I pray that they will never have to know or go through it themselves.

Satan is so skillful in his attacks on the men and women who try to serve God. I've watched it down through the years and learned to be on guard. When nothing else works, Satan worms his way into their hearts, whispering of great passions, of great loves.

So many marriages have been destroyed, and children forever damaged by nothing more than Satan telling a parent that their own happiness is of greater importance than anything else.

If there is one thing I know, it is that lust is a powerful force. But I also know that true love can be even more powerful.

You proved that when you walked away. Despite your love for my husband, you walked away. You saved us. You and that great, loving, compassionate heart of yours saved us.

I will enter eternity with gratitude and praise for you on my lips.

Your forever friend,

Charlotte

Bertha folded the letter and slid it back into the envelope.

Charlotte had been a better friend to her than she had ever imagined. A great longing to see her sweet friend once again washed over her.

Unable to sleep, she went to the window. A storm had kicked up, and the rain was blowing against the panes.

"I did the right thing," she said, with a sense of wonder. "And it made a difference."

The letter Charlotte had written was still tightly gripped in her hand. Such a healing message. It was so much more than a letter of forgiveness. It was one of understanding and gratitude. It freed her from the cloud of guilt and humiliation she had labored under for so long.

Exhausted by all the emotions of the evening, Bertha slipped on her nightgown and slid beneath the sheets. She fell asleep with a heart lighter than it had been since the day she had first stepped onto Haitian soil.

CHAPTER 69

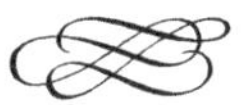

February was a much better month for Calvin and Alex. Once the landlord found out that he was renting to the newest Sugarcreek cop, he was thrilled and decided to do what he could to help Alex want to stay. He hired some Amish carpenters to redo the cabinets and floors. He also put up new windows and had every room in the place painted. Calvin got to help Alex pick the colors. His room was bright blue! Just like back home at Grandma's.

Alex wasn't sleeping so much anymore. They both got up early and got themselves ready like men. Alex said only sissies sleep late. Real men got up early and got on with the day.

Calvin very much wanted to be a real man when he grew up. So when Alex told him that a real man would also stop by the Sugarcreek Inn every morning to check on Aunt Lydia, that's what Calvin did. The fact that she had a good breakfast waiting for him was a bonus. He would have stopped in any way.

A real man would check in with her after school, too, Alex said. And so that is what Calvin did, as well. The fact that her face lit up and she was happy to see him, made the stop very pleasant. It was exactly how Grandma had always acted, like just the sight of him made her happy.

The fact that there was always a piece of pie waiting for him after school, or some cookies and a cold glass of milk, didn't hurt. He was always happy to be with Aunt Lydia.

Plus, she was teaching him things. Lots of things. He helped her do the laundry on her wringer washer in the basement. That was fun. He gathered the eggs from Anna's chickens. He liked watching Lydia quilt and was happy to thread her needle for her whenever she asked. He loved hearing stories about when she was a little girl. It seemed like her life had been much more interesting than what he had experienced so far, but thanks to Lydia, his life was getting more interesting every day.

All in all, it was a perfect arrangement. Calvin loved Aunt Lydia, and she loved him back. Maybe it hadn't been such a stupid idea for Alex to bring him to Sugarcreek after all.

CHAPTER 70

Rachel didn't have the trouble she thought she would at adjusting to being a stay-at-home mom. Even though working for a paycheck had always been part of her adult life, caring for two children and a husband wasn't exactly boring. She enjoyed little Holly so much, and as the days went on, she began to feel the peace that came from being able to have things organized around the house and a routine in place.

Holly had a bit of a schedule now instead of constantly being passed back and forth. Rachel was also able to be on top of Bobby's assignments at school and go to all his programs and teacher's meetings. Best of all, he seemed so happy about getting to come home to her every day.

Joe was more content, too. He got to concentrate on work instead of trying to help her cobble together their schedules to cover all the bases. Rachel had been a hard worker before she gave up her job, and she was a hard worker now, although she was able—at least for this short, sweet, period of time—to put her energies into her family instead of other people.

Of course, the restaurant was a family business with which she and

Bobby helped out every day. Little Holly did, too, just by being herself and a joy to everyone who knew her story, which was most of the population of Sugarcreek.

Apparently, Rachel's old job had made a big difference in Alex's life, too. It was becoming more and more evident that he was a great choice as the latest Sugarcreek cop. He had even begun learning Pennsylvania Deutsch from Lydia. It helped that he had been exposed to it for a time when he was a child. Calvin was learning it, too. It had gotten to the point that they were both speaking it more and more with Lydia and to each other.

Lydia boasted that Alex was achieving an even better accent than Rachel.

"You've lost that lilt, Rachel," she said, "The one that the older Amish generation has. Alex said that if he's going to learn this language, he wants to learn it right."

Rachel and Joe agreed that if Ed truly needed her for an emergency, she would still go, but she hoped there weren't any emergencies for a while. After so many catastrophic and traumatic events these past three years, she was ready for things to be calm for a very long time. She had helped keep Sugarcreek safe for many years. Now it was someone else's turn, and she was happy to abdicate.

"We need to take a picture, Sweetie," she crooned to the baby. Dane had told Rachel that he would rather she not bring Holly to see him or even tell her about him as she grew older. He didn't want her knowing that her father was in prison. He thought it would make her feel less of herself. But he also said he wouldn't mind getting a photo every now and then.

For all he had done for this baby girl, and all he had sacrificed, Rachel felt it was the least she could do.

Sometimes men didn't survive prison. She wanted to be able to tell her daughter that her biological father had known all about her and had loved her.

Of course, there was a slight danger in allowing him to see

pictures of his daughter. Even though the papers he had signed were legal, there was always in the back of her mind, the problems that could arise if he changed his mind. But there was more danger—in Rachel's opinion—in not allowing him to see her. He had given the baby to her and Joe because he wanted Holly to be safe and loved and have a better life than he had endured as a child. As long as he knew absolutely that she was well cared for, Rachel was fairly certain he would be okay with the arrangement.

She knew it would be a good idea as well as a kindness to send regular letters and photos of Holly to Dane. She would send pictures of Joe, as well. Dane had been impressed with Joe's athletic prowess and a little in awe of the thought of his daughter being raised by a world-famous ballplayer. If there were photos of Joe holding and caring for little Holly, it would help reassure Dane that he had made the right choice.

CHAPTER 71

It was a delicious feeling, walking into Bertha's beloved Sugar Haus Inn after living in Florida for two months. The place smelled of vanilla sugar cookies, which was understandable since Lydia was pulling a baking tray out of the oven covered with cookies shaped like stars. Several cooling on a dish towel had already been sprinkled with white confectioner's sugar.

"They are starfish to celebrate Anna's return!" Lydia said. "I'm so excited to have you home!"

And it was so good to be home! The familiar house with light streaming through its large windows, the comfortable-looking rocking chair in a corner, the sight of her beloved sister. Lydia, wearing her lavender dress and white apron, sprinkled with errant confectioner's sugar.

"I am so glad to be back," Bertha said. "But first, I have something for you."

Anna, who had been hiding directly behind her, jumped out and shouted, "Boo!"

"Oh, my goodness!" Lydia feigned surprise as Anna stood there, grinning at the success of her favorite joke.

Then, suddenly, Lydia's pretend surprise turned real.

"Anna! Let me look at you!" Lydia exclaimed. "You look wonderful. So much healthier!"

It was true. The long, slow walks every day, along with frequently stopping to bend over and pick up shells, had done good things for Anna. That, along with the fewer calories available at Rosa's house had helped her lose weight. The fresh air and sunshine had impacted her emotional health as well. Anna looked like a younger, healthier image of herself.

"The new doctor was right," Bertha said. "Anna needed to go to the seashore for the winter."

"Cookies!" Anna exclaimed.

Bertha and Lydia exchanged looks.

"Only two cookies, Anna," Lydia said. "Then I need to put the rest away."

Bertha expected a small tantrum. They had never limited Anna when it came to Lydia's cookies, but she got a surprise.

"Okay," Anna said, simply. "Wanna see my shells?"

"I can't wait to see your shells," Lydia said. "Let's go into the living room. There is a surprise waiting for you and Bertha in there."

"A surprise?" Bertha said.

"It came this morning," Lydia said. "Come see."

There, on the coffee table in front of the couch, sat a large vase filled pink roses.

"For me?" Anna asked astonished.

"That's what the envelope said," Lydia said. "For you and Bertha."

Anna had never received flowers before. While she exclaimed over and smelled each rose, Lydia handed Bertha the small, white envelope with their names written on it. Inside was a card.

Dear Anna and Bertha. Welcome home! I hope you had a good trip back to Ohio! Does your Sugar Haus Inn have room for two visitors for the entire month of April? My daughter is in great need of a vacation, and I am in great need of more time with Bertha.

Love, Anthony

"It looks like Anna isn't the only one who had a nice time in Florida!" Lydia said. "Who is this Anthony? Is there something you want to tell me?"

"Yes," Bertha said. "I want to tell Rachel, too. Would you call and invite her over while I unpack? I need to tell both of you the story of my first months in Haiti. It's been a hard journey, but God, in His great compassion, has given it a happy ending."

AUTHOR'S NOTE

Of all the characters I have created over the years, Bertha remains my favorite. I think it is because she is so very flawed in spite of her stellar intentions, and I identify.

Some of Bertha's behavior is contradictory. She is consistently upset that her niece, Rachel, chose not to become Amish despite the fact that Bertha left the Amish religion for many years to become a nurse. Her own choice in her youth makes perfect sense to her, but Rachel's decision to become a cop irritates Bertha no end.

Bertha is blunt, frequently impatient, and even though she is an Amish woman, her sewing and quilting abilities are dismal. She's also not thrilled with the idea of cooking. Given a choice between going out to a cold barn to milk the cow, or staying inside and baking cookies, Bertha will choose the cold barn every time.

And yet, in spite of her flaws, my Bertha sometimes does things that are truly extraordinary; like taking in a homeless man and his son, or writing twenty years of letters filled with healing to the prisoner who killed her brother, or turning away from the only man she will ever love because she refuses to destroy his family.

Many people ask where my ideas come from. The genesis of this story came from the work my husband and oldest son did in Haiti through a church group called Hope for Haiti's Children. We have continued to help support this group, which has an impressive 100% transparency and accountability rating from Charity Navigator.

As always, my goal as a writer is to entertain, inspire, teach, and leave readers—as they finish the last paragraph of the story—not with just a happy ending, but with a feeling of hope.

-Serena

ALSO BY SERENA B. MILLER

Love's Journey in Sugarcreek Series

- The Sugar Haus Inn (Book 1)
- Rachel's Rescue (Book 2)
- Love Rekindled (Book 3)
- Bertha's Resolve (Book 4)

Love's Journey on Manitoulin Island Series

- Moriah's Lighthouse (Book 1)
- Moriah's Fortress (Book 2)
- Moriah's Stronghold (Book 3)
- Eliza's Lighthouse (Book 4)

Michigan Northwoods Historical Romance

- The Measure of Katie Calloway (Book 1)
- Under a Blackberry Moon (Book 2)
- A Promise to Love (Book 3)

Uncommon Grace Series

- An Uncommon Grace (Book 1)
- Hidden Mercies (Book 2)
- Fearless Hope (Book 3)

ALSO BY SERENA B. MILLER

The Doreen Sizemore Adventures

- Murder On The Texas Eagle (Book 1)
- Murder At The Buckstaff Bathhouse (Book 2)
- Murder At Slippery Slop Youth Camp (Book 3)
- Murder On The Mississippi Queen (Book 4)
- Murder On The Mystery Mansion (Book 5)
- The Accidental Adventures of Doreen Sizemore (5 Book Collection)

Uncategorized

- A Way of Escape
- More Than Happy: The Wisdom of Amish Parenting

ABOUT THE AUTHOR

USA Today Best Selling Author Serena B. Miller has won numerous awards, including the **RITA**, the **CAROL**, and was a finalist for the **CHRISTY Award**. A movie, Love Finds You in Sugarcreek, was based on the first of her Love's Journey in Sugarcreek series, *The Sugar Haus Inn,* and won the coveted **Templeton Epiphany Award**. Another movie based on her novel, *An Uncommon Grace,* airs on Hallmark regularly. She lives in southern Ohio, in the country, surrounded by three hard-working sons, three talented daughters-in-law, six utterly brilliant grandchildren, and five lazy porch dogs. When she isn't writing, researching, or traveling, she spends her time playing with grandchildren, failing at yet another decluttering mission, or sitting on the front porch counting her blessings.

For More Information, Please visit
serenabmiller.com

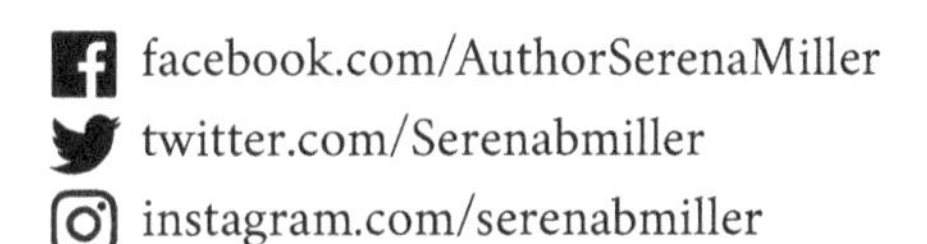

CPSIA information can be obtained
at www.ICGtesting.com
Printed in the USA
LVHW011209131220
674071LV00002B/258